October

ALSO BY ZOË WICOMB

You Can't Get Lost in Cape Town
David's Story
Playing in the Light
The One That Got Away

October

A Novel

Zoë Wicomb

THE NEW PRESS

NEW YORK
LONDON

Requests for permission to reproduce selections from this book
should be mailed to: Permissions Department,
The New Press, 120 Wall Street, 31st Floor, New York, NY 10005.

Grateful acknowledgment is made for permission to
quote the following copyrighted material:
Home by Toni Morrison, copyright © 2012 by Toni Morrison. Used by
permission of Alfred A. Knopf, an imprint of Knopf Doubleday Publishing
Group, a division of Random House LLC. All rights reserved.
Home by Marilynne Robinson. Copyright © 2008 by Marilynne Robinson.
Reprinted by permission of Farrar, Straus and Giroux, LLC.
"Poem in October" by Dylan Thomas, from *The Poems of Dylan Thomas*, copyright
1945 by the Trustees for the Copyrights of Dylan Thomas, first published
in *Poetry*. Reprinted by permission of New Directions Publishing Corp.
Kanna Hy Kô Hystoe by Adam Small,
copyright © 1965. Used by kind permission of Adam Small.

Published in the United States by The New Press, New York, 2014
Distributed by Perseus Distribution

LIBRARY OF CONGRESS CATALOGING-IN-PUBLICATION DATA
Wicomb, Zoë.
October : A Novel / Zoë Wicomb.
pages cm
"Distributed by Perseus Distribution"—T.p. verso.
ISBN 978-1-59558-962-0 (hc. : alk. paper)—
ISBN 978-1-59558-967-5 (e-book)
I. Title.
PR9369.3.W53O28   2014
823'.914—dc23   2013024379

The New Press publishes books that promote and enrich public discussion and
understanding of the issues vital to our democracy and to a more equitable world.
These books are made possible by the enthusiasm of our readers; the support of
a committed group of donors, large and small; the collaboration of our many
partners in the independent media and the not-for-profit sector; booksellers,
who often hand-sell New Press books; librarians; and above all by our authors.

www.thenewpress.com

Composition by dix!
This book was set in Adobe Caslon Pro

Printed in the United States of America
2   4   6   8   10   9   7   5   3   1

For Theo McClure

This house is strange.
Its shadows lie.
Say, tell me, why does its lock fit my key?
—Toni Morrison, *Home*

Home. What kinder place could there be on earth, and
why did it seem to them all like exile? Oh to be passing
anonymously through an impersonal landscape! Oh, not
to know every stump and stone, not to remember how the
fields of Queen Anne's lace figured in the childish happiness
they had offered to their father's hopes, God bless him.
—Marilynne Robinson, *Home*

And I saw in the turning so clearly a child's
Forgotten mornings when he walked with his mother
                Through the parables
                    Of sun light
            And the legends of the green chapels

            And the twice told fields of infancy
That his tears burned my cheeks and his heart moved in mine.
—Dylan Thomas, "Poem in October"

ACKNOWLEDGMENTS

I gratefully acknowledge the generous fellowship at the University of Macau, which enabled me to finish this novel.

Many thanks to Sophia Klaase, whose photographs have been an inspiration; to Frances Cairncross as well as Alice and Johnny Green for kindly allowing me to escape to their cottages in Galloway; and to Professor Derek Attridge for his support. I am also indebted to Henrietta Dax, Annari van der Merwe and Lynne Brown for their help in Cape Town.

Special thanks are due to The New Press, to Diane Wachtell for her support since the beginning and to Jed Bickman and Sarah Fan for preparing this novel.

And for everything, thanks, as always, to Roger Palmer.

October

Mercia Murray is a woman of fifty-two years who has been left.

There is the ready-made condition of having been left and that, as we know, as she knows, involves a death of sorts. But that is a less-than-helpful metaphor. For all the emptiness, there is her broken heart and an unthinkable amount of tears. As a thinking woman, Mercia goes over every gesture, every word that was uttered at the time, in search perhaps of ambiguity, but reflection reveals no hidden meanings. She has been left, and that is the banal truth. Thus, moving from the passive voice, from the self as subject, her thoughts stumble over the question: whom has she been left by? Well, she can hardly say that Craig has left her, since the man who spoke and acted was not the Craig she knew. Thus another ready-made: Mercia has been left by a stranger. Which should mean that there is something unreal about her grief, but that does not stop the tears from flowing, the heart from bursting.

Mercia has a best friend, her younger colleague Smithy, who says that time will bring an end to the suffering. When Mercia, slumped on the sofa, stops crying for a second to send a scornful look, Smithy warns that ready-mades cannot be sniffed at, and that there is the danger of becoming addicted to grief. Many a left one will not let go of the condition, will cosset a heart that lurches about to the broken rhythms of sobbing.

Smithy claps her hands and says, Let's get organized. What do you have to do this week? Let's clear lectures and supervisions for the next three days so you can get some healing sleep. Which makes Mercia sit up. Good old considerate Craig, she says wryly, not a stranger after all. See how he chose a Friday afternoon to tell me. All packed up and gone within a day, leaving me with a long weekend for grieving. By tomorrow I will have cried my heart out, so no need to miss a single class, she sobs.

There's my girl, Smithy says, and pulls out of her bag the peaty, medicinal Bruichladdich that they discovered on a trip to Islay. This will put hair on your chest.

Jacques Theophilus Murray is a bad egg.

Unlike an egg his badness is not contained, concealed within a sound, flawless shell. He is a drunk, and wears his drunkenness on his sleeve, which is to say that there are bags under his eyes, that his face is a flushed mass of veins barely concealed by his dark brown coloring, and that Meester, a pillar of respectability in the village of Kliprand, has suffered the humiliation of his son spending his days in the new, unfortunately named Aspoester bar that has opened in the village. Jake wears his trousers low down on his hips, showing the crack of his buttocks. Which may be the fashion nowadays amongst well-to-do young men, but he is neither young nor well-to-do; there may well be a whiff of urine; and, in fact, the trousers reference the skollie gear of his youth.

When Jake wakes on the morning of the first of September with an evil taste in his mouth, his first thought is of oblivion. What would he give to sink into the softness of a feather pillow, down into deep forgetful sleep, but there is no pillow under his throbbing head. His mouth is parched; he stretches out his hand for the jug of water—Sylvie always puts a jug of water by his bedside—but there is no jug. Light drilling through the curtains, blood-red curtains for fuck's sake, pierces his eyes, so that he turns onto his stomach. Already the heat is oppressive. He must snatch more sleep, but then a groan escapes as he remembers what has to be done on that day. Already it is late; he can tell from the light; and there can be no more than say nine hours of daylight left.

On that first day of the month he must kill Grootbaas, Meester, his father. In the kitchen, Sylvie has a fine butcher's knife, which she keeps razor sharp. He need look no further. He will plunge the knife, twist it into the bastard's heart.

Sylvie is in the kitchen feeding the baby. She knows nothing of Jake's thoughts, but the baby, Willem Nicholas Murray, known as Nicky, who has woken up late after a night interrupted by his father's shenanigans, must sense the patricide, for hearing Jake groan in the adjacent room, he spits out the nipple and purses his full rosy lips with distaste for the nasty world of adults.

Nicky is nearly five years old and given his rude health and firm tread is by no means a baby. Some busybodies would say that he is well beyond breast-feeding. Sylvie has thought of weaning, but what harm could a suckle at the beginning and end of the day do? Besides, the boy would make such a fuss. But what now? Has the little one decided for himself?

What's up with you? she asks. But Nicky stares at his mother and refuses to speak.

Sylvie has much experience with sheep. She has since childhood reared lambs, has cradled hanslammertjies in her arms, hand-fed them milk from a bottle and teat, knowledge which she expects to transfer readily to child rearing, but this one has flummoxed her since birth with his contrary human ways. She tries the left breast. The child turns away with unmistakable disgust, so that she puts him down on the old sofa and buttons up her blouse. He does not protest; instead, he stares at her with wide-open woeful eyes. Nicholas, she says, trying out the controversial name. The child, normally a chatterbox, does not answer.

She has insisted; it was only right that Nicky should have his grandfather's name. Jake had no business registering the first name as Willem, a common Afrikaans name at which she still smarts. Why not at least William? Jake was of course drunk, but for all her scolding he just nodded knowingly, and spat, Call him Klaas if you like. And count yourself lucky I didn't call him Theophobe. Which sounds quite respectable to Sylvie. She has a feeling that Jake does not care for the boy. She knows that to be a sin.

Sylvie is unnerved by the child's silence, by his unflinching stare. Standing like the countrywoman that she is, her left arm is tucked back, the left hand stretched across her back to clutch at the right elbow. The right hand rests on her chest. In this manner, an expert on the television said, countrywomen announce at the same time their humility and their steely determination to see things through. Sylvie listened with interest; she is not averse to explanations that show her to be part of a wider world, only what a pity that the program was in English, which she does not follow with ease.

Thank God, the boy shuts his eyes abruptly and turns over, draws up his knees as if to sleep. Now Sylvie will have to deal with Jake, who is stumbling about behind the door. Damn, damn, damn the devilish drink. She has never been read to as a child the terrifying tales of monsters and giants who chill the blood, but who get their comeuppance in the old end. Behind the door Jake grows vast and evil, a giant-devil capable of anything, so that she flinches. Perhaps it is she whom he will kill today.

Thank heavens she baked yesterday. Sylvie takes Jake a placatory cup of coffee and peanut-buttered bread as well as some panados, and gently pushes him down, back onto the bed.

Here, she says, you'll feel better after more sleep.

You get that knife sharpened, Jake says quietly. Today, no later than today, I'll kill him.

Sylvie laughs mirthlessly. He's dead and buried, Jake. How

many times do you want to kill him? He's saved you the trouble, remember?

Would you like sausage and beans for supper? she asks, in the knowledge that the way to a man's heart is through his stomach. She has made the sausage herself, and would stretch the dish with salted, wind-dried intestine. What Jake imagines they live on, Sylvie has no idea. Her part-time job at the butchery is poorly paid and Jake has been on sick pay for two weeks. What she does suspect is that he has been lost for good to the evil drink, that she will never have him back, and although she knows that there is nothing a girl can do to change the course of events, she should at least make an effort to challenge Lady Fortune. For all her social fears, Sylvie does not take things lying down. She has after all nursed him back once before, rescued him from death's very door, and that only six years ago. But today he is impossibly evil.

You've crept out of a reed hut to ruin my life, Jake replies calmly, and reaches for his bottle. He coughs violently, then a horrible gurgling sound escapes from his throat.

See, she says, it's not nice to drink from a bottle, not healthy, and points to an empty glass.

Jake picks up the glass, a tumbler, turns it this way and that, for all the world as if he were checking for any smudges, for evidence of her failing as a wife, before aiming it at the wall.

Ouch, Sylvie laugh-cries, holding her head, as if she's been in the firing line. This is no way to behave. If only you could pull yourself together and stop this childishness, this badness. What an example for Nicky! I'm not used to such behavior. Also, I didn't grow up in a reed hut, she adds, my AntieMa's house has a good zinc roof.

So why don't you fuck off to AntieMa. Or to Kiewiet Street. Fuck off and take the little bastard with you. Get out.

Sylvie sighs. She hopes the child has not heard. She may be a nobody, but she hasn't bargained on raising a child on bad language. Sylvie knows that Kiewiet Street is shorthand for Meester, whose name Jake will not, cannot utter. But surely he has not forgotten that Meester is dead, that the house is now being sold?

At the kitchen sink, instead of doing the dishes, she stands clutching her right elbow in her left hand, staring fixedly ahead. Just her luck that Jake is not only a drunk, but is also losing his marbles.

It is in the small, dark hours that things get tough, and Mercia must find ways of stemming the phantasmagoria of grief. The conference paper is finished, needs to rest (like pastry, she advises her students, acquiring new properties in left-alone time) so that it becomes more legible for the final edit, and now she should perhaps try her hand at . . . memoir. Oh, there is cause for pause. Mercia is skeptical of the genre, has misgivings about the contemporary turn to memoir, would not dream of reading such a thing. A cliché, of course, this kind of writing deemed suitable for a woman who has been left. Which means that she spends some time hunched over the screen, blank save for the word memoir at the top of the page, typed first in plain text, turned into bold, then into parodic italics.

Mercia's youthful idea of herself as a poet, she thinks, has in fact been a false start at autobiography, and meeting Craig, a real poet, has mercifully put an end to that folly. Then there was much raking of fingernails across her scalp, much doodling in the margins, as you would, not knowing who you are. But now, in a forest of midnight loneness, in the crazed hours of grief, she grows bold. If she thinks of such writing as private, not for publication, then really she is free to write; there need be no thinking through the reason or purpose, no need to retract her views on memoir, and more importantly, no repetition of the angst-ridden biting of the pencil. There is after all a screen, ready to receive an image of herself, but also to protect, to conceal.

Mercia has no intention of wasting her research day on this project. The memoir will be strictly for midnight. And so her fingers fly across the keyboard; words flow effortlessly, for rather than start with the self, there are her parents, Nicholas and Antoinette, both dead and representable. How little, really, she remembers or knows about them; how much there is to invent. She saves the file as Home.

In the past friends have said wistfully—even Smithy—How far you have traveled. You should write your story.

Mercia has met this with embarrassed silence. They are mistaken, also about the source of her embarrassment. Yes, she has come a long way geographically, crossing a continent, but what people really are alluding to is what they believe to be a cultural gap, a self-improvement implied in the distance between then and now, the here of Europe seen as destination. In that sense, Mercia is not conscious of having traveled any great distance. As she once deigned to explain to Craig, her humble origins left little room for improvement. Besides, autobiography is what people like her are expected to produce, and thus for Mercia not a possibility.

Craig has been gone now for eighty-seven days and sixteen hours.

❧

Nicholas Theophilus Murray was a good man, a decent colored man, with a name that he had never disgraced—unthinkable, he was a Murray, of civilized Scottish stock. He neither drank nor smoked. A good man need not rely on anything other than himself. Nie Klaas, he jested, cracking his name in two. No Klaas, so ever my own Baas, and he thumped his chest proudly.

I am Meester, he announced when he first arrived in Kliprand as a young teacher, and Meester was what everyone called him. Within weeks he became a deacon in the Sendingkerk with its new modern building in the center of the village. There he devised plays for young folk, Old Testament narratives turned into dramatic dialogues, with brimstone homilies for keeping the youth out of the bar and on their toes. His thoroughly up-to-date Moses would strike a papier-mâché rock and declaim the commandments, bringing tears to the eyes of old and young alike. But the truth was that even respectable, churchgoing people were all too fond of the devilish drink. Which saddened Nicholas, not least for the fact that the bar was a humiliating window at the back of the Drankwinkel, where they waited (how could they?) until every white customer had been served. Really, it was this abject behavior that made him think of the Namaqualanders as hotnos.

Not that Nicholas had any objection to a decent tot of whisky or brandy, or even a beer stout; he was not narrow-minded, and a drink on festive occasions, birthdays, New Year and so on—though not Christmas—was not a problem. For such rare occasions he favored brandy, something with a good name like Oude Meester. Wine, like the cheap Oom Tas or Lieberstein favored by the people, did not so much turn his stomach as turn his thoughts to dignity, a reminder to straighten his back and lift his chin. So that Jake the reprobate said that in spite of Grootbaas's belief in his own rectitude, it showed that everyone slumps and slackens, and from time to time finds to his horror that his head is hanging. Like shitting, he added, everyone slumps, so that Mercia shut him out with palms pressed against her ears.

Nicholas was not a vain man. He wore a goatee and a moustache that marked his respectability. For some time it had been white with age, in other words, what is known as distinguished in a man. Thus he did not long for the days of youth when he courted the beautiful Antoinette with his raven-black hair; rather, it was the sprinkling of salt and pepper of his forties, when poor Nettie had already departed, that brought a tug of nostalgia. Youth, he knew, was overrated. Being hotheaded and impetuous, a young man could not know where he stands, or indeed at times how to stand, his hands darting in and out of pockets searching for a comfortable place.

How well Nicholas remembered his youthful arms dangling awkwardly, or how shifting his weight from one hip to another brought no end to uncertainty. Then, neither Klaas nor baas, it was a matter of tottering and stumbling on shifting sands. No, it was in the middle years of salt-and-pepper respectability, when Nicholas stood firmly on the rock and uttered his words with precision, that he knew who he was. That, he thought, was also when a man was most attractive to women, for he could not fail to note their interest. Not that he'd had much to do with women. With the help of God, Nicholas had found a wife whose price was above rubies, a good woman who produced two healthy children, but who died all too early at the age of thirty-nine. Yes, he had been tested by God, but that premature death had not encouraged desire for another marriage. He was perfectly capable of boiling an egg himself, of raising his two children, and the good people of Kliprand helped out from time to time, for Meester was a good man.

Nicholas believed that there was a handsome solidity, as well as virtue, to be found in a disciplined man given to gravity and kindness, but irrevocably single. So people said that Meester was a good man and that a good man, as everyone knows, is hard to find. Which for some with a literary bent might signal a well-deserved murder, although it would be foolish to expect a match between life and art.

It is not the case that Mercia neglects her duties. She works as hard as ever on lectures, tutorials and supervisions. Given who she is, she expects no allowance for slack, but it is the case that her research project on postcolonial memory is slowly being supplanted by the memoir. Mercia reassures herself that the funded work is well ahead of target, that for once she ought to let go since the personal writing gets her through the pain; it won't be long before she is back on track. She must make allowances for herself—it is not so surprising that her habits are being amended. For instance, if academic life has left little time or inclination for contemporary fiction, a recent review has persuaded Mercia, titillated by the title, to order the prize-winning novel *Home*.

The book arrived at the same time as Jake's letter. News from home was always disturbing, making any kind of work impossible, thus she started reading the novel, partly to put off reading the letter and thinking about Jake, darling Jake, her no-longer-little brother. As it turns out, Mercia is consumed by the novel. All evening, she reads, until late that night, barely stopping to eat a hurried supper. In the morning, a glance in the mirror confirms that she looks awful, unwashed and haggard, much like the fabled writer she once would have liked to be, stumbling out of an attic, disheveled and blinking in the northern light.

Mercia may not be as good as the glorious sister in the novel, but the correspondences are there, including the ironic depiction of home. Strangely familiar, this story of siblings, brother and sister, that turns out also to be one of father and son. But theirs—Mercia and Jake's story—is from a different continent, a different hemisphere, a different kind of people, a kind so lacking in what is known as western gentility. Theirs is a harsh land that makes its own demands on civility. Their father too, a good man, even if he does not know how to show his love for an errant son. By the time she gets to the end of the novel she has doubts about her own memoir. Is hers not redundant for the telling?

Mercia, an English teacher, an academic, necessarily thinks of texts and their families, thus she will suffer with the anxiety of influence, but more importantly, she no longer feels like carrying on with her story. There is, as she has always suspected, in the face of fiction and its possibilities, no point in telling the true tale; besides, she can't vouch for the truth, since already there is more invention than memoir. For her story is also Jake's, and has she not always, or in some ways, avoided Jake's story, avoided being caught up between him and their father?

Jake's letter, still unopened, landed in her house as a caution against writing, against the presumption of knowing (it is as if she can hear his voice)—and from such a distance too. There is also the small matter of the research for which she has been awarded a sabbatical, and which will not brook delay whilst she messes about with memoir. She does not delete the morning's work as she promised herself; instead the file, Home, is saved and closed. Will she open it again? Mercia thinks not. An aberration, that's what it is, another ready-made response to being left. She ought to have known from the uncanny flow of words. For heaven's sake, she has after all no interest in this genre that floods the markets, or supermarkets, these days. All the same, she does not delete the file.

Now, whilst there is still the business of adjusting to being alone, unloved, Jake's please-come-home letter has arrived. He has never written before, never replied to her occasional, dutiful accounts of her life in Glasgow. There are neither recriminations nor a reminder of her rash promise at their father's funeral to return, just the brief note, a single page on which is hurriedly scrawled, without salutation: Come home Mercy. Then plaintively, You haven't been home for ages. There is a gap, as if time has passed and he has deliberated over the next line: The child (yes, that was how he referred to his son) needs you. Please come and get the child. You are all he has left. It is signed Jacques, which she has never called him.

Mercia knows of course about the boy, Nicky, who at the time of the funeral had been packed off to his granny. She thought it strange, but it was so much easier not to ask questions. Strange too that she has not been shown any photographs; she cannot remember how old Nicky is, has no idea what he looks like, does not understand how he could possibly need her, but then people seldom say what they mean. Mercia knows Jake's letter to be histrionic nonsense. Has he returned to drinking? If there really were a problem, an emergency, he would have called. Nevertheless, she may have to heed his request and go home, or rather, visit. Maybe that is the place where she might stop crying—at home, a place where a heart could heal.

The thought of the Cape as home brings an ambiguous shiver— the small town in Klein Namaqualand, Kliprand. Hardly more than a village. *How could anyone want to live there? Why would anyone stay there?* These are questions that Mercia too must ask, although in those parts the words live and stay are interchangeable. South Africans, having inherited the language from the Scots, speak of staying in a place when they mean living there. Which is to say that natives are not expected to move away from what is called home. Except, of course, in the case of the old apartheid policy for Africans, the natives who were given citizenship of new Homelands where they were to live. But they were required after all to work and therefore to stay in the white cities from which they had been ejected. *Come stay with me and be my slave . . .*

In Glasgow Mercia insists on the distinction between living and staying; she is only there temporarily; it cannot be her home.

She visits Kliprand often, but knows at the same time that to stay there would allow the soul to die rather than to live. Which is how Mercia and Jake had always thought of the place, although they would have balked at the word soul. The soul of black folk? Or rather, Jake corrected her on an earlier visit—colored folk like them who once adopted soul; nowadays it is better to come clean as colored, he laughed. Typically, he would not expand, could never allow himself to see a thought through, so she exclaimed provocatively, Mayibuye Africa!

Bu-ullshit, he said, turning bull into two syllables.

Nicholas, now dead for several months, had never made a distinction between living and staying. A son of the soil, he called himself, without irony, which was to say a good person. To stay put was virtuous; to stay there was to be alive. Like the great old thorn tree that he planted on his arrival at the gate of the dip-kraal, now rooted in the history of the place, he lived and naturally, necessarily, stayed.

Mercia thinks of her father as still being there. Like the thorn tree. Stricken with guilt, she had come for the five days it took to manage the funeral that Jake and his wife seemed incapable of doing.

I know, her father used to say at the end of each of her visits, I know in my heart that you'll come back home one day.

Yes, she agreed at first, as soon as this monstrous government is overthrown. After the end of apartheid she had nothing to say, would smile sheepishly at him.

Home to stay!—the opening words of the father in the novel, which strikes a chill in the fictional daughter's heart, as it does Mercia's. The chill is laced with guilt. Oh, if only she had spent some time with him before he died.

Bu-ullshit, Jake said, the old bastard was well past his sell-by date.

Ag, Jake, don't be so disrespectful, so unkind, she pleaded.

Respect! he snorted. I've never forgiven him for the beatings. And neither should you.

Was it grief that made Jake speak so cruelly? She was his sister, the one he loved, so why did he seem intent on hurting her? And why did Jake not want her to stay at his house? She saw his wife Sylvie only briefly at the funeral, had not seen the child at all. But Jake shook his head, stared vacantly.

Man, he said, you won't like our way of doing things. Just count yourself lucky that you don't stay here, in this mess.

Mercia assumed that he was speaking of the state of the country, of the disappointing aspects of the New South Africa. Perhaps you have unreasonable expectations, she said, given how much of the old South Africa is still in place. But Jake would not be drawn.

I'll be back soon, she said rashly. I'll come home for the summer, the winter I mean, so just you get yourselves ready.

There was something unspeakably forlorn about Jake. For all his callous talk about their father, he seemed more distressed than he would admit. Jake needed her, but then, Jake had always needed her, Mercia thought guiltily.

Whatever, he said.

So, fashionable expressions nowadays spread even to unlikely places like Kliprand, a place she thinks of as the bundus or whatever the contemporary word for such places might be. At least Jake did not say Bu-ullshit. Which she hated.

For Mercia there could be no return to the pays natal where the same old dabikwa trees lean to the west and ghanna bush turns gray and crumbles in midsummer. Jake too had gone to Cape Town for good, except that he succumbed to drink. Mercia wept as her father told of how he had become a drunken vagrant, found in the Cape Town docks sleeping rough, and racked with pneumonia. Nicholas had fitted the back of the bakkie with foam and an old traveling rug, and fetched Jake from the gutters of the city; he nursed him back to health in the room that the children once shared. Then Mercia wept on Craig's shoulder, stricken with guilt for not being there for him, her baby brother, abandoned to the city's cold wet winter. But their father said that Jacques had only himself to blame, that Mercia should not spill any tears over a good-for-nothing. As for the rug, he was sad that after all those years it had fallen apart, a thing to be thrown away. Their mother, Nettie, had bought it when the children were infants, and he did not like throwing Nettie's things out, but, he tutted, it was soiled after the journey. A disgrace.

Mercia has never minded Jake being Nettie's favorite. She struggles to summon a memory of their mother, but a flash of blue striped fabric is all she can muster. That, and yes, a cake for Jake's birthdays, dried fruit and the smell of clove and cinnamon and nutmeg rising from the oven. Is it an actual memory? her own? Or is the smell entwined with that in the novel she is reading, where the house is filled by the mother with fragrant food? Mercia recollects the message of that fragrance: *this house has a soul that loves us all, no matter what.* She shakes her head. Again, the soul! She ought to have known the memory to be false. It is just as well, if she can't distinguish between her own history and someone else's fiction, that she has abandoned the memoir.

With a sabbatical awarded for the autumn semester, Mercia cannot leave for the Cape right away. There are a number of administrative duties to fulfill over the summer, the re-sit examinations to manage, and her monograph has to be advanced in order to finish it by the end of the leave period. Much as she hates not going away over the summer, there is only just enough time to catch her breath. The memoir has been a foolish distraction.

In the past Mercia has rushed off to escape the disappointing weather. Now the gardens in Glasgow compensate for staying put. With the enduring summer light comes wave after wave of bold efflorescence, which anyone would prefer to drought-stricken Namaqualand. Mercia watches over the fading of glorious forget-me-not, the powdery fragrance of lilac, species after species of flowering rhododendron, and the trellises spangled like so many stars with clematis. She awaits the explosion of flame-red poppies, the roses that will stay in bloom until the autumn. That is when she ought to be away, in the month of October, when the sadness of retreating light strikes.

At home, in the Southern Hemisphere, with the sun well on its way to the equator it will be warm, at least during the day. How effortlessly the word comes: home, the place she has not lived in for more than twenty-six years. Hot, oppressive, and heavy with the memories of growing up under the eagle eye of the old man, Our Father, Old Who-art-in-heaven, as the seven-year-old Jake mocked irreverently, but whispered all the same. Home, no more than a word, its meaning hollowed out by the termites of time, a shell carrying only a dull ache for the substance of the past. But living in another country, in a crazy era, Mercia is not yet ready for its collapse.

How the Old Ones would have danced around the strange word, home, poured into it their yearning for a break from the mud and wattle and hide shelters of hunter-gatherers who followed their herds, who muttered under the breath their supplications to the moon, who relied on the seasons to assuage the restlessness of the soul by moving on. Even before the word, there would surely have been old women who sucked their gums in despair and dreamt of living as staying, dreamt of seeds taking root in the earth, growing into ripeness, even as a headman announced the decision to decamp. If nowadays ambition cannot accommodate the old notion of home, there has surely always been ambivalence, the impatience for something new, for moving on, across the world, whilst at the same time, at times, feeling the centripetal tug of the earth.

Always in the period before going home, Mercia finds her nose twitching to various smells: onions sizzling in a pan, a patch of dug earth, or infuriatingly, something she cannot identify that nevertheless transports her to the Cape. From which she chooses to infer that the world is much the same all over, that we necessarily rely on nostalgia, the trace that connects us to the past. If the novel that Mercia is immersed in speaks of the soul finding its own home if it ever has a home at all, she must add that in places like Kliprand, where the idea of home is overvalued, laden with sentimentality, the soul produces its own straitjacket. Then she swallows, once, twice, to relieve the lump in her throat.

When Mercia and Craig decided to buy a house together, she wrote to her father in carefully chosen words: I am throwing in my lot with a Scotsman, hitching up with a man called Craig McMillan.

Nicholas, who naturally read that as marriage, took what was for him the unusual step of telephoning. Were there any problems with this man, Craig? he finally asked. Does he have children? Is he divorced? And Mercia, having said no, prised out of him the problem, the question he could not quite bring himself to ask: Why has Craig not managed to get a woman of his own kind? What was wrong with him?

Mercia, not having the will to deal with such self-hatred, resorted to humor.

Nothing much wrong with Craig, she assured him, it's just that he has only one leg and one eye, and it so happens that Scottish women are mortally afraid of men who do not have thumbs.

Her father said he was sorry, but he would not manage the trip overseas to give her away. He hoped that Jake would do. Jake, he assured her, was quite respectable these days.

Mercia refrained from saying that she was not for the giving. Instead, she wrote, no, no need for Jake to come, that neither she nor Craig was keen on weddings, an ostentatious waste of money, leaving him to infer that it would be a simple registry office marriage. She dropped the flimsy blue aerogram hurriedly into the post box, suppressing guilt. She had not actually told a lie, had merely nudged him into believing that they were to marry. And really, there was nothing to be gained from hurting him with the truth—that she had no interest in marriage. The absence of a ring would be easily explained. She had never worn rings, chose not to draw attention to her ugly hands. As it turned out, Nicholas was still anxious.

It was good, he said hesitantly on her next visit home, that she had chosen a man from Europe, but he hoped that she would be careful, vigilant against anything shameful.

What on earth did he mean?

We-ell, he said, people say that European men, at least here in South Africa, are disrespectful, that they hate themselves for going with nonwhite women. He hesitated before adding, and that's why they beat their wives, for separating them from their families and their country. So Nicholas could only hope and pray . . .

Mercia laughed, relieved that she could set his mind at rest. Are you mad? Do I strike you as someone who could be beaten? No one, she assured him, would as much as try. When apartheid came to an end, and it wouldn't be long, Craig would come to meet them, and he could see for himself that she was not living with a brute. She felt his anxiety, and so said nothing about his use of the word nonwhite. She shudders to think how her father would have interpreted Craig's leaving. Would she have told him at all?

Jake, overdressed in a dark pinstripe suit and carrying a leather briefcase, laughed uproariously. Mercia could do with a good hiding, he said. I thought, Grootbaas, all those beatings when we were children were meant to prepare us for marriage. Now Mercia knows what to expect, and I'll know what my wife will feel when I beat the shit out of her.

It's no laughing matter, the old man said. I have set you an example. You do not as much as hurt a hair on the head of any woman, let alone a wife. When your mother and I—

Jake interrupted, holding up both palms. Oh please, not another sermon. Look, I promise to choose a wife like Mercia, one who can't be beaten.

Do you like my gear, Jake said mockingly, once their father had left. This nonsense, it's what Grootbaas rigged up for me, and you know what? I didn't have the nerve to say no. So here I am, Mr. Bigshit, I mean Mr. Bigshot, driving a Chevy in my suit and tie. I'm in the liquor business, the only secure business in South Africa, one that will never go under. Your people over there in Britain will pretend to boycott South African products, but you know what? My shares in liquor are doing just fine. So now, and he held out his wide lapels parodically, I'm a proper playboy, hey.

Then he looked her up and down, puzzled by her plain skirt and T-shirt, the scuffed flat shoes. Aren't you supposed to be some grand professor or something? So what's it with the clothes? Do you think you have to dress down for us? Are we not good enough for you? For a proper hairdo and makeup? We're not plaasjapies anymore. I'm a city playboy, don't you know.

Yes, I mean no, not at all, Mercia stumbled. I teach in a university, that's all, not a professor. At any rate, not yet. And you, playboy of the Western world, she sighed, for peering ahead, squinting through time, she saw a flash of axe being wielded at their father's head.

For some time Jake had addressed their father as Grootbaas, a name the old man found amusing. But Mercia knew that Jake simply could not bring himself to call him Father, saw that the child's fear and dislike of Nicholas had not dissipated with time. Surely that was childish, she said to Jake, surely you can see him as a product of his time?

Mercia was shocked by the bitterness of his reply. Let me be. You left home, you got away, so no need to bother your head with me. But don't expect me to stand in for you, to be the dutiful child.

On the sideboard there is a photograph of Jake clutching at his mother's skirts. A plump child, but in those days, in those parts, not wanting to look impoverished, it was known as healthy and strong. The mother is of another era. Her dress sports a bow at the throat, the skirt skims her ankles, and her hair is raked back severely into a bun. Good hair all the same. No hot iron, her husband would proudly offer apropos of nothing, has ever touched that head. If nowadays it is the look of a prude, it is worth remembering that then the severity signaled that she was a good woman. There is further, bucolic virtue in the hand that rests on the haft of a garden spade. There is nothing of the raciness one would expect to find in one called Antoinette.

Some who come across the photograph are surprised. Has Jake not claimed that his mother died in childbirth? That he was responsible for her death?

Nowadays, a disheveled Jake shrugs, Whatever, who gives a shit. And if the speaker is one of those smarty-pants Cape Town types, he may throw in, shockingly, Jou ma se poes, and cackle at the sharp intake of breath. That is Jake's new thing: being a foulmouthed, lowdown, drunken colored.

Sylvie is furious; she has been betrayed. It further infuriates her that he would never use such language in Mercia's presence. What use is it being married to a Murray who has sunk lower than the lowest farm laborer?

The poor Antoinette might as well have died in childbirth for all the trouble the boy had been. Fat, in spite of being breast-fed, and jolly as an infant, he was much given to laughter, a levity that turned out to be a precursor to lewdness. At the age of two and a half Jake discovered his penis, which he whipped out at every opportunity, both in public and private, causing his parents unspeakable shame and distress. For all the punishment, the child simply would not understand that he was doing wrong. Once he found the matted doughnut around which Nettie wrapped her hair into a perfect bun, and balancing it over his erect peetie stumbled giggling into the room where a meeting of deacons was being held. They took him to Dr. Groenewald, whose assurance that the child would grow out of it Nicholas thought to be mealy-mouthed. In the meantime, he recommended, circumcision was worth a try, advice that Nicholas scorned. God could not possibly approve of bits of the body being lopped off. He would rather rely on the solution of regular beatings.

On Sunday nights before supper their father held aloft the aapstert whilst he reiterated the sacred duty of chastising his own flesh and blood. That was what the God of Abraham and Isaac and Jacob commanded. Nicholas did not relish this task, but in addition to whipping them at the time of actual transgressions, he would beat both children for the secret sins accumulated through the week, for those that only God knew of. Mercia complained that she did not even have a peetie, which earned her an extra blow; they were not to speak of the organs.

Nettie thanked the Lord when Jake grew bored with his peetie. She suggested that they now could drop the Sunday thrashings, but Nicholas explained that that would be wrong, that it would encourage other secret sins. Jake, who retained no memory of the peetie days, did his best to justify the punishment, and with hearty laughter boasted of his misdemeanors. Thus his mother came to understand the necessity of the aapstert, even if she thought the instrument brutal. Would a stick not do, she asked, but Nicholas said no, that animal hide, used also by the police, was the material for correction, that they were the unfortunate parents of a miscreant.

Nettie worried about the boy's waywardness, and in the short week that it took for her to die, got Nicholas to promise that Jake would be shepherded through school and sent to university to study medicine, that he should start by teaching the boy Latin. Which Nicholas hoped to achieve by keeping up the regular beatings of both children.

Jake was eleven years old when he completed primary school, and took the aapstert to the cemetery behind the hill. He checked the graves, mounds of baked red earth studded with white stones, and the rough wooden crosses with names of the departed and dearly beloveds in crooked writing. There he found Antoinette's, away from the rest, where the veld was left to encroach. Jake pulled out his mother's cross, and alongside her grave, covered with soutslaai and vygies, used it to dig a long, slightly curved channel in which he laid out the aapstert. With his bare hands he scraped together the red earth to mark the curve of the grave.

The very name, aapstert, was proof of his father's folly. The whip was of course not the tail of an ape, who would have bared his teeth and hissed rather than part with his tail; rather, it was the cured hide of a common donkey's tail, a stupid obedient animal that bowed to its fate. Jake would not wait for the earth to settle. He collected white stones from the hill and arranged them to write the letters along the curved grave: DONKIESTERT.

He remembered just in time to replant Antoinette's wooden cross. The very next day an unseasonal rainstorm washed much of the mound away, but the leather switch lay snugly in its grave, under the mangled letters of dislodged stones.

That Sunday night Nicholas looked behind the door where the aapstert was kept, found it gone, and found Jake with arms folded, looking him squarely in the eyes. It's dead and buried, you'll never find it, he said calmly. Nicholas clenched his fists, shook his head, and proclaimed: Gods water oor Gods akker. Mindful perhaps of Nettie's misgivings, he asked no questions and never again mentioned the aapstert. Jake could have sworn that, for all the show of disappointment, Nicholas was relieved. But, if the Sunday-night ritual was stopped, Nicholas did not now hesitate to remove his belt and thrash the offending child within the proverbial inch of his life.

Not even a full day has Mercia been here in Kliprand, and already she would like to wash her hands of these people who are her own, would like to pack her bag right away and leave. But that is not possible. One does not walk away from family. Patience and kindness, that is what family lays claim to. Which may mean that one should not come to see them in the first place.

Mercy, that was what her father called her. You'll be a professional, an angel of mercy, called to minister to the sick and needy, he pronounced. Nice and smart, that nurse's uniform of starched whites and good brown walkers, perfect for an angel of mercy. Of course, being a clever girl, you'll be promoted to matron in no time. Which sounded fine until Mercia reached her teens and thought with distaste of a matron's headdress, clearly modeled on that of a nun.

Nonsense, Nicholas said, nursing was not only a good

profession, it was also a noble vocation. Mercia's argument that
a vocation could by definition not be imposed by another did not
sway him. What did was the confident assertion that she'd be a
doctor instead. Nicholas had expected Jake to be a doctor, that's
what he promised dear Nettie, but really, he had his doubts about
the reprobate boy. Anyway, so much better if there were two of
them. And if Mercia's Matric results showed her to be outstand-
ing in languages, she allowed herself to be bullied into registering for a science degree. After a BSc her father said, she could
transfer to medicine at the white university.

It was less than halfway through the year that a disheartened
Mercia gave up. Could she not start again the following year on
an arts degree of English and history? Nicholas tried once more
to sell the noble vocation of nursing, before giving in.

When Mercia gained her doctorate her father shook his head:
a doctor of literature who could not even cure a headache? He
hoped she would not go about calling herself doctor, making a
fool of herself. Doctoring books, he said wistfully, well, what
good could that do? He supposed if one day it brought a steady,
well-paid job . . .

It was shortly after her mother's death that Mercia announced
that she would no longer answer to the name of Mercy.

Jake complained. No man, Mercy man, it's too late now. How
would a person remember to call you by that mouthful of a name?
Anyway what's in a name? In that little add-on?

Everything, she said, and stuck to her guns until everyone
learned to say Mercia. An entirely new name was really what she
had had in mind: how much better something plain, like Mary or
Jane; she hated both Mercy and Mercia. But her father exploded,
an outrage it was to her mother's memory, so that she abandoned
the idea.

Now that she is an older woman, she ought not to care. That label after all supersedes a name, wipes out presence itself, as she has found even in her privileged position. An older woman is not only left, but left behind, which she supposes refers to reproduction, as if that is what every woman wants. Here, back home, it is clearer than ever that a child would have been a horrible mistake. Not that she has ever had any doubts. But then, once upon a time she was sure of Craig, sure enough not to marry—oh it does not bear thinking about.

And once, in bygone days, Mercia was a place, an English region, the name for border people, which she supposes has its own resonance for certain South Africans like them, or for that matter her own liminal self. Nicholas and Nettie would not have known these meanings, on that dry Namaqua plain would not have known of the lush Trent Valley, the land of the Mercians. No, more likely they were guided by the word mercy, guided by a cry that must have issued from every soul who set foot in that godforsaken place. But Mercia cannot take her cue from mercy, since there is for her no deity who will or will not, according to his caprice, dispense the stuff. Given the Christian fondness for abstract nouns, the virtues as names, she supposes that she has come off lightly after all. Imagine being called Charity, Prudence, Sobriety, or Virtue itself. Names for girls. Names that boys happily escape.

Mercia—she has always hated the name, and attached to Murray it sounds too foolishly alliterative, an aural joke, thus a good enough reason to marry and take a stranger's name. Which she now supposes she may well have done had there been children, but not having the stomach for reproduction, and with Craig's claim that he didn't care for children, it seemed too self-loathing to take another's name. Abbreviated to Mercy, the name puzzled the child, for whom words, if not names, had meanings.

What was the child to make of Mercy? That as an embodiment of mercy she, like a god, would be the one to dispense it? Or was she to inspire mercy in others, which gave her license to offend? Would she have wanted mercy from Craig? That too does not bear thinking about.

Here in Kliprand, trapped in this cramped house where Jake lies in a darkened room, it would seem that she must be the angel of mercy, though what quality of mercy she cannot imagine. All she knows is that it won't be easy, that its twice-blessed promise has to be taken with a pinch of salt. Rather, it will be a haphazard affair, like groping for an herb or spice in a dark cupboard, any herb or spice for flinging into a tasteless stew. Mercia does not see herself as being up to the task. No, it's ridiculous. Jake can't expect her to take the child.

The child seems about five years old, but how would Mercia know, having had so little to do with children? There is the full mouth and the brow of the Murrays to identify him as one of them, but he is very like his mother, more's the pity. It puzzles her, Jake's retreat to Kliprand. They have always talked about it as a place to leave behind, so why has he stayed and taken this Kliprand girl as wife? Mercia corrects herself; she must not be unkind or snobbish, must also try to see things from the mother's point of view. It is difficult though, given Sylvie's eagerness, the way she presents the child like a trophy, as if reproduction were a feat.

The child is uncomfortable. His eyes flit between his shoes and Mercia's face, but then, as if preparing himself for combat, he boldly returns her stare. Shame, his eyes sparkle; he is a little boy with an irrepressible brightness about him. The brightness tugs at her heart, or is she being unsettled by the word that has crept up on her? For it suggests to her that he is doomed, that he will pay for the sins of others. Mercia wishes that her father's horrible notion of sin would keep out of her consciousness. The boy is bright, new as a penny, but then one would imagine that all children are necessarily bright and new, that is, until they are scuffed or battered by parents. Who may not mean to, as the poet has it, but nowadays even that sounds optimistic.

For all his brave stare, there is something about the child, something that casts a shadow, a guardedness perhaps, and there is, if she is not mistaken, a faint trembling of his chin as if he is summoning the courage to speak. Like an old man he runs his hand across the tight black curls, then settles his shoulders in an extravagant gesture of nonchalance.

Nicky, this is your auntie Mercy. Give Auntie Mercy a kiss, his mother commands. Mercia winces at the woman's loud voice.

No, he says. Upon which his mother slaps him decisively about the legs; she will not have any rudeness from him. The child does not flinch. He steps forward and formally holds out his hand for Mercia to shake, so that his barely proffered cheek discourages kissing. The gesture relieves for her the shock of the smack. Should she say something? Let the woman know that it is despicable to beat children? But then, what difference would it make; the mother—for that is how she thinks of Sylvie, formally, in terms of the biological relationship—would pay no attention, would think of Mercia with her fancy foreign ideas as meddling. Oh yes, Mercia all but hears her say, there overseas where people still are decent, children may know how to behave and so, of course, do not need the belt. But here, in this godforsaken place, nothing other than a smack will keep a child on the straight and narrow, prevent him from diving straight into indecency and drunkenness. Things have really gone wild in this New South Africa. A person can't allow any rudeness at all; give them a pinkie and they grab the entire hand; and besides, what did Mercy know about being a parent?

The trick is not to give the woman too many opportunities to air her views. But the smack, the affront, smarts in Mercia's own flesh, so that she drops to her haunches and pats the boy about the legs where she imagines the imprint of his mother's hand lingers under the synthetic fabric, a gesture that the mother understands only too well.

It is I, his mother, Sylvie says, only I, who have to see to him, make sure he behaves, right from when he was only so small, and her flattened palm skims the imaginary head of a smaller child. This Nicholas boy is now stubborn, even as a baby he always wanted his own way. Takes after you people, the Murrays, so I have to make sure from the start that he does as he's told. And my word, you just have to beat him before he'd listen, enough to break any mother's heart. That brother of yours does nothing, doesn't care, leaves us to find our own way, just as long as he has his bottle. She giggles. Like a baby really, before her face straightens and resumes: that is why the child must now look to you, the auntie, for help, for direction to his life. As I said to Nicky, just because your father is useless doesn't mean you don't have family to keep an eye on you. Auntie Mercy—you are all he has left.

Sylvie knows that this is what Jake calls whining, but she can't stop herself from piling grievance upon grievance, from uttering the thoughts that nibble day and night with no hope of abatement. If it were not for her part-time job at the butcher's shop, what would they eat? And the worry about the child—whether his father, now apparently confined to bed, can care for him even for the few hours that she's at work. Then there are the years to come, clothing, schooling and all the gedoente of growing up. God alone knows what they'll do, she and the child, what will happen to Jake, who is surely drinking himself into an early grave. If she could keep Nicky on the straight and narrow he could be a doctor, a real doctor, she adds pointedly.

Mercia tries not to look at the woman's arms, the emphatic hands held up in a gesture of helplessness. She imagines those elbows poking out of a tub of minced meat, as Sylvie kneads, her arms coated in grayish grease, whilst an even, steady sausage of

speech issues from the girl's mouth. She is embarrassed, critical of her own snobbery, but really there is no chance of cor-
recting herself while the girl shouts as if she were in another
room.

Mercia recalls the wording of Jake's brief letter: You are all he
has left, which the mother echoes. There is no telling whether he
had consulted with Sylvie, but now it does seem as if Sylvie too
wants to wash her hands of the child. What on earth is Mercia to
make of these people who belong to her? She cannot suppress her
disgust at the fecklessness, the shamefulness of having a child
whom you then hand over to someone else.

Still on her haunches, she says to the boy, quietly, Would you
like to take me for a walk, show me the veld? She points ahead
to the kloof that plunges into the foot of a hill. Let's go, you can
be my guide, she says in her halting Afrikaans. How odd that
Jake's child should speak Afrikaans. What it surely shows is that
Jake does not speak to him at all. How has her kind, loquacious
brother come to be such an irresponsible father?

The mother intervenes. Answer your auntie. I don't think he
can hear your whispering, she says. The shadow of a smile hovers
on Sylvie's face; it is clear that she knows exactly why Mercia has
lowered her voice. The girl may be vulgar but she is certainly not
stupid.

But I don't know the way, I don't know what's there, I've never
been to the veld, Nicky says earnestly, and looking at his feet, I'm
not allowed to spoil my good clothes.

In perma-pressed long trousers and a long-sleeved shirt buttoned to the throat, the child is overdressed, a parody of a businessman. He wears Mr. Price's cut-priced shiny black school
shoes and socks. Not surprisingly, he is damp with sweat.

Oh, Mercia says airily, we'll make sure your clothes don't get messed up; between us we'll manage. Sometimes you may think you don't know the way, but actually once you set out find that you can follow your nose, find that you know it quite well.

Imagine, the child not knowing his own patch! Surely a child's physical world should not be so circumscribed, especially here where you can see for miles across the veld. She smiles at Sylvie. We won't be long, she says hurriedly, before the woman finds in the arcane field of motherhood a reason to object.

She takes Nicky's hand. The little warm hand in her own flutters like a bird before he withdraws it. As soon as they are out of earshot language tumbles helter-skelter out of his mouth. It's a very long journey but he'll have no difficulty getting to the top of the hill; in fact, the goats usually go to the left of the clump of castor oil bushes so there's sure to be a path, but he wonders if Auntie Missy will make it. He wonders about the kloof. Is it the case that a kloof comes like a thunderbolt from the top, splitting open the hill and mangling its foot, or is it rather that the kloof starts in the hill, slowly as a trickling baby stream, before it grows and claws out the earth? Mercia explains about erosion brought by the rare rain—as a child of the hill the kloof nevertheless mangles the parent's foot. And they laugh.

What does Auntie Missy think they'll find in the kloof? He's heard there are caves, so would there be giant goggas, or snakes? The penny-bright eyes widen, his arms stretched out theatrically in measurement of a snake, and his mouth falls open at the terrible thought.

Well, she says, it's only just October so there may be a few sand snakes about but they're not poisonous; we'll just keep out of their way. More likely that a troll has made his home in the kloof, but Nicky hasn't heard of a troll, doesn't know the story of the Billy Goats Gruff. She adapts it, turns the bridge and the green meadow into a cave where the goats want to shelter from fierce sunlight. If only she had brought him some books. It turns out that Nicky knows no fairy tales at all, has neither been told nor read stories. His mother has told him a couple of things about Uilspieël, but stories about a funny man doing stupid things do not please him. He hasn't got to know any fairies because he's been trapped indoors, Nicky explains. There was heavy rain a little while ago and he was not allowed out for days. Look, he shows her the swirls of washed sand, traces of small winter streams that feed into the kloof. They stoop over the striations, the tender ridges of sand, and walk on the shrub in order not to spoil the memory of water.

Mercia explains that most likely there'd be no more rain, that seasons come and go as the earth spins around the sun, that now it is spring in the Southern Hemisphere. Miraculously a verse from her childhood returns, in pristine Afrikaans, and he recites after her: Dit is die maand Oktober, / die mooiste, mooiste maand! / Dan is die dag so helder, / so groen is elke aand, / So blou en sonder wolke / die hemel heerlik bo, / So blomtuin-vol van kleure / die asvaal ou Karoo.

The child declaims like a preacher, then once he has mastered the verse he stops at the fourth line, tickled by the poet's claim that the nights are green. So wit is elke aand, he improvises, and laughs and laughs. Might as well call it white. He knows lots more colors—red, yellow, black—but purple would be best: yes, and starting again he folds in the color: so pers is elke aand. Now it is his poem, he says, and looks up at Mercia for her agreement.

When Mercy loses her footing on a ridge, he tugs at her arm. Just as well he is there to rescue her; he doesn't suppose that she does much exploring of the veld overseas.

There is something of an overhang ahead, barely a cave, but the child is enchanted. It is a ready-made house, look, a roof that will never leak, and is also shaded against the sun. He darts ahead of her, scooping up a handful of freshly dried goat droppings, nice and round and light as a feather. These goats, having killed the troll, have a good place to hide. Now he knows to follow the goats; they know a thing or two, and he fills a trouser pocket with the pellets. Then he whoops with excitement. The cave is deeper than it seemed, and ahead, in the farthest recess, is a clump of flowers, their starry white heads burning in the dark.

Chincherinchee, Mercia pronounces carefully, and explains how the rare rainwater coming down the hill—see, see the crack at the back of the cave—has found a basin in which to rest, how the roof delays evaporation so that the bulbs can swell and sprout. The child chuckles with delight at the plants, leafless, with pure, starlike flowers.

Yes, it is wonderful, incredible, she agrees, that is why the Greeks called it bird's milk. Ornithogalum, she sounds the word, syllable by syllable. Mercia says that she likes to think of their South African name, tjienkerientjee, of which the English name is a transliteration, as a Khoe word for stars, but she doesn't know. It is of course a lily, like kalkoentjies. Has his father shown him kalkoentjies in the veld? she asks. The child's face clouds over, the fleshy mound of his chin twitches.

My daddy, he says hesitantly, is sleeping; he's too tired to go to the veld.

Or that is what she thinks he says, since Afrikaans does not have the progressive to distinguish sleeps from is sleeping. Nicky adds, My daddy can get lots of turkeys from the shop. Big ones with tails that make so, and with outstretched arms he struts, drawing arcs above his head.

She laughs. No, not the bird, kalkoen. Kalkoentjie is also the name of a red lily you find in the veld. In spring.

• • •

Jake would have been about seven years old when he came back from minding the goats with an armful of flaming flowers. Breathless, he had run all the way to present the treasure to Mummy. They were hiding, he said, in the shade of a cliff; he had never seen anything as wonderful in the dead old veld. There were of course the vygies with their little pink or yellow daisies dotted here and there across the gray bush, brazenly staring at the sun, but this—Nettie called them kalkoentjies—was a flower plant all by itself. A slender green stem grew straight out of the earth without proper leaves, he explained, sprouting bracts from which blood-red petals like little tongues leaned out, and look, the lower bracts had not yet opened up, their blood-tipped fists barely poking out from the green sheath.

There was no vase in their house; instead, their mother used a preserving jar so that the stems showed through the thick glass. Bent, but fresh and bright green. Jake was a clever boy, she said, to have found that treasure of kalkoentjies. She took one out of the water, held it up once again to admire the form. Elegant, she said, that's what it is, and how heavenly it smells!

The image is indelible: Nettie bent over the flower in the dappled light, and the little Jake looking up adoringly to say after her: Elegant, that's what it is.

Why are they called kalkoentjies? Mercia asked. It doesn't sound elegant at all, and they look nothing like turkeys.

Nettie didn't know. Ask no questions, hear no lies, but she carried on smiling, twirling the flower between her fingers. At the age of eleven Mercia had heard plenty of lies without asking any questions at all, but it was best to protect her mother from that.

When Nicholas came home he looked at the kalkoentjies sternly, as if the flowers had misbehaved. They are good, sweet-smelling flowers, he acknowledged, but they will die in this jar of brack water long before God has meant them to die. Jake started saying that there were bracts still unopened, that the flowers . . . but the words dried up under their father's fierce eyes as he reached for the aapstert behind the door, so that the children whimpered with fear. The goats, he hissed, your duty was to the goats, and you've let them down, just left them who knows where. You've shown yourself to be as unreliable as any Kliprand hotnot. A failure. I'll have no failures in this family.

No, Mercia screamed, please, don't punish Jake. I'll take the hiding. Which she got anyway for trying to interfere, but that could not prevent the seven lashes that God had ordained for Jake. Their mother stood with her back against the wall, arms folded, tall and expressionless. She could not possibly have approved, so why had she said nothing? Jake was after all her favorite, as anyone could see.

The next day Mercia found Jake holding the bunch of dripping kalkoentjies by their stems, ready to crush them underfoot. She snatched at the flowers, but Jake smashed the jar all the same. Later he claimed it was an accident, that he had run into the room, and taking off his hat had swiped the jar that must have been on the edge of the cupboard. Then he fetched the aapstert from its hook behind the door, but their father thundered that he was to put it back, that only God decided on chastisement. Their father heaved with rage, which surely showed a rift between him and God.

Nicky is lying on his belly, sniffing at the chincherinchees, a spot of pollen yellow on his brown nose. He says it has a quiet smell, nice and fresh. How did the bulbs get there in the first place, how

did they know to hide here? Mercy shrugs her shoulders. Then
it must be God, the child says, when things can't be known it's
because of God.

Or perhaps the troll, she laughs. Once you learn to read, you'll
see that things you don't know can be looked up in a book.

Ah, he says triumphantly, but Mamma says God also made all
the books. Will God mind if they pick the flowers?

Her heart breaks for the repetition, the foreboding, and breaks
again as he says, I could take it back for Mamma. Something
screams in her head as she says quietly, There are two ways of
thinking about it. On the one hand: how beautiful these white
flowers would look at home in a vase, how your mamma would
love such a present; on the other hand, they'll die so much sooner
before they were meant to and, besides, any other children who
come to explore here won't be able to see them.

So what shall we do? the child asks.

That is for you to decide, she says to the beat of a sledgeham-
mer in her head and the roar of blood in her chest. It is not in her
power to ward off disaster.

I could pick just one to show Mamma, and when it's in a glass
at home I'll try to remember the whole big clump of flowers, and
Nicky bowls his arms for holding a huge imaginary bunch.

But as he squats by the clump of chincherinchees, wrinkling
his nose in search of the delicate fragrance, looking intently, he
says that he wouldn't forget. There is a long spike with a head
carrying lots of little starry flowers, each with a central sac of
yellow pollen, all bunched together, a basket of petals. A green
spike so, so long, and he holds his hands an exaggerated twelve
inches apart. Yes, he could easily remember that and he could tell
his mamma, explain the chincherinchees to her; she is good at
seeing things he talks about, although the smell would be hard;
he doesn't suppose she'd get the smell at all. He, Nicky, would

remember it, even once he got home, but carrying it over to her exactly, that he couldn't be sure of, that he would just have to try. He digs into his pocket for a handful of goat droppings. These drolletjies, he explains, would help the plants to keep healthy. He is not so very keen that other children should find this cave, but if they do at least the chincherinchees—he says each syllable carefully—would be looking their best, and the children wouldn't dare to pick them.

Does Auntie Mercy know that drolletjies make things grow better? he asks, sprinkling a handful at the base of the clump of flowers. He would keep a few in his pocket to help him remember.

In her own pocket Mercia finds a paper tissue, not entirely clean, which she uses to wipe a smudge from his face and to dust down his shirt and trousers. It is not possible to remove the stain of earth on which he has lain. Then she remembers, unsolicited, the official name: *Gladiolus alatus iridaceae;* she had looked it up many years later. Why is it this name rather than the homely Afrikaans, kalkoentjie, that makes the eyes prick? Does Mercia know that what threatens are tears of self-pity, that she is touched by her own difference, her distance from home? It is the thought of the child by her side that stanches the tears. This is no time for sentiment, no place for crying, she admonishes herself, and so she launches into a description of giant gladioli you could buy at florists' in town. Is that, she wonders, why Sylvie prattles? Does the heart command speech in order to clear a path for the child? This place, home, is a place for doing and thinking at an angle, a place where speech, triumphing over genteel silence, has many different functions.

Back home, Sylvie dusts roughly at the boy's trousers. Ag, liewe Here, look how he's got himself in a mess, she complains, but at least he's safe, and she ruffles his hair, as if indeed the child has been taken on a dangerous outing.

Mam-ma, he squeals, squirming out of her grip, I saw the magic flowers in the troll's cave. Like white stars in the dark.

Oh yes, Sylvie says, you found tjienkerientjees. Why didn't you pick some for Mamma? They last very, very long in water.

❦

In spite of Mercia's explanation about seasons and her reassurances to the child the previous day, it rains. And that in October, the lovely, loveliest month.

Sylvie laughs; she is a sugar lump; she dissolves in the rain. If it weren't for the important job of making boerewors today, she'd wait until the rain stops. Mercia must now know that that is her job. Hers is the best boerewors in Namaqualand, a recipe she worked on for months until it was just right, an improvement on old Lodewyk's slapdash mixture. In that case, Mercia says, she'll drive Sylvie to Lodewyk's butchery, prevent her from dissolving, and the girl crows with laughter, but then she bundles the child on her lap in the front seat, which Mercia will not have, so that the mood changes. Sylvie shakes her head, Ai Yissus! she complains, such fussing, as she straps Nicky into the backseat.

At the stoplight Mercia points out to the child the wayward behavior of water on the windscreen. There are steady rivulets trickling down the glass, then for no apparent reason they stop in their tracks, momentarily, before a radical change of direction. The boy is mesmerized. He strains forward in his seat. Look, look how it turns on its heels, he shouts, as a rivulet skids horizontally across, refusing to roll down in an orderly, or rather, expected manner. The chaotic flow of water on the windscreen keeps them entertained, so that she does not have to speak to Sylvie.

Nicky says that Auntie Mercy has brought this good, cool weather. He loves rain, and one day he'll have a car so that he can watch at close range the water tumbling about on the glass, changing its mind. But his mother says that changing your mind is not something to be admired. You've got to stick with things. There's no other way. Make your bed and lie in it.

So why, Mercia wonders, is Sylvie prepared to give the child away? But that, she revises, may not be a fair question. The poor have always had to gird their loins and harden their hearts, packing off their children to be raised by grandparents. Or handing them over to more prosperous family members in the hope of better lives for their offspring. It was not so long ago that the barbaric Homelands policy for those less privileged than coloreds was justified by the belief that black people do not care for their children in the usual ways. Just look at how they pass them round! Wages from the cities easily compensate for leaving behind children in the desolate Bantustans! Distancing herself from the cant, Mercia still cannot help thinking that Sylvie ought not to part from her child.

Mercia imagines Nicky in their apartment in the West End of Glasgow. Or rather, her apartment. There is Craig's study, left untouched, next to the living room. South-facing and bright, and a good size, the best room, of course, for Craig the poet. But it is unreasonable to be bitter; it was after all her idea, for what better use could have been made of that room?

Now she perches the child on that desk, a child looking up in wonder at the high old ceilings with intricate cornices, the ornate ceiling rose from which hangs a tasteful glass globe of diffused yellow light. She brushes out the image. Whatever is she thinking of? With her fastidiousness and need for silence, how could she have a child in her house? A boy somersaulting over her leather sofas? For there is no question of confining a child to one room, she imagines. Not like a man who keeps put, bent over a computer, his desk faced out toward the window.

Craig took only his books and office chair. Even his favorite Howard Hodgkin print from a recent exhibition is still on the wall above the mantelpiece. A clean break, with nothing to remind him of a life spent with her. Mercia swept in a single movement, and without looking, the girlish paraphernalia from the mantelpiece into the bin, wondering why he had not done that himself. Did he imagine that she would keep it intact? The desk she has left, in the same place, against the window, with the stain of overlapping circles on the right where Mercia, having slipped in quietly, would leave a mug of coffee. Often, as she withdrew her hand, Craig would take hold of her wrist, squeeze absently, before she tiptoed out.

What Mercia ought to do is to turn it into another, cozier living room, have the chimney swept, shift the television into the study, console herself with a fine Ziegler rug. But who needs a second sitting room? Perhaps the apartment is too large for one person. There certainly is room for a child who could transform Craig's study himself with gaudy, boyish things, who could scrub out the coffee stains, but she supposes a child should choose a room. Together they could go about the apartment, rearrange the entire place, marking out their separate spaces.

Mercia tries to say it out loud, in several formulations: I will take Nicky. Nicky can come and live with me. I will look after Nicky. But this one stops her. How? How will she look after Nicky? The business of raising a child may be no more than commonsensical; still, she flinches at the thought. No, she concludes, it is too much to ask of her. They cannot expect her to make a sacrifice like that. It is one thing having a tolerable or even an enjoyable outing with a child, but quite another to have him for keeps. Of course, she would support the child financially, put him through school and university, but that is as far as she could go, besides, a child should be at home with his mother. That is what home is for. For children, who have no choice in the matter.

That evening Sylvie announces that they will have to move to one of the government's RDP houses. Jake has not been paying the mortgage and has ignored the bank's warnings of repossession. Sylvie's tone is bitter. Jake has no right to do this. The house is not just his to knock down as he pleases; the deposit from Pa, as she now refers to Meester, has also been given to her, Sylvie, security for her and the child, that is what Pa said in her very presence. The pittance they'll get from the bank will slide straight down Jake's throat. It's a disgrace. Whatever will people think of them coming down in the world like this?

There is a colony of RDP houses on the horizon stretching eastward from the town's rubbish dump as far as the eye can see. Only the Gifberge rise beyond it. What amazes Mercia about RDP housing, or rather about the architects of these dwellings, is that in a country where land is plentiful, houses are virtually butted against each other with barely any space between the boundary fences. There is no question of a small patch where people could grow vegetables, a few mealies and pumpkins to keep the wolf from the door. How strange that the architects of these townships, living as they no doubt do in comfortable houses lost in large gardens, and well out of sight of their neighbors, should imagine that the poor want to huddle together in cramped conditions, that they do not want to grow vegetables, let alone flowers.

Now you must know, Sylvie says, these houses are already falling apart. But what can you expect? The state of the country, with nothing working! The blacks now wanting to kill all the coloreds, even swarming into Kliprand, into the RDP houses. Who knows what will happen to them in such a place?

Precisely, Mercia retorts, if you don't know what will happen there, there's no basis for racist assumptions. And people can't swarm into their own country; they belong here. Namaqualand can also be their home, she hears herself saying.

The girl laughs mockingly. Ooh, you Murrays have such bakgat ideas. Jake also says she should stop talking like a white person, but true-as-God she, Sylvie, knows of a woman who's been raped even though the family's keeping quiet, and there was a murder reported only a few months ago. Imagine, a murder in Kliprand!

It is Mercia's cold stare and exaggerated sigh that make her return to their housing plight. If only Jake would pay the bond, but she supposes now that he has given up, now that he has made himself ill, he can't. Her voice creaks with self-pity.

Mercia knows that she is required to come to the rescue, and that after all is not as tall an order as taking the child. There is the money from their father's house, she says, she could do without her share. Jake can have it all to pay off his mortgage; he should have told her. There really is no need to live in RDP housing.

But you don't understand, Sylvie says. She smiles, evidently pleased with herself as she explains. Jake doesn't want your father's money. He *wants* to live in an RDP house; he wants all of us to live there; he wants to punish all three of us.

Mercia stares at her coldly. She cannot speak with this woman, does not want to hear her analysis. She says, I see, and goes to her room, or rather Nicky's room, which he has had to give up for her. In that room there are no books. The walls are bare except for a hideous picture on the wall connoting cutesiness—a small blond boy holding his peetie to aim an arc of pee into a flowery chamber pot. It is in an ornate plastic frame of white and gold. What does Nicky make of it? Could it be that he sees himself in the image?

Mercia switches on her computer and stares dolefully at the screen. She wishes herself far away from this place called home. Never again will she complain about the pressures of academic life, the nightmare of trying to write. Being with family is far more stressful. She thinks of the parallel construction, being with child, and winces.

Earlier this year, after Nicholas's funeral, when she spoke about working on her laptop, Jake asked, Do you call it work, the stuff you do? And a laughing Sylvie interjected, You should come to the butchery on a Saturday morning to see real work.

I'll do that, Mercia said stiffly, I'm happy to find out about the different ways of working. Mine may not be the chopping up of carcasses, but it's work all the same. Why, she wondered, has Jake taken to championing the working person? Is that what has driven him to marrying the girl?

So are you trying to make a *name* for yourself? Jake asked.

Ah, she mocked, I've been given a crap name so perhaps that is what I'm trying to do, blazon my name across the world so that its crappiness might efface itself. Then she said soberly, We try to think things through, think about texts and their language and interpret the world, nothing to do with making names for ourselves, and besides it's such a small world, so many people working in my field—yes, working, she repeated—that it hardly signifies. Actually, nobody reads this stuff. Perhaps a handful of students, if you're lucky.

Jake threw his head back and laughed heartily, healthily for a man who seemed to be shivering, a man she thought who may well have returned to excessive drinking.

Then why not rather write a book for real people about real people? he asked.

You mean a book about people like you? It's been done, she said curtly, done to death.

Ag don't be cross, Mercy man, he said, and handed her a large brandy.

Why did she not question his drinking?

Mercia could not be sure that it hadn't been ushered in as long ago as the millennium itself—the screaming of women in extremis. Was it her new single condition that alerted her to it? Only days after Craig left, in a hotel in Paris, she lay awake, wondering when such requirements for women might have been established.

Fortuitously, there was the conference to keep her occupied shortly after Craig's announcement. Surely you'll cancel, Smithy said, no one would expect you to honor that commitment. But Mercia was determined, glad that there was a paper to revise and travel to manage; she even looked forward to questions after her presentation, something she had always found terrifying. It will keep me on my toes, she said; it will make a change from crying.

Determined also to focus on other, less familiar areas, Mercia agreed to chair another panel and so keep at bay Craig's words that otherwise would mill about her head like midges. But who could have anticipated the sound of women screaming? As she arrived in the late afternoon and threw open the hotel window for air, the small courtyard trilled with a mewling that bounced promiscuously from wall to wall, echoed and amplified gleefully until the final shriek. At night, the sound came from the rooms on either side, the screaming of women. Mercia was not mistaken. Sound had, of course, always leaked from hotel rooms, but it surely had been muted, discreet, as people did not wish to be heard. But this, for her, was a new phenomenon where the female of the species announced her unbridled pleasure. How long had it been going on? It was not as if over the months, the years, she had noted an increase in volume; no, this seemed new, and ubiquitous, the world of couples and congress having taken over. And not having known about it, was that too a mark of her failing relationship?

Two weeks later, as she escaped from the emptiness of the apartment to Berlin, her expectations of screaming women were soundly met. Mercia imagined that the international magazines, the Dutch, German, French and British *Elle* or *Cosmopolitan*, or whatever they were called, had been pounding out advice for the twenty-first-century woman: the no-holds-barred shrieks of fulfillment to replace the old angst-ridden Munchian woman, she of the silent scream. Was management doling out prize-winning badges at the breakfast tables? Smithy, who had been prevented from coming along by her younger child's whooping cough, laughed at her account. Och, you're a prude, she said, let people be.

Hotels then were for a while at least to be avoided. They were not places in which to learn to be alone, in which to stop crying.

Craig had found someone else, he said, after the throat clearing and required preamble of his respect and devotion to her, Mercia, and he lowered his eyes to scrape together with the edge of his hand bread crumbs on the breakfast table.

Found someone else! Why was that thought to be ameliorative? What prompted the search? she asked. How long had he been looking? Her questions were met with silence. Craig herded the crumbs together into a neat pile. It had not been easy for him; he had suffered beyond measure, but he had come to a final decision: he would leave, and do so that very day. There was nothing to discuss, nothing to be gained from painfully raking over their relationship.

In the study Craig's books were already all packed up in boxes. Mercia, awash with tears, swallowed repeatedly to find her voice. She said, Yes, okay, of course, she understood, but then could not stop the bile from entering her words. Someone younger, more attractive, someone less preoccupied with her work, with a job that allows for leisure time; indeed—yes, she said that word, indeed—someone with an eager womb? She did not know where that had come from. Craig started, looked up in alarm. Not a young, glamorous, size-ten blonde by any chance? Mercia continued. She hoped that that would be received as self-parody. In the last couple of years she had gathered a few inches around the waist. As had Craig.

Craig shook his head sadly, with disbelief, as if he had expected better of her. As if she had not expected better of herself! Only days later she could have added: and someone who screams. Smithy reported that the woman was not so young after all, looked about forty. But that was no guarantee against screaming. Was it not these days incumbent upon the aging woman to perform youth regardless? Besides, forty was young. A decade or so at that stage made all the difference.

If only Mercia had not referred to the woman's hair, for according to Smithy, who had walked into them at the Film Theatre, she was in fact blond or blond-streaked like the majority of women in Glasgow nowadays were. Oh, it made Mercia sick, her own delicate tiptoeing around markers of race, required to prevent others from thinking her sensitive about color. She had no such difficulty, thought that if there were a problem, it belonged to her beholder. No doubt a matter of multiple mirrors. Craig would have been the one person to know that she was comfortable in her skin. But that Craig has vanished, has left behind only the question of whether she had invented him.

· · ·

Mercia lies awake in her brother's house. On the far wall, in a chaste single bed, under easi-care sheets, she listens to Sylvie's screaming. It is less embarrassing than puzzling. The girl is hardly a reader of *Elle*, but then the style columns in the age of globalization probably in no time at all filter such matters through to villages via *Sarie*. Sturdy Sylvie, not yet plump, with her strong legs and high Namaqua behind, is still youthful. How much longer must she suffer the attentions of a drunk, dysfunctional husband? There will be no escape for a girl of her kind, Mercia muses. She should try to muster sympathy for Sylvie. She does not wonder why she thinks of Sylvie as a girl.

Mercia has much to be thankful for. She knows that she will come to terms with being alone, which is not to say that she does not miss the Craig she knew, that she is not still engulfed by sadness. But she has tried to make the most of post-Craig life by immersing herself in work. How Craig would have laughed at that. Not possible, he would have said, for her to be more immersed in work. Did he resent that? Let others call it complacent, but nowadays she counts her blessings, names them one by one: a research grant and sabbatical; conferences at which to present papers; an invitation to Yale; the monograph on postcolonial memory to finish; and almost certainly a professorship the following year. The book will surely bring further invitations from prestigious institutions abroad, travel to new cities, new countries—even if it does mean hotel rooms in which postmodern women scream.

But how do the poor manage? Must Sylvie put up forever with the attentions of a husband who seems to not like her anymore, if ever he did, and who in his few waking hours shouts abuse at her? What a relief for her if Jake were to find someone else. But there is no knowing what Sylvie's screaming announces. Mercia shudders at the possibility of the girl being grateful for Jake's drunken attention. She would like to take her firmly by the shoulders and say loud and clear: it's over; save yourself, go away and leave him to his drink. But where would she go? Where do people like Sylvie go? Is it in order to leave that she has to give up the child?

Mercia's Afrikaans is rusty; her ability to make small talk rudimentary; and small talk would surely have to precede such big talk. It is of course not only a matter of language. Everything in her dealings with Sylvie is uncomfortable, creaking with embarrassment. A problem of class, Craig had proffered after her last visit, without the benefit of having met the woman, but what did he, a Brit, who had visited the country only once, know about the complexities of rural colored life?

It is midnight. Mercia props herself up in the sagging bed and kicks off the hideous nylon cover. Since her arrival in Kliprand she has been plagued by menopausal hot flashes. But there are drugs, she consoles herself, and there will be freedom from the monthly discomfort. She fans herself with a newspaper. Burying her head to weep into the easi-care pillowcase is not an option; instead, she must press on. Mercia reaches for her laptop. Too agitated to carry on where she has left off, she could at least revise the last chapter.

❀

When Mercia arrived in her hired car that afternoon, Jake was in bed. Sylvie brought the message that he was unable to rise, that he would see Mercia the next day. Mercia said, Nonsense, she had come all that way, and with a brief knock on his door, barged in to his bedside.

Jake made as if to sit up, but fell back against the pillow. Mercia all but choked with nausea at the stale air, but so shocked was she by his sunken eyes, his skin a sickly yellow-brown with lack of sunlight, that she laid a hand on his head, pressed his bare shoulder. What had happened to him? There had been no mention of illness.

Jake, you didn't say you were ill! she exclaimed in alarm.

He laughed weakly, pulling up the covers. Yissus, Mercy, so you got here. Welcome to Rainbowland. Then he pulled the sheet over his head, and turning his back, muttered, Yissus, my head. I can't. Got to lie down, I'll catch you later. And tell that bitch to keep out.

Appalled by his language, she backed out of the room without a word.

So what's the matter with him, Mercia asked Sylvie, what does the doctor say? Why didn't you say anything about his illness when I called?

Sylvie looked at her intently, as if to ascertain what she knew, so that Mercia panicked. Is it AIDS? Is that why you won't say?

The girl laughed. That's what they think overseas isn't it, that everyone's got AIDS in South Africa. No, with Jake it's just the drink. Nothing wrong with him.

Mercia squirmed with embarrassment. She would have to leave further questions until later.

Having prepared dinner, Sylvie refused to rouse Jake. He'll just swear at me. Effing and blinding, that's all he has to say. He doesn't eat, that's why he can't get better.

They ate in awkward silence the festive food that Sylvie heaped onto their plates: a mound of braised mutton, yellow rice with raisins, potatoes and sweet pumpkin. Tomorrow, Sylvie said, I'll make sousboontjies. Jake is now very fond of the beans. Perhaps that will bring back his appetite.

The child, who sat in an armchair with his food on his lap, piped up, I also like sousboontjies. I don't eat pumpkin.

Wouldn't you like to come and sit with us at the table? Mercia said, but his mother replied that he wasn't one for sitting up, that slouching was his thing, and as for pumpkin, there was no way of getting him to eat it. See how stubborn Nicky is, he's his father's child all right, no question of that, and she shook first tomato sauce, then chutney over her meat.

Mercia stared at the child, who looked so like his father and his grandmother Nettie. Did Jake have nothing to do with the raising of his child? And how was Mercia to eat all that over-salted, sweetened stodge? Would she have to eat such heavy dinners every day? What would she do in this strange house? How was she to speak to the girl? What could she possibly say? She said, Ah, I remember Mrs. Ball's chutney, that's what we used to have, and I still miss it.

The girl looked panic-stricken for a moment. O Gits, I haven't got any; this isn't Mrs. Ball's. I'll get some tomorrow. Jake, you see, doesn't like it much, but I do.

Oh no, Mercia protested, I didn't mean that. This chutney is fine, I mean, it's lovely, but also, there's no need to do without because Jake doesn't like it. When will he have his dinner? He must be persuaded to eat. It can't do him any good lying in that stuffy room. Driven by embarrassment, the words spilling from her lips could not be stopped.

Lately, Sylvie explained, Jake has more or less been confined to bed. His legs, they're bad, and his chest is kaput. He can't breathe; he has no appetite, no energy. And he won't let me clean or open the window even. I'm not used to living in a mess. Lowering her voice she added, He just drinks and drinks like there's no tomorrow. Anything he can lay his hands on. He used to stagger out to the bar but in the last few days he's not had the strength. He goes berserk if I don't get home on time with his bottle.

How strange then that Sylvie thought there was nothing wrong with him. Tomorrow, Mercia resolved, when Jake roused himself, they would talk, and she would get to the bottom of this.

Mercia said she was sorry but such a huge plate of food was beyond her; she could eat only half of it, delicious as it was. Girls like Sylvie still had the capacity to digest, but when you reached Mercia's age, you had to be careful.

Girl! Sylvie shrieked, I'm thirty-eight.

How Jake slept through all that screaming was a mystery to Mercia. The girl, or rather woman, had only one register, declamatory, as if the most mundane statement had dramatic potential in the telling. And the volume was deafening. How could anyone bear it? Mercia found her own volume dropping in the presence of such declaiming, so that the girl—she must think of her as woman—often had to say, Excuse me, I didn't catch that. Why did Mercia do it? What would it cost to let go and shout along merrily? But that was as far as she went—the posing of questions.

Sylvie carefully transferred the food from Mercia's plate into a Tupperware container and placed it in the fridge. That will do for lunch tomorrow, she said. Mercia wondered if she should offer to help bathe the child, but it seemed he would go to bed just as he was, dusty legs and all. Should she not have read him a story? Is that not how children go to sleep? But the child called a hurried good night and crept into the dark room where his father snored, surely, Mercia thought, with an unpromising night ahead. Of course, she knew nothing of children, felt a certain fear of the boy, but the mouth and eyes were so like Jake as a child, so like her little brother with his snake belt bunching together the too-large khaki shorts into which he would have to grow, that she offered to share her room, said she didn't mind Nicky sleeping with her, but his mother said no, that he wouldn't like that.

· · ·

When Mercia staggers out in the morning, Sylvie brings in from the yard something in a checkered cloth that she drops hastily onto the kitchen table. Ouch, it's hot, she cries. The smell of wood smoke wafts in with that of freshly baked bread.

I thought you'd like roosterbrood for breakfast. It's quick to cook on the coals, she explains. I kneaded last night. She leans over the latched lower door and shouts for the child, Nicky. God knows where he goes, she complains. So early in the morning and already he's disappeared.

Mercia slides a knife through the grilled bread and stuffs butter into the envelope. Butter on roosterbrood? Sylvie says boldly. Her voice contains a hint of scorn. It appears that only namby-pambies, or is it the gluttonous, would butter such bread.

Ag ja, Mercia says. She relies heavily on Ag ja. There is little else to say but then, as she bites into the warm bread, she exclaims with delight, It's sourdough, isn't it. She had forgotten about the sourdough of her childhood, had believed it to be the invention of metropolitan master chefs. Yes, Sylvie says, if you like you could take back some of my culture in a Tupperware, just add flour and warm water and leave in a warm place. Her voice gathers volume as the emphatic Namaqua speech takes courage from her sister-in-law's ignorance.

I've never made sourdough, Mercia confesses. She knows that this would please the girl. I've no idea how to make it, but you can buy a sourdough loaf, expensive it is too, at my local organic bakery in Scotland.

Which surprises Sylvie. She wouldn't have thought that country bread would be available overseas. It sets her off into explaining how some people use raisins, but that the ordinary potato makes for a much better rising, fermented with less sweetness, although a teaspoon of sugar certainly hurries things along nicely. Look, she says, there's nothing to it. You boil the water, leave it to cool, but make sure it's still hand-hot, then put in thick slices of raw potato. I don't even bother to peel the potato. In three or four days or perhaps five, there should be a gray fermented mess, and only then do you add flour and wait for—

Mercia interrupts. Oh no, what a palaver, that's way too much trouble. The bread from my local bakery is very good. Even in the olden days my mother only made sourdough when she ran out of fresh yeast. Then we were so far away from shops. No need to go to all that trouble nowadays.

Sylvie looks at her askance. What a strange thing to say after she stayed up the previous night to knead, and rose early to make a fire so that there'd be something warm for breakfast. Well, so much for the blarry woman's grandness, for all that education. If she does not think that warm roosterbrood is a treat, why does she not at least pretend that it is? That's what she, Sylvie, would have done. That's how AntieMa had raised her. What on earth would she have to make for breakfast tomorrow if roosterbrood is not good enough?

Sylvie leans over the door and shouts again for the boy. Ni-icky, she bellows. Blarry child, she'll kill him for running off like a wild thing. And she notes with something akin to pleasure that Mercia winces at her words, that she stops short of pulling a face.

I'll go and see Jake, Mercia says, and pays no heed to Sylvie's anxious attempts to stop her. In the fetid room, she calls his name, but Jake refuses to reply, pulls the cover over his head. When she shakes him by the shoulder he calls out: Leave me alone. My head, I can't speak. I'll get up later, when I feel better.

Defeated, she leaves the room.

❀

Jake's house, at the fringe of the township, is one of a short strip of buildings that peters out into a field. Sylvie says there is talk of further building on the field, which is a shame because she relies on the council renting it out for grazing. Four of the sheep nibbling at the stunted shrubs belong to her. Look, she says, that two-year-old dorper, the Bleskop with the marking on the rear is hers, given to her by Meester—Pa, she corrects herself. And now she has the additional sheep, one of which has just given birth.

In spite of the apparent lack of new spring growth, the lambs are gamboling in that desolate veld, and Sylvie points excitedly at two leaping joyfully over ghanna bush. See, there, right there, she says, those are hers, the ones who now fix their mouths on either side of the dam's udder, tugging fiercely at her teats whilst their stunted tails wag furiously with pleasure. The dam, poor thing, flicks her ears and stamps with impatience, tries more than once to move away but the lambs, firmly clamped to her udder, draw their feet nimbly, if comically, along and move with her. Only when they relax their greedy grip on the teats does the dam manage a hasty getaway, but with her lumbering bulk the lambs quickly overtake her and clamp their jaws once more to the tired udder.

No escape there, Mercia says with disgust. And they're so big—should they not by now leave the poor mother alone and graze by themselves?

Sylvie shakes her head. This is her territory, and she delights in the fancy woman's ignorance. No, man, they're only a couple of weeks old. And they do graze, she explains, but the lambs still need milk as well, mixed feeding, just like any baby. See how they wag their tails, well babies do much the same—they murmur at the breast, make funny noises when they first start on solids too.

Her thoughts flicker guiltily to Mercia. They really ought to have slaughtered a sheep for her visit. That was what one did in the past when people came from the city, from afar to stay; it was what AntieMa always did at New Year when Ousie came from town. Then it was all go, a whole day of hard work with nothing wasted: the intestines cleaned in order to be stuffed as sausages; the colon, clogged with fat, dried for a crackling fry; tripe and trotters scraped clean with a razor blade; and the salted meat hung out in the evening breeze to dry. Only when the sun rose would it be brought indoors, packed in a basin and left in a cool dark room, covered against the noisy mumbling of blowflies, who would lay eggs and spoil a whole carcass within a day. Then there were the delectable organs that could not be wind dried, liver, heart, kidneys, spleen, sweetbreads, and best of all the special treat of braised brains. Which meant nothing short of feasting, and passing on parts to neighbors, although AntieMa argued against giving anything to Oom Hansie, who sat under the tree; he shouldn't be encouraged, she said haughtily. But Ousie always managed to wrap up some liver in greaseproof paper for the child to slip to him.

Sylvie assures herself that things are different these days. She could not be expected to lose a whole sheep, what with Jake not eating at all, and the faint guilt dissipates as she thinks of the woman looking down her nose at roosterbrood.

They are standing in silence on the verandahless stoep, where Mercia, not knowing what to do with herself, not knowing how to get away, has turned to a neglected geranium, stooping to pinch off dead leaves.

Ai tog, Sylvie sighs, waving her arm vaguely at the field, it's not much of a life, nê.

Mercia straightens to look at the girl, whose head is tilted to the sun. It is as if she sees her for the first time, as if, brushing aside the prattle, there is a new face strangely luminous, every fiber lit with sadness.

Is the girl finally going to speak of Jake's drinking, of his inability to get out of bed? But no, when she turns, once more composed, it is the sheep she speaks of.

Once upon a time, she says, they would have been wild, doing their own sheep thing, and then people came along to domesticate them. Seduced them with ready-made food in winter, and that was the end of them. Fed and fattened so that they have lambs, and then the slaughter.

It transpires that there is no stopping Sylvie when it comes to sheep. Or goats, for that matter. She tells of being just a little girl when she was given her first kid. Funny, it was Oom Hansie, did Mercia remember the old man who used to sit hammering and sawing under the old thorn tree? Dead now from the drink, and a broken heart people used to say, but anyway, he had a nanny goat for milk and it was he who gave Sylvie the day-old lamb, still unsteady on its feet. The dam had died shortly after giving birth and the little thing had to be fed by bottle. How she loved its wagging tail as she held it close. It would suck at her fingers when the bottle was drained and follow her around. Mary, she was, with her little Bokkie, like the English rhyme they recited at school, and sometimes she couldn't help wishing that he were a lamb with fleece as white as snow. Anyway, he had beautiful brown patches on his neck and on the left, no, she frowns thinking again, it was on the right, all the way down to his foot. Even Bokkie's droppings were perfectly formed little pellets that smelled of earth and wild thyme—sometimes, musically clattering onto AntieMa's linoleum—which she hurriedly had to clear away. But then, Bokkie's time came and there was no arguing with the old girls. Could she not herself be slaughtered instead? she asked AntieMa. She prayed to God, but unlike Father Abraham who was offered a ram caught with its horns in the thicket in order to spare Isaac, God would not provide a substitute for Bokkie.

Sylvie giggles. She supposes God could not very well give her a boychild, and one with horns to boot, to slaughter instead. You do know the Bible story of Father Abraham and the sacrifice of Isaac, don't you? she asks, and Mercia nods curtly.

Sylvie does not speak of her fears for Bleskop, who sooner or later will have to be slaughtered. It was not as if she herself did not eat mutton, but not yet, she prayed, not even for the grand sister from overseas could she bring herself to do it. She had, of course, to ask Jake if she should slaughter for Mercia's visit, but Jake, rude as ever, snarled, Just keep your hands off my sister, she's got nothing to do with you. Do what you like with your fucking sheep. Uncouth, that is what he has become, so she gave herself permission to save the sheep. Instead, she would rise early to make a fire and cook the roosterbrood, which, it turns out, does not please Madam. Unless, and she glances sidelong at Mercia, she really is clever enough to see through the substitution.

It's so much trouble, she explains, forgetting that she is echoing Mercia on sourdough. The business of slaughtering, I mean, when you could just buy from the butcher. I hope you don't mind, she adds timidly. Lodewyk's mutton is good, comes from the same local Namaqua sheep.

Mercia has no idea what she is talking about. No, of course not, she says. Whatever the problem is, she does not want any further trouble for the girl, whose sadness is barely hidden in all this prattle about sheep. Mercia says that she is there to help, to see what could be done to relieve the burden. How will they sort out Jake's problem? she asks.

Sylvie, it seems, is not ready to speak of Jake. She laughs. Look, she says, pointing to the field. The dam must have made herself scarce, for the stupid lambs bleat loudly, disconsolately, until the mother popping up from a donga can take no more and baa-baas in return. All right then, come along, she baa-baas, and then the whole aggressive business of feeding starts all over again, the tugging at the teats.

I could watch them all day, Sylvie says, I know their bleats as well as their mother does. That pair, and she points, had some trouble being born. Had to pull the second one out myself, she says with pride. It will be very hard to slaughter those.

You don't do it yourself, the slaughtering, do you? Mercia asks with a shudder.

Yes, of course, I wouldn't let anyone else kill my lambs. Learned when I was young. Didn't you, from your father? Meester, Pa, used to slaughter, and when I was a child I used to help, holding a leg for the chopping off of the head.

Mercia finds this talk horrible, but suspecting that Sylvie thinks her a namby-pamby, she looks the girl resolutely in the eye as Sylvie speaks of kneading away with your fist the skin from the carcass.

Not at all difficult, and a nice, hissing sound, Sylvie says. Then, of course, I was sent to work in Lodewyk's butchery. If you want to eat it you should be able to do it yourself, that's what I always say.

It is this, Mercia thinks, the sanctimonious nonsense that makes her vacillate wildly for and against Sylvie. For all her belief in female solidarity, she simply cannot take to this girl. As for the snobbery that Jake attributes to her, well, at least it is not the whole story. She is relieved when Nicky turns up, gamboling too, like a lamb. Hurry, Sylvie calls out to him. We have to drive the sheep over the hill, into the next camp. This patch has been eaten and trampled bare.

The little boy frowns. A man, he says, could just run into the midst of them and shout and frighten the daylights out of them. Then we'll see them jump over the fence. A man could get a big stick.

A man? Mercia repeats with distaste.

Oh yes, his mother smiles, already he thinks he's a little man.

I wouldn't encourage that, Mercia retorts, and turning to the boy says that being mannish and frightening animals with sticks is not humane, is not what good people do. She'd rather he be a decent little boy.

His mother says nothing, smiles, and pats the boy's head as if to say that he should not mind his auntie, that the woman for all her supposed cleverness knows nothing of either children or sheep.

Mercia spends most of the day in her room reading and writing. Although there are several articles she ought to look at, she wishes she had brought along the novel, *Home,* to read again. The strange room is unsettling; she cannot start a new chapter; instead, she revises again an earlier one. If Jake is not ready to see her, she has no intention of wasting her time, although her patience is wearing thin. To stretch, she steps out and finds the girl flustered, waiting to speak to her. Why did she not knock? But Sylvie ignores the question. She says that she will have to leave for work in the next ten minutes. Jake is still asleep so she can't leave Nicky. She'll take him to her AntieMa, perhaps Mercia remembers her old aunt? Mercia nods. Sylvie has run out of time, so Mercia must please find herself something to eat for lunch in the fridge, and perhaps get something for Jake as well. He eats so little, perhaps he could be persuaded by her.

It is preposterous. Mercia takes in the neatly pressed hair, the memory of a bruise yellowing below her left eye. Nonsense, she says, I'll wake Jake; of course he should look after the boy.

Oh no, the girl begs, please, and her voice is strained. He'll be in a black mood if he doesn't sleep it all off; please I couldn't leave the child when he's like that.

So Mercia relents. Fine, she says, but you're making it difficult for yourself. Look, I'm here; I'll stay with Nicky. No really, she says as Sylvie looks doubtfully toward the room where Mercia has been working. I can do that any other time. No problem in taking the afternoon off, and you can rely on me to give Jake a talking-to when he deigns to get up.

Mercia has a vague memory of Sylvie's auntie, by now surely an old woman who could not run after a child wagging his tail. Besides, that is no way to raise a child—the scolding and shouting of country folk.

❦

Sylvie was raised by her parents, Ma and Pappa, and the sisters, AntieMa, Nana and Ousie, who all lived in a ramshackle little house at the edge of the location. Pappa had been injured in the gypsum mine, so he limped about the homestead, growling and sucking at his pipe while he tended goats and grew pumpkins. Ma shuffled through the dark rooms, her head swaddled in two large doeke tied the old-fashioned way in an invisible knot above her left ear so that her long, withered neck seemed unable to carry the weight.

Ma was sick with a permanent bad head brought about by disappointment, which was why she was sad and cross and wary of sin. And why they all had to walk on tiptoe. She had already reached her fifty-eighth year and was waiting for the Goodlord to fetch her. The child had in mind an outing that would make Ma laugh, or at least smile, one that you earned after fifty-eight years of pursing your lips. It would be like the olden days that Ma spoke fondly of, a trip to the town with her legs swinging carefree from the side of the mule-drawn cart, her top doek flying in the wind, with the Goodlord merrily cracking his giddy-up whip. That would be why Ma so looked forward to being fetched.

To help Ma overcome disappointment, Sylvie pounded tobacco into a rough snuff. The old woman inhaled, pinching each
nostril in turn, then she would sneeze and blow her nose into
large khaki handkerchiefs that the child washed on Saturdays.
As Sylvie grew older she undid Ma's doeke in the evenings,
combed and plaited her short hair into little horns, no matter
that they would be lumpy under the doek, for there would be the
second cloth to smooth them over, but still Ma did not smile at
her like a real mother. Instead she issued warnings against sin
and urged the child to be frugal.

See, she said as she dug in her apron pocket for a crust saved
since breakfast, now I have something to dunk into my morning tea.

Sylvie decided that Ma was her stepmother. Otherwise, she
would have been called Mamma. What had happened to her real
mother? Ran away with a smous, AntieMa teased, and next year
when he returns with his donkey cart full of muskmelons and
pumpkins and cards of buttons, he'll take you back with him to
Boesmanland. So you had better not ask any more questions.

Oh no, the child said. She wouldn't go with such a person.
Never. But Nana said she should not give herself airs. Sylvie
tossed her head imperiously and said, But I prating the Ingleese,
and the sisters laughed behind their hands the suppressed laugh
of women staving off sin.

The child was too old-fashioned, AntieMa said, with her nonsense about stepmothers. So she sat her down and explained that
yes, Ma was not her only mother, that they, the sisters too, were
her mothers. Sylvie said it was okay with her, as long as the smous
was not involved.

Once, when Nana took Sylvie along to her place of work as
housekeeper, the English Madam said she was cute, a sharp little
girl whom she hoped would be trained as well as her aunt. As

long as her family had a decent Willemse girl to help in the house everything worked out smoothly, Madam declared. But Nana said that they were planning for Sylvie to train as a teacher, that they had a sister in town with whom she could board. That was all very well, Madam said, but in town cute girls soon become fallen girls, and Nana blushed.

Sylvie's jobs included helping Pappa in the garden and tending to the animals. And it was Pappa's job to administer hidings for her many misdemeanors. Like bouncing on the kaffirmelons or knocking on the pumpkins in the hope that a fairy godmother would pop out, and worst of all for running off like a wild thing so that she could not be found. Such wildness, Ma said, had to be beaten out of her.

Pappa, more often than not distracted, would slowly take off the belt that he wore along with braces and, leading her outside, would make her lean against the henhouse for the thrashing. Sylvie would throw back her head and howl loudly, and the hens came out cackling, but so weak and listless were Pappa's strokes that the belt would often bounce against the wall. Besides, he did not seem to believe that his trousers would stay up with braces alone, a matter of much concern, so that his left hand tugged and clutched at the scuffed corduroy waistband. His heart, the child knew, was not in it, and she howled all the louder.

My hands are not as strong as they used to be, the old man complained, holding them up this way and that in wonder. Which made Sylvie wonder whether he had given up the fight against sin, whether he too was waiting to be fetched by the Goodlord. After the beating he would pat her backside and ruffle her hair, but once inside, he complained to Ma that she was a noisy child, that her howling would send him to his grave.

When the old people died within a year of each other, Sylvie thought in terms of numbers. There were fewer of them, which surely meant that things would lighten up. And for a few days she was fooled by the shutters that AntieMa had pinned back, by the air that rushed through the unglazed windows, and by the door left ajar, through which a girl could slip out, quiet as a mouse.

❀

On the wet sand where the sea had retreated far away on the other side of the Solway Firth, favoring the English towns of Maryport, Workington, Whitehaven, light bounced and frolicked. They walked gingerly across the abandoned seabed, holding hands in case of quicksand. Tongues of light licked at the liquid sand. The sky bore down upon the earth, repeating its white cloud in the mirror of seabed. Mercia was afraid. She had heard of the rogue tides rushing in, so that the murmur of water announcing its return drove them up to the hill.

Coward, Craig said. See, the water is nowhere near.

The clouds dispersed and sunlight dazzled both from above and from the reflection below. Cocooned in sunlight. Craig said it was the perfect place for their old age, the climate marginally better than the city to the north, the sea air good for the brittle bones of the elderly, and yet so close to Glasgow too.

Mercia protested. Best not to think of old age; time should be resisted; best to imagine it could be kept at bay.

Control freak, Craig laughed. Look, pal, it's nothing to be afraid of. Wrinkles are no big deal. The middle-aged are in any case invisible to the young, who believe that they've bumped into ghosts as they stumble into us. That's why we shiver in our youth. Think summer. Summer's the new autumn, as the advertisers would say. In our autumn days we'll put on our wellies and wade into the water, hand in hand. Stuff the mermaids and the peaches. The young are welcome to those.

How Mercia loved being called pal. When Glaswegian bus

drivers or workmen said, There you are, pal, or, Got the time, pal? she was named, felt the warmth of an embrace, a welcome that came close to a sense of belonging. Whatever that was, Mercia was careful to add. And Craig teased, Oops, we mustn't let go of the exilic condition now, must we? But she knew that he knew what she meant.

That night, with the water miles away, a full, lascivious moon stretched out on the sand, gazed up narcissistically, moonstruck, at itself, the light so bright that their shadows stretched before them. They walked for miles across the abandoned seabed, rested on a rock and waited, watched the moon as she slowly skated across the sand, tugging at the tide.

Just the two of them, Mercia and Craig, doing as they pleased. Not kept indoors by children. Over the years, discussions about children had come up from time to time, more often than not sparked by a rude, demanding child. Not, of course, that all children were horrid. Smithy had two little ones whom Mercia adored, but why should that influence her decision? Mercia would not be bullied by her body, by the demands of Mother Nature. If the tides of blood produced no urge for a miniature Mercia, so be it. There was no reason to question her lack of interest. Many women nowadays felt the same.

And no urge for a miniature me? Craig pouted.

Mercia said she found the idea of a flat-nosed, freckled, red-haired, frizzy-headed infant perfectly resistible. She preferred the sound of chickens pecking about the place, which would be feasible if they lived there, by the sea.

Craig said, Ditto. He didn't feel one way or t'other; he was a bloke, immune to the moon. Although, if Mercia really wanted such a thing, he could be persuaded, could think himself into the unthinkable. By which he meant the chickens she had been banging on about ever since they had met.

. . .

Mercia could not help herself. She was drawn to places where they had been together, where they had planned their future, not doubting their control.

Unhealthy, masochistic, Smithy maintained, why not come away with her and the children instead? They had rented a farm-house in the Trossachs with plenty of room, and Ewan wouldn't be able to come until halfway through.

I had in mind that you'd come along, she said. Think wind-swept walks in the hills, back to blazing log fires, delicious food washed down with the blushful Hippocrene, and then being beaten at Scrabble. Oh, I know you wouldn't manage a whole week of vegetarianism, so we'll allow you to bring along your own frying pan and pig chops.

Mercia was grateful for the offer, but declined. It was just that she believed the Solway, a place where she and Craig had so often been together, would help her to get used to being alone. That was where she should learn how to shape a new life. Nothing bet-ter than confronting things squarely, so she must return to that time, traverse the same places where she had imagined things to turn out so differently, test the solidity of the same stretch of wet sand. Confronted with the same thorny gorse crowding the pathways, she will turn the past into something she does not crave. Only there can memory be neutralized. Yes, the cliché of time healing the wound may be true, but she would accelerate the process, add to the medicine its old mate, space.

Mercia spent four days on her own at the coast. She could not help sketching out different scenarios. If they had had children, would Craig have left? Would he not have had a fling and re-turned to the fold? She wept for the shame of it: yes, she would have endured that, would abjectly have put up with it. Which led to the conclusion that she had been right about not having children.

Things will get better, are already better, she consoled herself. Spring will do the trick, even if in these parts summer held off indefinitely. Already bluebells burst in waves of blue in the woods, and gorse crowded the path in a sea of bright yellow, hiding its thorns, the honeyed coconut smell hovering above the brine. The clichés of the countryside sprang into life, with lambs gamboling on brand-new legs, yes, actually leaping joyfully in the reluctant sunlight.

Just you keep it up, this friskiness, for soon you'll be slaughtered, Mercia muttered. She wondered at what stage a gamboling lamb became an edible lamb. At least she was brought up to eat mutton, full-grown sheep, rather than babies caught in joyful midair leap.

The coast had also been a means of escaping Jake's letter. Emptied by grief, Mercia had so little to give. Was she not the one in need of comfort? The impossible flashed before her: an older, fictional brother who would touch the top of her head with four fingers, stroke her nape with his thumb, and take her home.

Jake's letter was no doubt written in the early hours, in a struggle with insomnia, with a hangover perhaps, when things get distorted. In which case it was kinder to ignore it. A nuisance that in this day and age Jake did not have e-mail, not since he returned to Kliprand. For all the hastiness of his scribble, for all the desire he might have had to fish the letter back out of the pillar box, here on the coast it turned into an arrow pointing home. His request was preposterous, and she had no intention of making any reference to the child, but she would have to respond.

Back home in Glasgow, she telephoned. It was Sylvie who

answered. Everything was fine, she said in her emphatic voice. Jake was not there, was at Aspoester's, the new bar, but she would tell him of Mercia's plans to visit. Later in the year, in spring, would be a better time to come. When the Namaqua daisies were out.

Did Sylvie not know of Jake's letter?

It is day two and still no Jake. Of course, he is there, in the sagging bed, in the room with curtains drawn. Mercia has heard him in the night stumbling to the lavatory, then the slam of the fridge door, but during the day he lies low in the dark, fetid lair and ignores any attempt to rouse him. Sylvie sneaks in to feed the monster, carries in mugs of sweet black coffee and the occasional bread with peanut butter which he may or may not eat.

Mercia is furious. It was not at all convenient to come at this stage, and Jake could surely have written or telephoned to say that he has changed his mind, that he does not want to see her, even if such a cry for help is indelible. She does not know what to make of the claim that he is too ill to speak to her. Jake has always been difficult, contrary, has delighted in being the good-for-nothing villain, but his villainy had been directed at their father. With her, Mercia, he had always been gentle, had appointed for himself a place in her heart, had wanted her approval.

In the old house built of clay bricks baked in the sun on the riverbank, the children shared a bedroom. Mercia longed for a room of her own, but Jake was content; he believed that he would not be able to sleep without her. It could not have been beyond their parents' means to add a room, but their father had in mind a grand future for his children, and to that purpose they were to make sacrifices and lead frugal lives.

Sometimes, on winter nights, after the animals were tended

71

and the supper dishes were cleared, Father grew less stern and read to them from the abridged Dickens novels that Mercia loved and did not mind hearing again and again. She traced with her finger the line drawings of Miss Murdstone's wicked face, of hungry Oliver, and Pip as a young gentleman. Oh, it was Pip with whom she identified—his betrayal of Joe quite overlooked—Pip who escaped to a grand life in London. Miss Havisham too was captivating, also in the drawing where she presided, tall, dignified, imperious in her moth-eaten frock, over a magnificent crumbling cake. The table was laden with unidentifiable dishes, but unmistakably grand and bounteous, bound together as they were with the gossamer of spiderwebs. Mercia would practice their words in many fancy voices: Please, sir, I want some more; Barkis is willing; Play, boy, play.

There was also the Children's Bible and the magic of Moses's bush that burned and was not consumed. In grave tones she repeated over and over God's words to Moses, I am who I am, for they were regularly tested on the wonderful stories from the Old Testament. In the light of the paraffin lamp and with coals glowing in the pan, God's strange message, "Tell the people of Israel I am has sent me to you," was doubly mysterious. Their father said that God's words were not to be questioned.

Mercia does not remember Jake enjoying the stories. He sat stiffly, on the edge of his chair, as if bracing himself for an unexpected blow. In a sense he was right: there never was any knowing how they might trespass, do or say something wrong; they lived in a state of perpetual fear and guilt. But she, Mercia, transported by stories, was prepared to take the evening's suspension of harsh parenthood at face value. Fagin's den grew right there in the shadowy corner of the kitchen where the paraffin flame darkened the glass; Nancy's faded frock rustled; and Sikes's dog barked ominously in the distance.

At night when their candle had to be snuffed as soon as they were in bed, Mercia listened in fear to the distant barking of real dogs. Or worried about the church bell, which rang in the night when someone died. Then she was pleased to hear Jake muttering in his sleep. She believed the bell to ring all by itself, or rather be rung by a fierce bearded God, far fiercer than Father, who glowered through the corrugated zinc roof, and she would hide in vain under the covers as he thundered his demands like any common robber.

Guilt—that was what defined their childhood. Guilt ran like a dye through their days, streaking the most innocent of activities, tingeing all with fear of trespassing and disappointing their virtuous parents. Were there no golden days of childhood, no forgotten walks through parables of sunlight, when after rare rain they scampered about in a fresh, new world? Jake was emphatic. No, never, that Mercia was mistaken.

But Mercia, who fashioned her own private world, remembers otherwise. On lovely days cooled with cloud, she stepped out of the real to play alone at her secret place, a thornbush decorated with the silver paper rescued from Christmas sweets. In spring tiny green leaves burst from the gray stems, and later, at the end of summer, red berries shone as brightly as the silver paper. With twigs she swept a clearing around the bush, and there, hidden in an embankment, escaped from them all, even from Jake, whom she did not tell of that home.

Mercia had stolen a cracked inkwell from school so that she could cradle in her hand its exquisite shape, the clean lines of white porcelain that tapered to the base, and at its mouth the curve of the rim, rounded to fit a slot in the school desk. She had washed the well clean of ink and kept it hidden in her thornbush home. Never again would it be an object for use, no, from that day she renamed it a vase. Mercia did not mind the crack at all, as she placed in it a sprig of flowering Jan Twakkie. Her collection of stones was kept in a special oval tin that once contained canned fish. Father had hammered the edges down smoothly, so that she would run her fingers around the rim, marveling at the lack of corners, the lovely shape with its matching name: oval.

There were also Sunday afternoons when the children played together between rows of rustling mealies. Then they would strip barely bearded cobs and chew at the sweet milky seeds. They'll know, Jake said earnestly; they know everything we do or think, and that's why we'll be beaten. They know the bad things we don't know that we've done or thought, the things we will do tomorrow and the next day. Jake said he hated Grootbaas, that he wanted to be bad bad bad beyond the old man's imagination.

Look, he said, I'm a mealie, as he stripped off all his clothes and rolled in the dust. The only reason they won't admit that they know I've been bad is because they're ashamed. That's grown-ups for you, frightened of nakedness. But what the old boy will do all the same is beat the shit out of us. He'll find a reason.

And he did. Waited for them on the stoep with the aapstert swinging from his left hand. From his right hand he sipped noisily from his afternoon cup of coffee. There was no escape from those Argus eyes, from his omniscience. A father who loves his children knows everything, he claimed, like God. Knows when they've been bad. He did not want them to turn out like the people of Kliprand, like the dirty, drunk Bassons. Jake rolled his eyes at Mercia. He would rather not be loved. Besides, he admired the Bassons, who spent their waking hours around a fire in their kookskerm without a roof, happily without chores. At weekends their tin guitars tinkled across the veld, and the dust rose as they danced the kabarra.

For Jake, that is all their childhood has been: the fear of Father and God. In that order. Why was it impossible for him to summon the cool of summer evenings when they finished the chores, the sheep and chickens put to rest under flaming skies, and the sudden dip of the sun that would plunge all into darkness? Then they sat outdoors and listened to the swallows swooping in and out of the eaves. In December they sang carols, their mother teaching them to harmonize, and they laughed at the old man's off-key voice. Hark the herald angels si-ing. The beauty of the word, hark, that made you sit bolt upright and feel the quiver of bats as they dived. Then Father, scrambling for his rightful place, would say, Look at the stars. Come and find the Southern Cross, the Three Kings, the Bear.

When the sun's lingering on Capricorn brought the fiercest heat, Mercia and Jake would sleep under the stars on the old wooden trailer, and watch the Three Kings beaming and bending over the newborn Christ child. Jake was her darling baby brother whose antics made her laugh, for whom she feared, and as the fresh morning air arrived the children snuggled close together under the yawning stars.

Mercia drifts from the southern December to the lingering light of the Scottish summer. After all these years the slow inching of day to darkness still brings melancholia; for all its reliability still creeps upon her as a surprising ache of weltschmerz, until darkness finally engulfs the day. Now sitting in Sylvie's yard, she thinks of that dusk-bound sadness as a longing for the African night, for blackness that like a screen is swiftly, securely drawn across the sky, obliterating the day in a quick, decisive death— obliterating guilt.

Oh, she hears again Craig's lilting brogue, his steady hand mixing her a drink. Your sundowner, Madam, he would jest. Wrong hemisphere, she'd groan. Sundowners were for Europeans trying to adjust to the swift descent of the African night. Over forgetful drink, they flocked together to counter angst and fear, for otherwise the world would yawn with the descent of darkness, showing its inner space, and who could stand that? Certainly not those who had left home in search of a better life in the colonies.

And you? Craig asked, the people of Kliprand, too indigenous to be afraid of the dark?

Precisely, she laughed peevishly. Not a problem in your own, your home hemisphere.

Mercia wonders if that perhaps is what children are for, to ease the shift from day to night through bustling, tiring chores. No, of course not; she knows that dispensing care is not the business of a child.

And now, where is Craig? As she catches a star skidding across the familiar southern sky it feels as if her barely mended heart will break once more.

Oh, this can do no good, this harking back, broken—a far cry from the summery hark of angels.

❦

Jake the monster is bellowing from his room, throws what sounds like a shoe against the door, barely audible above the voices of the soap opera that Sylvie is watching. Transfixed by the television, she doesn't hear him. Mercia rises. It is preposterous, Jake behaving like a child, refusing to get out of bed. She barges into his room and gropes for the light switch. A bare bulb casts dim, eerie light onto a figure she cannot bear to look at. He is lying on his back, his hands on the bedcover are shaking; his eyes are screwed shut against the dangling lightbulb, his face yellow-brown and bathed in sweat.

It's evening, time to get up, she says briskly. I've come all this way and you haven't as much as looked at me.

Jake opens his eyes and looks at her, squinting. Get me a drink, he growls. He tries to lean down to retrieve a wine box from the floor but doesn't manage. It's empty, he says, that bitch hasn't brought my drink.

Forgotten your manners, have you, dear ogre? That's no way to speak of your wife, Mercia says. Stop this ludicrous behavior right now. You're an adult, so get out of bed and see to your own needs. And while you're about it, pay some attention to your child. He didn't ask to be here.

Jake clutches his aching head. My child? Well, neither do I want him here. It's all down to that bitch and her scheming. Please man, Mercy, he pleads, get me a drink, anything. He tries to get out of bed but falls back with exhaustion. Perspiration beads on his upper lip, and his thin arms tremble.

I'll get Sylvie for you, Mercia relents, but only if you promise to speak politely. And to see a doctor tomorrow. You're sick, you need help, Jake; you've got to stop drinking.

Yes, yes, yes, he says. I promise. You're right. I'll do whatever you say, just get me a drink now.

Sylvie is irritated. He can wait, she says, now speaking quietly, her eyes fixed on the television screen. He's a liar. You mustn't believe a thing he says. Promises! She laughs bitterly, then stops to concentrate on a woman on the screen who speaks indistinctly through dramatic sobs.

Ag no shame, Sylvie tuts, it isn't that poor Thandi's fault, then she returns to the real-life drama at home: I've heard plenty of Jake's lies. The only promise I believe in is that he wants to kill us, me and Nicky. It's just that he doesn't have the strength, but he'll think of some way to do it. Just you wait and see when—

She stops in midsentence as the camera returns to the sobbing woman, but when the advertising jingle starts up, she says, He killed your father, you know.

• • •

Jake did not aspire to doing well at school, but without much effort he excelled in mathematics and science. Which he resented
for the pleasure it brought their father. See, he said bitterly, how it
encourages the old man to make up more and more rules: in bed
by nine, up at five; nothing other than mealie porridge for breakfast, which made Jake gag; no sweets; no pocket money; no radio during the week; only study, study, study. No this, no that, a
mouthful of homilies, and stupid idioms: spare the rod and spoil
the child; a bird in the hand is worth two in the bush; make hay
while the sun shines; honor thy mother and thy father that thy
days may be lengthened in the land of the Lord; and the usual
nonsense about gratitude. Oh, it made him sick. If Gentle Jesus
were meek and mild how could it be good for a child to be bullied and beaten? How could the *Hit Parade* or pictures of John
Travolta or Grace Jones that he had put up on the wall be bad?

He loves me yeah, yeah, yeah, Jake intoned slowly, solemnly,
parodying the old man, old Who-art-in-heaven. He said the old
man was pure evil. Even God could not have been as petty as
their father. If that was what paternal love was, please could he be
an unloved, abandoned orphan? The very word, love, made him
want to reach for a knobkierie; he would club to death anyone
who claimed to love him.

Jake did not despise their mother for her silent complicity, for
agreeing with the old man. Yes, Nettie knew how unreasonable
the old man's rules were, but he believed her hands to be tied, that
she too was subject to Nicholas's wrath.

Jake's revenge came in his first year at university, some years
after Nettie's death. I don't think, he said languidly—stretching
rudely at the breakfast table, savoring the effect and calculating
the hurt—nah, I don't think I'll be bothering with the kak of
exams this year.

Nicholas frowned, cleared his throat; he surely hadn't heard correctly. What was that? Ignoring the rude word, he asked, Do you mean you'd like to go back to bed like a lazy hotnot and sleep till midday, rather than do your duty?

Precisely, Jake retorted, glad you understand that this is it. I'm finished with university.

He pushed back his plate of mealie porridge and leaned back, tilting his chair. Jake was proud of his defiance. He laughed uproariously when the old man said that he was not too old for a hiding.

Jake could no longer bear to be dependent on their father. I don't want the vark's money, he explained to Mercia, and university loans are only for those who become teachers. Can't face that, so I'm off. Plenty of jobs in the liquor trade, and it suits me fine that the vark's disappointment is such that he doesn't want to have anything to do with me. Serves him right for ramming down my throat that he'd sacrificed himself for us. All those pathetic tales of a snot-nosed barefoot child with no schooling, pulling himself up by his own bootstraps, dragging himself through night school, the scrimping and scraping by and going without in order to fulfill his promise to Mummy that we'll go to university—I've had enough of that.

Boring an index finger into his right temple, Jake mimed their father's madness. Old Who-art-in-heaven's off his head hey, stupid, thinking that if you shout the word gratitude long and hard enough at children that's precisely what they'll feel. What kind of gratitude is that that has to be implanted by the giver? Mercy, you too should leave, he urged, get out of his bullying grasp.

But I'm at the end of my honors year, she said. It wouldn't make sense.

Oh no, he mocked, the old boy will have an idiom for it. Don't cut off your nose to spite your face, he intoned. No man, Mercia, he said, shaking his head. It's a matter of principle. Besides, the price for this grand education is eternal obedience. No thanks, he can stuff it up his arse. Jake spat a spectacular far-reaching arc of spittle through his front teeth. Look where obedience has got him. A bloody apartheid collaborator. I'm surprised he's not stood for the tricameral colored parliament.

Grateful that her exams were no longer the topic, Mercia said that it wasn't fair. Yes, the old man was flawed, but he was their father, and who was without flaws? He belonged to another generation, and the truth was that she did feel grateful to him for living a life of frugality and penny-pinching in order to pay for their education. And Jake's assessment of his politics was unfair. He was not a revolutionary, it was true; he kept his head down, keeping out of the way of what he saw as trouble, but he had taught them self-respect, never to capitulate to whiteness.

Oh yes, Jake snarled, self-preservation all right. And what about Africans? Did he teach us to respect the people of this country? Or the people of Kliprand? What does he mean when he says they're not our kind of people?

Then Mercia refused to argue with him. Jake was intolerant, did not appreciate the difficulties of a previous generation who barely managed to raise their heads above water. You don't understand how difficult it is to think outside of the dominant ideology, she sighed.

Ideology! Bugger that claptrap, he snarled, that can't be an excuse. Others managed, why can't he?

Mercia clutched at straws. Could their father not be thought to mimic obedience to the state? Which made Jake laugh. The old man simply did not make sense, he said, toeing the apartheid line, and at the same time crediting himself with independent thought, with being different.

It was true that Nicholas insisted that they were different, that living amongst the Namaquas did not make Namaquas of the

Murrays. The people around them were not their kind, and thus Nicholas taught his children to speak English. Which meant that they were not to play with others who spoke Afrikaans. Besides, the children had each other, and friendship was a dubious category that only led to evil. It would be friends who would persuade them to smoke or drink alcohol, lead them astray to do or think the countless bad things that young people were prone to do. It was, according to their father, important to remember that they did not belong there.

Then where did they belong? they wanted to know.

Nicholas was puzzled by the question. Why belong to any place or any people in particular? They simply belonged, a word that need not be followed by where or to. For a moment Mercia feared that he would say: I am who I am. But he explained that Kliprand was inhabited by uncouth, uneducated people. Yes, their home was there, but the Murrays couldn't possibly think of belonging there. As long as they could fit in anywhere with decent people, also city people, that was the important thing, that was where they would be at home. By which, of course, he meant English-speaking coloreds with straight hair, skin color being less important than hair, the crucial marker of blackness. Jake guffawed. Did Nicholas not know that all coloreds had European ancestors? If it were only those with visible genetic links that counted, he would happily grow his hair to accentuate the frizz. Which he did.

Thus the notion of home was revised. Decoupled from location and belonging, and crucially from community, it was shrunk into a prefabricated rectangular structure of walls that could be dropped down anywhere as long as it was surrounded by people who looked like them, people related to them. As for Nicholas's own family, they were raised in respectable God-fearing countryside, Nettie's at a mission station founded by real Europeans, and even if the Malherbes were Afrikaans speaking, they had good European blood.

Okay, Mercia conceded, the old man was deluded, poisoned by an atrocious apartheid ideology, but he was still their father, a man with many admirable qualities, in short, a good man. As his children, did they not owe him some loyalty, even love?

That's just moffie talk, girls' stuff. Certainly not what the mighty Shakespeare thought, Jake, who had studied *The Merchant of Venice* at Matric, retorted. You should know this. Because Shylock is greedy and evil, his daughter doesn't owe him any loyalty. And not a word of remorse. "In such a night did Jessica steal from the wealthy Jew, and with an unthrift love did run from Venice," he quoted. Mercia envied his ability to remember.

Ah, she said, a good example of the ideology you call claptrap. Shakespeare shows this anti-Semitic nonsense to be wrong, shows us that Shylock is a victim of prejudice and hypocrisy. But Shakespeare himself, trapped in Christian ideology, asks us to approve Jessica's theft and disloyalty. It's interesting that she should fall in love with a Christian, but one would expect ambivalence, not an outright rejection of the father; love shouldn't clench the heart in such an unnatural way.

Crap, Jake said, confidently. The story shows ultimately that Shylock's rubbish, so he deserves rejection and humiliation. Listen, I can't believe people get degrees for this kind of foolish reasoning. I'd say, pack it in, Mercia, you could have a decent job all the same. Please don't take his money. Together, the two of us will manage. Old Who-art-in-heaven hasn't earned our love. You too must be sick of hearing about saving and sacrificing himself for our education. It's plain old meanness and megalomania.

Try to understand, she pleaded. His own father wouldn't let him go to school, sent him out to plow the land. You shouldn't rely on dictionary definitions of meanness. People who have little, or who are threatened, necessarily guard their pennies. Frugality is not the same as meanness, and Father is never mean to others. He's never refused to help people out in this community. Take Scottish meanness. The tag tells us more about the culture that assigns the label and has no ability to see things from the point of view of another. They do not understand that frugality, practiced by and for the self, can go hand in hand with generosity directed at others.

Craig used to joke about being the penny-pinching Scot. Aye, we have to weigh ourselves down with two bottles of wine, a box of chocolates, flowers and a paperback when we go to someone's house for a bite to eat, so as to prove to the English that we're not mean. The wine, of course, is also to keep up with the label of drunken Scot. Aye right, it's a burden, so it is.

Then his eyebrows would shoot up comically, perfectly shaped arcs, beautiful as a girl's.

❁

The little girl in a blue gingham dress that Antoinette fashioned out of her own frock that no longer fits sits proudly on her father's shoulders as he goes about tending to the animals, checking on the broody hens, and collecting eggs from others.

Look, he says, how different the little bantam egg is, and he helps her down to peer into the nest. She wants to hold in her hand the perfect oval miniature, and he gets it for her whilst the little hen cackles angrily.

Is it the same as other eggs inside? the child asks, cupping the delicate shell, tinged a deeper brown.

Father says yes, later they'll crack the egg, examine the yellow yolk and the white albumen. He knows that Mummy will need some for supper, that she would be more than happy to add the bantam egg. Bantams are not much use, but Nettie so wanted a pair that he gave in, and really it is nice to see these swaggering little things boasting their difference amongst the Rhode Island reds. See, he says, how different types have different characteristics, different natures. Foolish to think that everyone is the same, or equal.

Mercia is allowed to carry the precious egg. Indoors, they crack it into a saucer. The tiny yellow center floats on the quivering translucent white. Yolk and albumen, she repeats after him. He writes down the words that she has to copy on her slate.

It was the screech of pencil on slate that returned Mercia to the garden, where Jake was smoking a furtive cigarette. He said, bullshit, that she romanticized. False memory, he warned, nostalgia for an affectionate father, for things that never happened. Had she chosen to forget the hidings and the terrible sermons?

But how could an adult hold such petty grudges? The trouble with you, Jake, Mercia remonstrated, is that you refuse to understand the pressures under which that generation was raised. Empathy, my bro, can't you summon empathy? The large families, the poverty, and lack of education. They did what they thought was best, and that is why you should forgive and forget. Larkin got it only partially right: yes, they were fucked up in their turn; it goes back and back, but it is unreasonably misanthropic to imagine that they add some extra just for you. The very fact that we can be clear eyed about their bad parenting shows that our lives are an improvement on theirs. Surely we inherit less rancor than they did. Come on, you too were a kid. You too must have larked about on the garden wall chanting, I'm the king of the castle. You too would have said, I'm going to jump, will you catch me? And of course, he did; there was no question. That is what a father is for.

Jake shook his head, stabbed a finger into the side of his head.

You're crazy, man, cut it out, you're imagining things. Let's go for a drink.

Mercia thought that Jake had taken some of her argument on board. On her last visit before their father's death, Jake seemed less exercised by him, appeared to have come to some understanding with the old man. Mercia wonders why it did not occur to her then that Jake's experience was different from hers, that perhaps as a child he was not indulged as she sometimes was. Nicholas would have believed it his duty to turn the boy into a man, to toughen him, and so suppress all that he believed to be girlish. Why had she expected Jake to melt at her soppy little tale about an egg? Why had she not remembered instead her little brother sobbing, having stubbed his big toe on a stone? Blood streamed from the toe as he hopped on one foot, trying to clutch the other. And Nicholas's stern voice: a boy does not cry. Get down on your knees, say sorry to the stones, and stop crying right now. Because of your careless rushing about, you've disturbed God's stones.

Yes, Jake was Nettie's child, one who found it difficult to recover from her death. He chose to believe that their father had killed her.

Don't be silly, the twelve-year-old Mercia said, how could he have killed her?

But Jake insisted that no one would want to live with such a brute; that his bellowing was enough to make their mother lie down and wish for death.

Oh, he was too young, too vulnerable, Mercia felt, to survive that death. How selfish of her to wish for a brother who would steer with his fingers on her head, thumb in the nape of her neck. Poor Jake. Too vulnerable for the idea of manliness that their father imposed on him. If only she had been old enough to protect her brother. Instead, she thought of the stepmother of fairy tales who would ruin their lives.

Please don't marry again, the adolescent Mercia pleaded after her mother died, and her father said no, that he would devote himself to them. And his reward?—Mercia's defection to Europe. If only she had not been so intent on escape. If only she had spent time with him during that short illness. If only Craig had left earlier, then she would have come home and eased things between father and son. As if they were children, she corrects herself. Why on earth would she who has chosen not to have children take on a motherly role?

Mercia regretted that she was unable to see Jake during his recovery at home in Kliprand. She had been engulfed with work, and reports from both father and son gave her permission to stay away. There seemed to be a truce as a no doubt chastened Jake submitted to his father's care.

When Mercia eventually cleared time to visit, Jake was sardonic. Well, who is the hypocrite now? He laughed at her solicitous questions about the Willemse girl he had married. Go on, let it out, he said, putting on a high-pitched mimicking voice to ask: What on earth, Jacques, are you doing with one of those people? I thought, he said, I was giving the old man a lashing here but no look, my leftie, egalitarian-minded big sister is the one to be appalled.

Mercia was disappointed to find the old rancor still there. Good God, she remonstrated, don't tell me you married the poor girl in order to punish Father. That would be so childish, and what's more, so cruel to Sylvie—and to yourself.

Jake cackled. Remember what Grootbaas used to say when we were little: don't show your teeth to those people—whatever that meant—they are not our kind. Well, there'll have to be plenty of teeth on display for all of you. Sylvie's pregnant.

Mercia mouthed her congratulations. She could only hope

that fatherhood would keep Jake on the straight and narrow, though really, it seemed irresponsible, the casual way in which he took to reproduction.

Ag man, Jake conceded, we get along, the old man and I. And he'll like being an oupa. Too old and decrepit he is now to think of whipping a child.

True, Nicholas was not well at all, but he brushed off Mercia's anxious questions about his health. Yes, yes, he said impatiently, he's seen the doctor. All he needs is his favorite chicken and barley soup that Nettie used to make. The old country convention of cooking the entire chicken leg, foot, claws and all, was repellent to Mercia, but no, he insisted that that was best. The strong flavor, he claimed, the medicine that would restore his health, was from the gelatinous stuff of the joints; he would eat nothing else. Mercia poured boiling water over the hideous claws and scraped off the yellow scales.

Her father, diminished, had a faraway look in his dimmed eyes, the old stentorian voice turned down. If he knew of Sylvie's pregnancy, he chose not to speak of it. Instead he reminisced about Nettie, about how lovely it would be if Mercia would come again with him to see the old place, the mission station where Nettie grew up. Oh yes, he wittered, Nettie also loved a good chicken soup with specks of yellow chicken fat and bits of tomato, not too much tomato, mind, just a speck of red, a couple of spoonfuls to bring out the chicken flavor.

Really, Mercia would have to stop him. She would have to speak of the child before she left. She winced at the thought of a baby—bald, helpless, mewling, waving its arms and legs involuntarily, like seaweed in water; she could only hope that it truly was the case that old people liked having grandchildren.

She tested the waters. You'll want to be well by the time the baby comes. Jake will need your help.

Yes, Nicholas said, without enthusiasm. I said I'd help with a house that his wife has an eye on. He was very ill, you know, with the drink. Perhaps a child will settle him. Nicholas shifted into the plaintive mode. I did my best, he started, and Mercia shut her ears—surely not the old litany about saving and sacrificing. Why don't we talk about chicken soup, she said.

Mercia thought that the house would please Jake, demonstrate their father's care for him. Sylvie was over the moon. Ooh, she crooned, patting her flat belly, how nice it will be for the baby to start somewhere decent, a nice little room with a real cot. I'll paint it bright yellow, and with nice sunny curtains . . . She looked up into Jake's stony face. Or, what do you think, Jake? Don't you like yellow?

Do what you like, he snapped.

Mercia intervened. That's no way to talk to your wife, Jake, but he interrupted. Just keep out of it, okay; you know nothing. I don't want the old man's house, and I don't know what's got into Sylvie. She'll take anything, sell herself for a pair of curtains.

Ag, Sylvie said, he's trying to be the old bad Jake. Look, I've cooked a nice tomato bredie, and she proceeded to set the table for two.

But aren't you going to eat with us? Mercia inquired.

Looks like she doesn't want to, so let her be, Jake said. We've got a lot to talk about; you've been away so-o long, he accused. His voice had softened so that Mercia did not insist. She thanked the girl for the food, and watched her leave the room.

So how's this Scotsman of yours doing? Jake asked. Is he giving you enough to eat? You're so thin. Not skimping on the food is he? And he roared with laughter.

Mercia sighed. It's not funny, Jake. And do try to remember that I work; I'm a senior lecturer and I don't rely on anyone to feed me. Craig is my partner, not my father.

For all the sparring and Mercia's exasperation, Jake became once again the exuberant brother of her youth, who made her laugh with his impersonations, his parodying of members of their family and of politicians. Was it really so long ago that they huddled together in a mealie field, where the sky above had shrunk into a narrow blue strip, the satin edge of a familiar blanket in which they wrapped up together, protected from the world of adults?

Mercia did not speak of the child, and neither did Jake. They ate and laughed and drank Sylvie's homemade ginger beer until late that night. It was only as she snuggled under the easi-care sheets and heard the girl bustling about in the kitchen that she wondered about Sylvie. What had Sylvie been doing whilst they sat at the table? Where had she gone? Had she been waiting outside on the stoep for them to finish?

If Sylvie had any memories of Ma and Pappa, whom AntieMa so piously invoked, she would not encourage them to lodge with her. The house was already chockablock with the mustiness of old people, relieved only rarely when Ousie came home, and that did not last beyond the day of her arrival, when the mustiness engulfed her.

Ousie worked in Cape Town and people said that she wore red Cutex lipstick. Not that she would have dared come home with painted lips, oh no, AntieMa would never have allowed her to cross the threshold in such a state. The Sodom and Gomorrah ways had to be left behind, but the sisters did not mind Ousie's wages as a nurse's aide at Groote Schuur; in fact, they boasted about her neat check uniform and the white cap that was nothing like a servant's. They said that Ousie was *trying*.

When Ousie arrived, always after New Year's Day when the Cape Town drunks were nicely bandaged up or safely behind bars, she brought a whiff of the modern that drifted around her person like perfume, guided the eyes to her white peep-toe shoes and the op-art shift that stopped just on the knee. AntieMa thought that a final band of black added to the hem would not go amiss, and Ousie nodded dolefully. There was no avoiding the improvement.

For the child, Ousie also brought clothes, which AntieMa inspected for decency, and often there was a hem to be let down, an extra buttonhole to be made. Which at the age of eight Sylvie was already capable of doing herself. Oh yes, AntieMa said, a girl-child must know how to do such things. As a good wife and mother your stitching must be near invisible.

Why did Sylvie not find it odd that they called each other AntieMa, Nana and Ousie, the names that she, the child, called them by? But Sylvie did wonder why she should have to be a wife and mother when none of the sisters, her sisters, was. But were they her sisters? Had Ma, whom she no longer could remember and who, AntieMa said, was as sin-free as the pebble-white hills, also been her mother? Or was she Sylvie's ouma?

Don't keep yourself old-fashioned, AntieMa, the spokesperson for all three, would reply, by which she meant that the child should not be precocious. There were things that you did not ask your elders. Sylvie knew that she was being fobbed off. AntieMa said: Of course Ma was mother to all of us, but we three are also your mothers. You, Miss Cheeky, have lots of mothers. Which did not sound grand at all. Lots of lace-edged hankies with embroidered corners, or flower hair slides, or a paper bag full of nickerballs—that would be something, but here was one example of lots not being so desirable. To have brothers and sisters, lots of other children in the house, that too would be good. But many mothers—whoever had heard of that? Lissie in her class claimed to have seen a picture of a giant woman, with a whole row of breasts and several feet, who would qualify as both one and many mothers. Nana said that other less fortunate children may not know of such a condition and therefore make up silly stories, but she, Sylvie, was just unusually lucky. And when Ousie came home they would have so much holiday fun that the sisters knew Sylvie would not spoil things by asking old-fashioned questions. And she didn't. Not even what Ousie's *trying* meant, what she was *trying* for.

See, they said, that was why the child had the beautiful name Sylvie, which meant Good Girl. She had always tried to be the Good Girl that AntieMa said she was—deep down. Except for the time when Sylvie took a sixpence that turned out to have been deliberately left under a chair by Nana as a test. Then AntieMa pursed her mouth and shook her head sadly. What could anyone expect of a child shot through with sin? she asked.

The Willemse sisters were respectable, and not bad looking either, but too full of themselves, people said, almost as snooty as the Murrays, whose house had a verandah and glazed windows. Which the light-skinned Willemses did not have, and neither did they have such good hair, such good blood, so why they gave themselves airs and graces, no one knew.

Ai Goetsega! the old people had sniggered, next thing they'll be taking on the English talk like the Murrays. Just as well they didn't have the book learning. Ouma Willemse, with her sour-fig face perched on a regal neck, would have nothing less than a teacher court her girls, and ones with hair to boot, so that the local young men gave up. Pride will come to a fall, they said vengefully, as one by one the men had been turned down, and now, look, a clutch of crooked spinsters with only the small child, whom no one could account for.

Where had the lovely child come from?

The Goodlord has given her to us, they said, and who could argue against such a gift? Which also meant that Sylvie could not leave home, would never be allowed to live in town. Her mothers had pledged to God that she would keep out of Sodom and Gomorrah.

When finally Ousie was of an age and had had enough of trying, she did the decent thing and came home to Namaqualand. Groote Schuur no longer was the glorious place it had been in Dr. Christiaan Barnard's day. (Ousie thought it only correct to call him by his full name and title.) The trained nurses were lazy, leaving more and more work to experienced aides, and there were too many cheeky African girls who would not take orders. Ousie was of the old-fashioned kind who expected Xhosa girls to look up to her. No, at forty-eight she was a Big Woman, and she had had enough. She would rather go home, tend to chickens, sell eggs, and possibly find work as a housekeeper in the dorp. This time Ousie's gifts were worthy of one retiring from city life. But that was it, she sighed, final gifts. She was tired; she had had enough of trying.

For Sylvie, there was a camera, and Sylvie did not tire of taking pictures of herself. AntieMa did not approve. Especially later when the girl started dressing up. It was profane, vain, and as the preacher said, vanity must come to a fall. Did the girl have no shame? All those tight, tight clothes that would give any healthy person the hiccups, the skirts too short and the necklines too low, enough to make her mothers choke with shame, but where was hers? Where was Sylvie's shame? And how could her sewing skills be put to such shameful use?

What do the Old Ones know? They are of another world. They have not noticed how the world around them has changed. Even Ousie for all her city ways is old, wears her colored cringe like a shawl tightly held around hunched shoulders, knows nothing of the world. They think of the new as tarred roads, water from a tap, telephone wires. They do not see that the young are new, that their bodies are fresh, that music beats in their blood, that with their heads lifted to the blue sky, their spirits soar way, way above the little church steeple. Hitse! This is the New South Africa. Even here, in what they call the godforsaken Namaqualand. But the young do not mind that God has forsaken the land. If that is how he wants to play it, so be it.

Here before her silver screen, Sylvie can be anyone at all, but today she is the Reckless One, the Daredevil Goosie who smokes and drinks and who is . . . yes, she'll say it: envied by all. The Good Girl, who has slipped in a teenie-weenie word to become the Good Time Girl. She has borrowed Tiena's cream canvas jeans and tucked her cigarettes into the right pocket. Just so, on the hip, which she thrusts forward, so that the packet of Marlboros (she always transfers her ciggies into a Marlboro packet) shows. Smoking Can Kill, it says. And you better believe it!

Hitse, all it takes is a skip, a leap or two into a pose—forward, backward, onward Christian soldiers—to be someone else. What does she care? Sylvie does not need a mirror for messing around with her mouth, pouting, or pulling it to the side, tilting her head like the girl with the glossy hair in the Clairol picture. She can stretch out her arm, point a finger, skim it across, taking in you and you and you, all of you stuck-up ones, who will say not a word against her, who wouldn't dare, 'cause why, she is the Reckless One who's seen it all, who doesn't care. Who has Three Mothers. Pity the camera can't record that movement of the arm swiveling across the imaginary crowd. Pity all has to be rehearsed, for there's the business of setting things right, then running to take up a practiced pose, breathless and just having to hope for the best, hope that the just-arrivedness does not break through the glossy print.

Sylvie has shooed them all out of the way, but Jakkie and Ky-tou can be heard messing about behind the house, so that it takes some concentration getting the haughty look. How does one stop oneself from laughing out loud? Perhaps it is too much of a sneer, but it will do, it will do for a Kool Kat. Then Oom Hansie starts up. Stationed at the gate of the klein-kraal, in the dappled shade of the thorn tree, he has begun his usual business of hammering, sawing, nailing down. Just as she thought that he had finished.

There is a large bird circling, right above her head for God's sake. Is it a bird of prey? a hawk? a buzzard of some kind? Come, she shouts, waving a fist, come and get me if you can.

Some will say, what about the flowers, the two pools of purple on either side of her. Well, what about it? A picture needs something pretty, some color. What is there to say except that every year, true as the clock strikes twelve at midday, these patches of dreary old vaalbos, so dead you can kick at it with shod feet and same difference, these two bushes go berserk, and explode, ag, like so many stars into this wild purple, pools of pure flower, with not so much as a tip of gray leaf showing. All around is gray, gray, gray dust, that is, not counting the common gousblom, a bleached yellow, so insipid that as a teenager Sylvie used to pop them into her mouth and swallow them whole whilst Jakkie and Kytou, still laaities themselves, looked on in awe. But here, where she has planted the vygie, its crazed October color bleats like a goat whose lamb is being slaughtered. Which she has always known is for her, Sylvie, and her alone. That is why she turned the patch into a garden, arranged the stones, which Jakkie helped her carry, into an enclosure. In the veld she dug up kanniedood and koekemakranka, and planted them around to show up the glorious purple. That's not a garden, Jakkie sneered, but what does he know? Jakkie's job is to do as she says.

If, as AntieMa sighs, the devil has blown into her blood, then that blood is the screaming purple of vygies here at her feet. More Namaqua Daisy than the bottle of sweet wine she could swig in one breath, in a single gurgle. Who amongst the meide could do that? Who could claim that pool of bold purple faces turned to the sun, daring it to scorch?

Sylvie stretches her arm, and with pointed index finger swivels it round once more. Not you, not you, not you. No one, 'cause none has dared to be Sylvie the good-time-girl, dared to plunge

into purple. What does she care about the blood of a boer from
long, long ago, the respectable blood that AntieMa bleats on
about? That is a stale story of aged, tired blood that has clotted in
varicose knots on the legs of old women.

Ousie says you have to press on and thank God for small mer-
cies. She says that she too can see goodness deep down in Sylvie's
soul; Ousie knows that in spite of everything Sylvie loves God,
that she is grateful for his mercy. Ousie makes Sylvie sit on the
floor, clamped between her thighs, as she rubs oil into the girl's
scalp, rubs the excess into the crinkly hair shafts so that they
glitter. Then Sylvie's head leans heavily, drowsily against the soft
thigh. Ousie shuts her eyes and, still rubbing, sings in a tremu-
lous voice:

> Jesus sal al jou sonde weg was,
> jou sonde weg was, jou sonde weg was.
> Jesus sal al jou sonde weg was,
> as jy kom kniel by die kruis.

Of all the hymns in the book that is the dreariest, can barely
be called a tune. But she, Sylvie, has knelt at the cross and in
the gloom of the church has seen it surge forward and retreat,
in and out of focus, breathing a purple light. The wooden cross
studded with amethysts from which light shot in all directions,
crisscrossing the ugly altar with shards of purple. Oh, she has
seen that purple light before, waiting by the thicket of thorn
trees for him to arrive, dressed in sin. As she was, dressed in sin.
Sin all bundled up in the heap of garments they shed like snakes
so that their bodies shone with purple light. It is a light that
AntieMa, Ousie, Nana—her mothers—have never seen, will
never see. It is for Sylvie alone. And for the cicadas who came
out to line up in the light and screech about God's love and sin.

Sylvie prefers the English word for SONDE, a neat, stylish word fit for Sundays: SIN. A looser kind of word that could shift back into Sense, Mind, Will. She bows. Ladies and gentlemen, I rest my case. But no, for them, the Afrikaans people, the hotnos, there cannot be a single, lightweight sin. No, always many, always heavy and fixed, always plural, creeping up on a girl, pumping her up with the bad. On days like today when her pool of vygies have burst into full purple flower she has no problem with sly sin. Let it lie in wait for her. God's sin, which he will not acknowledge as his own. It is the month October. Al die kriekies kriek daar buite, elke sprinkaan spri-ing. The hellfires have been eclipsed by a purple glow, and she, Sylvie, is not afraid.

Ousie says that if she prays for forgiveness she will be spared to grow old and wise, and understand the ways of the Lord. Sylvie lowers her head and nods. They have no idea. Old and wise? No, rather old and ugly with bulging veins of stale blood, and who would wish that? Ousie used to be young and beautiful. Glamorous in her peep-toe shoes as she swung, laughing and light as a feather, from the Bitterfontein train onto that dusty strip where their coach came to a halt. With the cardboard suitcase that the bedding boy, winking, handed down to her. Why had she come back to this?

Ousie is my mamma, the child, Sylvie, once chanted, and AntieMa said, Yes, she is; we are all your mammas. Now Ousie sings dreary hymns, dragging out the O of sonde so that it chokes like so many op-art dresses stuffed down her throat.

It is a shame about Sylvie's shirt. About the camera having fixed that moment. Not that she thinks the blue-green check does not go well with the jeans, but hooking her left thumb into the jeans pocket and easing her shoulder, the button has come undone and her bra shows. A clean white bra—her breasts, even if she says so herself, have always been lovely—but still, it spoils the pose. She had hoped for something else, something more sophisticated.

The October sun was already fierce, and she called, shouted at Jakkie to fetch her sunglasses in the wooden chest by her bed—there where she keeps the rollers and the hot comb. There's nothing like a squint to make a girl look as common as a goatherd. Jackie sauntered over from behind the house, distracted, strumming his ramkie fashioned out of a fish-oil tin, and she told him to hurry, hurry otherwise she'd lose the whole damn style. In the meantime, waiting, she wrinkled her nose, snarled, smiled, smoothed back her hair with a limp film star's hand.

Hurry u-up, she shouted, and it was Kytou who turned up with the glasses, which she had to snatch from him as he tried to balance them on his hotnos nose. Get, she said, voetsek, behind the house with you. This picture that she waves dry, this stylish Kool Kat Girl, is for her and her alone. Never mind about the button that has come undone.

Oom Hansie's saw moans in tune with the old thorn tree swaying in the wind. Sawing, hammering, nailing. Little tongues of light lap at the shade, at his velskoen, where he saws and hammers under the tree. That's now Oom Hansie, always by the klein-kraal where Sylvie's hanslam totters on brand-new sin-free legs, its tail wagging. The picture pulses with the sound of an absent saw.

Later Kytou can have his photo with her, Sylvie, and the lamb. Kytou is okay; he does make her laugh, and she'll let him wear the sunglasses for their pose.

It was not the job she had dreamt of, but after school, after all the things that happened, that filled their heads and leaked silent poison into the house, there was little else. It was Ousie with her town ways who came up with the plan. Not that anyone asked her, Sylvie; it was just announced, as she sat there cleaning the lamps with newspaper, getting the glass chimneys to shine clear as sunlight.

Sylvie was very, very lucky, they said, and her face fell. Oom Lodewyk would take her on in his butchery. Was she not the one who loved goats and sheep? AntieMa queried. Why then would she not be delighted with the plan? As if dead animals, carcasses, were the same as live ones. But she said nothing. All the things that happened was mos her fault and she should be grateful for something to fill the heaviness of those days, stifling with heat and the deafening shriek of cicadas.

No chance of getting to town, especially now that Ousie had come home. No chance at all. She would have to buckle down to the butchery, besides, there would be some money for herself, and perhaps she could have an account with the new Foschini that had opened in the dorp. Get some fashionable clothes. But AntieMa, by now fat as mutton and barely moving out of her chair, said that a decent girl brings home her wage envelope unopened, that her mothers would give her pocket money. Was there really no way of becoming an adult until you became a mother yourself? Sylvie did not think that she had the makings of a mother, the milky swagger, the whining voice. And who on earth would she team up with to do the mother-thing?

She would not let on to old po-faced Lodewyk that she found the meat cleaver scary. Steady does it, or bone would shatter into vicious splinters. Then it turned out to be not so terrible learning to make boerewors. Better than unpicking hems, lengthening skirts, and squinting over invisible stitching. Handwork, they called it at school. The good, the holy, done by hand alone. Busy hands to keep you out of trouble. Well now, with her hands she'd rather make sausages, boerewors. And what's more, it may be damp as babies, but she knows which she prefers.

Grind the meat in the big old mincer, add just the right amount
of salt, pepper, clove and coriander—although she cannot resist
an extra dash of coriander—then leave the mixture overnight in
the enamel tubs. No nasty cereals thrown in as they do these days
in town, nothing nasty like that pink polony. Sylvie would stand
over the tubs where time did not only pass, but slowly, wrapped up
in itself and taking its own slithery time, mixed things through,
drew the flavors into each other until there could be no telling
where one stopped and the other started. It was time that brought
something new called boerewors, and there was the wonder of it.
That too is how a person gets through. You put up with waiting,
with thinking of time working its miracle, changing one thing
into another, even when your hands are tied behind your back,
and when your mothers stand over you with three sets of eyes.

Sylvie does not like to think of large, greedy people gulping
down fried sausage without so much as pausing to think of time
trapped in that skin. Hers is the best boerewors in Namaqualand,
all because of the extra dash of coriander and the patience, the
waiting for time to do its blending business overnight.

She has finished with the sausage maker, the forcing of flavored, spiced mutton through yards and yards of skin. The same
mixture through two different sizes to make thick or thin boerewors, because people are so foolish as to believe one to be better, tastier than the other. The machine is washed, the mincer
cleaned and put away, and sausages hang neatly from the hooks
on the long steel rod. From the end of the steel pole the iron pail
hangs, nice and clean, scrubbed free of mutton fat.

When Sylvie first arrived it was a grungy thing, never cleaned
because old Lodewyk said that storing fat did not make it dirty.
Yes, she's made a few changes around here, and all for the better. There was no point in hardening her heart against the place,
standing stiffly at the counter, or sulking at having to use the

cleaver. Rather, she allowed herself to be drawn into the precision of severing a joint, cracking a rib, turning sheep's neck into neat chops, getting all to shine and sparkle. Now the place could not be faulted for order and cleanliness.

Sylvie sets up the camera as soon as old Lodewyk leaves wearing his black waistcoat, with a fake leather folder under his arm. The pompous old fool always dresses smartly to go to the bank, as if those boere-meneers would notice. Hardly anyone comes into the shop in the early afternoon; she need not fear any disturbance. A pity about the black doekie that she has to wear bound tightly around her head; she does not think her forehead is rounded enough for such severity, but never mind, there are always ways of flouting the rules, finding pleasure in transgression, even if the ones you trespass against do not know. Sylvie's black doekies have a secret splash of color, a patterned corner here or there, so that folded, a flash of floral is at the brink of revealing itself. A man, a dull man like old Lodewyk, will never notice. She whips it off, refolds it so that the spray of green leaves shows. A photo needs some color.

AntieMa thinks the doekie is an affront. The Willemse sisters never wore such things; their hair is not of the peppercorn kind that has to be tucked away. What's wrong with a white polystyrene hat like the boer butchers wear? AntieMa's objections make it easier for Sylvie to wear the doek. And Lodewyk does not deign to reply. He stomps and grunts. Typical of the Willemses. Full of airs and graces, and never satisfied.

Even if Sylvie says so herself, the sausages look fine, perfectly marbled with the red of mutton and the creamy-white of fat in just the right proportion. Dappled and gleaming, glory be to God. Sylvie sets up the camera and does the customary skip, a little good-luck akkeltjie before its knowing eye, before smiling, calm and composed, holding a rope of perfect sausage in her outstretched arms. In her left hand, the end is lightly pinched between thumb and index finger; the right hand is slightly raised with loops and loops of sausage draped over it. She throws back her shoulder triumphantly—tirrah—smiles broadly, in spite of herself, in spite of the pity of it, of her, Sylvie, the Kool Kat, the Wicked One, the Good Time Girl, beaming in a butcher's shop.

Her face is lit with pride. Only fear of someone bursting in prevents her from wrapping a length of sausage around her neck. Like a rich silk scarf. For it is a cold winter's day—people think it doesn't get cold in Namaqualand but Yissus, it can be bitter. Her fleece is zipped up to her throat. She could toss the length of sausage over her shoulder with the flip of her hand, just so, just like the film star on TV, the one in *Egoli*. Instead, this tame pose, but never mind, she smiles brightly, if out of breath, and click, click, it's done.

Think of it as an advert in *Huisgenoot*. Healthy boerewors for the family, recommended by a healthy, smiling young butcher. Sies-sa-aa! that's Sylvie. As long as no one mistakes her for a mother.

Sylvie has the perfect idea. Imagine, in the dark. On a summer's night. Stealing into Lodewyk's butchery. The moon just about skimming the window so that an eerie, film-set light is cast over everything. Over the streamers of sausage that gleam as moonlight lifts out speckles of shiny white fat. She, Sylvie, having stripped off all her clothes, would coil the sausage around her nakedness. Carefully, slowly, starting at her feet. Hitse! what a gedoente getting it round and round herself, coils of marbled sausage cool against her skin. Neatly, like an Egyptian mummy, a queen wrapped in time. And if the sausage skin should break? Ag, the sausage meat would stay, plastered to her skin, grafted onto her. Sylvie, the Sausage Girl, brand-new as a baby, at one with her handwork.

Oh, but she would need a better camera, a flash, and besides, you couldn't sell such a heap of used boerewors. What would she do with all that secondhand sausage, warmed by her flesh? Only good enough for the dogs. What a waste, what a dog's dinner that would be.

Sylvie stares with furrowed brow at the picture. Oh no siss, ooh siesa! The end of the sausage looped in her hand hangs down behind her right arm, just long enough to stick out, and she grimaces, like a—a thing.

As a child, Sylvie loved playing at the klein-kraal where Oom Hansie worked at weekends with his sawhorse and plane. There were the beautiful curls of pale, shaven wood to twist around her fingers, and she would pick up to examine in turn the chisel, the hammer, or the wide-toothed saw, but Oom Hansie did not mind.

Doff, doff, doff she drummed with her hands in tune with his hammering. AntieMa said it would do no good, that the child would get in the way, even hurt herself, that she should keep away from the klein-kraal. Hansie, she said, was being forward now that Ma bless-her-soul was dead. But Ousie came to Sylvie's defense. What harm could come of it? Hansie, she said, would always keep an eye on the child, would not be a nuisance. If the thorn tree was the place where he chose to spend his spare time, it was none of their business; the klein-kraal belonged to everyone. At least the child had in him a good example of useful work. AntieMa pursed her lips but gave in to the homily that presented itself. Idle hands, she intoned, make devil's work.

What was Oom Hansie making? Sylvie asked. The man mumbled something she could not follow. Later he gave her the three-legged stool with her name, SYLVIE, carved around the edge of the seat. Would she be allowed to keep it? Of course, he said, although she should ask her mothers. He said she was a kleinnooi, now with a throne of her own, and held out his hand to ruffle her hair, but she deftly slipped aside. AntieMa would not like that; AntieMa said there was no call for touching people, other than the circle of handshaking after the church service.

No longer did Sylvie sit cross-legged on the earth, her skirts tucked into her broekies. Oh no, she dragged her stool around the yard, sat perched on it, swinging her legs and surveying the veld. Fancies himself a carpenter, AntieMa sniffed, inspecting the stool. Not bad, she conceded, but it won't last, was bound to fall apart, especially with the child traipsing with the thing all over the yard. She would let Hansie know that they were not poor people in need of furniture.

Sylvie was in Standard Four when walking back from school with her friend Janie, they came across Oom Hansie, his hand raised in greeting. Kleinnooi, he smiled, and doffed an imaginary hat. Janie whispered that everyone knew the man was a freak, a madman and a pervert, that they should turn round and run. Which they did. But Sylvie was ashamed. She knew that it wasn't true, and when next she saw Oom Hansie with his hammer and saw she went to the klein-kraal, dragging her feet through the dried mimosa balls, up and down, until he called her over and said if she came next week he would bring something he had made for her. Not a word did he say about Janie, and so flooded was her heart with gratitude that she could not speak. She shook her head, then nodded. Yes, she'd be there.

Thus it was that Oom Hansie presented her with a chest, a wooden box made of slats in which he said she could keep her private things. Sylvie held out her hand formally to say thank you, then let out a whoop of delight. Yislaaik, she crowed, but she would have to find a pretty cover so that no one could peep through the slats.

The next day Oom Hansie brought a small Bokomo flour bag and showed her that if one unpicked the stitching on the sides it turned into a single length of cloth. If you washed it, he said, you could embroider in nice colors all around the faded images of corn on both sides. Green for the stalks, yellow for the cobs, which he warned would take some nifty needlework to pick out the individual kernels, and then any color you fancy for the surround, although it might not be desirable to draw attention to the cloth's origin by embroidering the words, BOKOMO.

Sylvie thought otherwise. She did not mind this handwork. It took a while to do the yellow corn, as well as a crocheted edging for the whole cloth in red. But the large letters of BOKOMO were easier, picked out in bright turquoise. Draped over the rough chest, the words became a special reminder of Oom Hansie. What did she care that AntieMa thought it common or backward to have a flour sack as a drape? As long as she kept her nose out of Sylvie's chest.

What do you keep in there? the old woman asked. It was a secret. She wouldn't say that all there was was a pale blue bird's egg and her Standard Three Reader with the story about a girl's red shoes that she had not returned to school. And a handful of boklam's perfect drolletjies.

Mist in the shallow valley crept up slowly like a thief across the field, toward the motorway. If you looked, it stopped in its tracks, guiltily. Like a game they played as children, What's the time, Mr. Wolf. Which, of course, was no good with only two of them.

Why was Mercia on a bus rather than on the train to Edinburgh? Ever conscientious, she worked at it, the being-left-behind, the management of loss and grief. Everything was different, and to maintain control, to keep on top of things, difference itself had to be cultivated. So why not the bus, why not see for herself why people of her kind preferred the train?

Now was the time, she said to Smithy, to assess all her habits, to check whether there was room for change. Craig's defection, his loss of interest in her, may well have happened because of her unexamined habits. A loved one may once have turned a blind eye, but in time would come to raise an eyebrow at slovenliness, at the old slippers and shabby dressing gown she clutched around her on a Sunday morning until well into the day.

Smithy threw back her head in laughter. He didn't leave because of your dressing gown, though he should have done. High time that went into the bin, so why don't you come shopping instead, but Mercia thought herself above retail therapy. Smithy was patient. She listened over and over to the same story, the same arguments. And the same question: was the old Craig for whom betrayal was unthinkable the same person as the Craig who had betrayed Mercia?

Heavens, Smithy, replied, who would have thought that you'd use the language of pulp fiction? It's not a question of betrayal, nothing to do with subjectivity; it's just what happens when your affections shift to someone else. Then Mercia would say triumphantly, so when women grow old and fat and ugly it's fine for men, themselves grown old and fat and ugly, to put aside notions of commitment and fidelity?

Neither of you is fat and old and ugly, but it appears to be what some men do. Who knows to what extent Mother Nature herself is responsible? Why, for instance, do men and women have such different libidos? When women are well past such things, men are still driven . . . Smithy was careful not to speak of reproduction.

Well, your Ewan wouldn't run off, would he?

They both laughed at the phrase, at the idea of Ewan running anywhere.

There's no knowing what an accident of time and place might bring. Someone may well one day step in his path and like what she sees just as he looks up at her in wonder, both smitten by the new. Then that will be it, the very Ewan who doesn't run.

How romantic, and how well prepared you are, Mercia snapped.

Mercia knew that there was no solution to such talk. Commitment and fidelity were themselves contingencies, but there was some comfort in raking over those embers, in trusting that they would one day according to the law of nature burn themselves out, collapse into ashes. Only a month ago she would not have thought in terms of ashes, so there was something to be said for the old, tired metaphors.

Jerking its way out of a narrow road, the bus jolted her out of the obsessive thoughts. Mercia had imagined that it would belt niftily along the motorway, had no idea that it would first bump through suburbs on the edge of the city, making her stomach heave as it then made up for lost time on the motorway. Oh, she had not been looking and now the mist has crept up, engulfing them.

Mercia started at the sound from the seat behind her. Hers was not the only heaving stomach. She had been aware of the little boy's voice, the chatter of one who has learned to make meaningful sounds and now was afraid of pausing, so that the words were a constant stream linked with because . . . because . . . because, used as a filler and in answer to his own questions. The young mother interjected with a soothing voice, reassuring him about the animals awaiting them in the zoo, the growling wra-wra of the lion; the hiss-ss of snakes. Christ, that was why people preferred the train. Mercia had not known that the bus went via the zoo. No wonder it was full of babbling children and mothers with flexible vocal cords, up and down the scales of infantile wonder and pious motherhood, backed by the rustle of snacks from backpacks.

Behind her there was the unmistakable sound of boaking, so that she jerked forward to avoid projectile vomit. The child cried, a slow gathering of sobs as he lamented the mess he had made, a mess that spread over the seat, over his mummy, over the animals in their lairs, over the entire day. He was sorry, he wailed; it was all messy, he wailed.

The woman's voice wormed and slithered soothingly. It was only sick, she said, only the crisps and juice come back up because the bus was bumping his tummy, and as for the mess, no matter at all, Mummy would clear it all up. How lucky they were that in the backpack there was a spare pair of trousers, and look, a whole packet of wet-wipes with which to mop up the sick. A plastic bag for the dirty tissues, ran her commentary, as she cleaned up. But the child, implacable, and evidently a cleanliness freak, would not be consoled; he had ruined everything.

Sweetheart, my sweetheart, the woman soothed, there is nothing in the world to worry about. Mummy will sort it all out. A little boy can't help being sick, the greedy lion cubs too have been sick, and that's because like the hungry caterpillar they've eaten too much—one piece of chocolate cake, one ice cream cone, one pickle, and he recited along between sobs: one cherry pie, one sausage, until the voice became inaudible as his face, Mercia imagined, was squashed into the woman's bosom.

Sweetheart, my sweetheart, sang the maternal voice, everything's fine. Shall we try to find the gruffalo at the zoo? Silly Mummy, hey? Doesn't she know . . .

There's no such th-thing, he sniffed and gasped, as the gruff-gruff-gruffalo.

Christ, Mercia'd had enough. She thought about changing seats. Then her own stomach heaved as she lurched into the past, once more a child groping for her mother's skirt, sobbing her sorrys and her incomprehension. She did not mean to drop a cup onto the cement floor. Why would she be beaten for an accident? How could anyone imagine that she wanted to see it in shards? She too loved the cool white of the glaze, the pretty pink posy on the rim. But there was no such thing as an accident, said Nettie. There was only carelessness, a disregard for her parents' hard work and sacrifice, which in itself was an offense before God, and which the child knew to be the case. The beating then stood for a lesson in care and vigilance.

The word, sacrifice, was firmly attached to God, who sacrificed his own son for the sins of the world, although it was not clear how that connected with grown-ups' sacrifice for their children. They did not explain how or what they sacrificed. The seven-year-old Mercia thought of a stack of firewood, the smell of a burnt offering, but why did it induce guilt? Besides, her mother did not make sense. How could there be no such thing as an accident? The word existed, and carelessness what's more was clearly not the same as doing something on purpose.

Was the fire Mercia allowed to go down, having forgotten to feed the woodstove, more deserving of a beating? She had ruined the bread and so was a good-for-nothing, ungrateful child, idle, with her nose buried in *Die Jongspan,* her mother said. She could not be trusted with anything when there was something to read.

That brought an end to *Die Jongspan,* which they decided was an unnecessary indulgence that filled a girl's head with too many stories. Over and over Mercia read the few remaining back issues of the magazine until she knew by heart all the jolly escapades of the boer children, the chicanery of Reinhart the fox, and the adventures of Jakkals en Wolf.

The bus stopped at the zoo, and for a second Mercia toyed with the idea of getting off. Precisely, she castigated herself; it was just as she had always thought—children inspire sentimentality. She kept her eyes down. She did not want to see the woman and child, did not want to host an image of them. No image, no redux.

At the bus station Mercia welcomed the long walk to the National Library. The howling wind would blast the cobwebs out of her head, the unseemly, blubbering mummy-longing, inspired by no less than an incident of vomiting. Christ, a broken heart may demand new directions but there was no need to regress to childhood.

How little she knew of this city only a few miles away. Mercia smiled at the old rivalry, remembering Craig's joke about the best thing to come out of Edinburgh being the train to Glasgow. Whilst living with Craig, she refused to think of Glasgow as home. Now, rehabilitating, did that not demand that she take a stand? Was there not the risk of being irretrievably lost? between cities? between continents? What a day for being assailed by non-sense. Mercia had to remind herself that she had only been un-settled by a pious mother-and-child display. Grieving for Craig need not turn her into a fruitcake.

What will you do now? Smithy had asked, and she knew ex-actly what Smithy meant. Had she, Mercia, not been going on for years about Craig being all that kept her in Scotland? That she would have liked to return to South Africa after the demise of apartheid? She only hoped that she had not used the horrible words—her parents'—of "sacrificing herself" for Craig. Said maybe in jest, but horrible all the same. Returning now, as a woman who had been left, smacks of defeat. To Smithy Mercia said that it was too soon to make decisions. Her work was there at the university; it was no time for further upheaval. She had no intention of missing out on a hard-earned sabbatical.

The rain came suddenly, viciously, and Mercia was wearing unsuitable shoes. She'd had enough of that malarkey, of the bus and its adventurous route; like a grown-up she would get the train back to Glasgow, forfeit the return bus ticket. In fact, she was cold, wet and weary, in need of a coffee, and reluctant to go to the library. There she was, so close to Harvey Nicks. Why not, for once, do the unexpected? Why not get out of the bloody rain, forget about the library, and take in not only a coffee but also some shopping instead?

Mercia felt a little tremor of guilt at wasting her research day, but she would make up for it, has surely already made up for it in the sleepless nights when she worked around the clock. She was contemptuous of the notion of a makeover, especially for the woman who has been left, but she could do with something new. A quick flip through racks of overpriced clothing designed for un-dernourished children was discouraging. A glamorous assistant came along and said, Yes, her intonation halfway between statement and question. Later, l'esprit de l'escalier provided Mercia with: Glad you're in agreement/I haven't yet spoken/Is that a greeting/Yes indeed—but at the time, affronted, she grabbed at a couple of garments and announced, I'll try these. She stared in dismay at the figure of a fifty-two-year-old in the mirror. Like the favored photograph of themselves that people carry about for decades in their wallets, Mercia had identified with an outdated image of herself. What did it mean when friends said she looked remarkable for her age?

Only a burka would do, Mercia said to the unsmiling assistant as she handed back the clothes.

It was still early enough to get a train back and start work as if the excursion to Edinburgh had not taken place. The train passed through the small towns of Linlithgow, Polmont, and yes, Falkirk too. No escape from home there at the foundries of Falkirk, she smirked, as the train pulled in at the station. The black and white station signs carried a reminder, as did the hanging baskets of petunia and begonia, ugly municipal combinations of pink, orange and purple.

Falkirk was the name stamped in relief on the three-legged cast-iron pots at home, pots manufactured for the colony, for Africans to cook their staple mealiepap over an open fire. Nowadays, for the experience of traditional potjiekos, the three-legged pot straddling its fire has found its way to fashionable braais. Once at a barbecue that Jake had organized, Mercia asked about the word, potjiekos. She had never heard it before. Where did it come from? Who used it?

Jake laughed. Give us a break, man. We're free in the New South Africa to do as we please, invent if we want. Just look at you, definitely an example of the pot calling the kettle black.

They ate heartily the perfectly ordinary stew from the

three-legged pot, the potbellied omphalos of authenticity, itself a potbellied word. And there where it was cast, in the foundries of Falkirk, a sudden burst of sunlight accompanied the rain, so that the water dripping from trees glittered like Christmas streamers as the train pulled out of the station. Jakkals en Wolf gaan trou. That's what they said at home when rain and sunlight commingled. An unlikely marriage between jackal and wolf, right out of *Die Jongspan*.

When the train arrived at Queen Street station, Mercia was unable to leave her seat. Her heart seemed to break over and over again, and that when she thought she was well on the way to recovery.

❀

It is midnight. Mercia, sitting at the table in her pajamas, looks up in the dark at Jake, who stumbles into the kitchen. She sees a wounded animal. His disheveled hair has not been cut for months; he is unwashed, an old mangy lion without a tail, dragging his left leg. She jumps up to throw her arms around him, but he pushes her off roughly.

No man, Mercy, leave me alone. If you don't have a drink for me, just leave, go home, and he turns on his heel, shuffles back to his bed.

When Mercia returns to bed, she closes the chapter she has been working on, and opens the file, Home. If she can't speak to her brother, she could at least write about him, about growing up in that place. That would be her only way of reaching Jake.

Antoinette, the name of a French queen—whatever possessed her parents?

For people like them, plain folk, names must transcend their condition; a name must ring with grandeur, and so earn respect. A grand English name, as they thought it to be, would cancel out the Afrikaans surname with its reference to madness; it would influence the life of a girl with few resources, and help in the tricky business of finding a husband, for who nowadays would want a Kaatjie or a Grieta. Certainly not a teacher, or rather a principal, for that was what the Malherbes had in mind for their only daughter.

Antoinette, who passed her Junior Certificate with flying colors, had learned about the French Revolution. Her parents would not have known of that queen's unfortunate death, and she did not tell them, but since her schooldays she has refused to look at a fowl or a sheep held down on a block with a chopper hovering over its head. Her father complained that all that schooling had given her airs. Why, with such a grand name, he whined, had she chosen to call herself Nettie?

Surely no one named Antoinette could help thinking of the guillotine, Nettie explained to her husband, who, delighted by her knowledge and identification with Marie Antoinette, agreed to spare her the sight. She did not admit to a distaste for meat, and as a good wife gritted her teeth to prepare dinners. Nicholas could not be expected to tolerate a fastidious palate, so it was a question of subterfuge, God forgive her, of strategic dishing that would allow her to eat as little meat as possible. Prolonged cooking guaranteed detached bones that could be buried under rice or potatoes accompanied by just the sauce or gravy, bones that she would then uncover for display. Like a dog, she thought. For Nicholas, like her father, was strict, a good man, a man of principle who would not tolerate fussiness. It would take some drilling to find the well of kindness that she knew was there, in his heart. And frugality helped. He praised her for the way in which provisions stretched well past the weekend, even if the meat cooked to death was not always to his taste.

When Nettie's first baby lay squirming helplessly beside her, the mother looked on in terror. Was it really hers? What, dear Lord, had she done? And whatever came next? Where in God's name was Mother Nature, whose job it was to flick the hidden switch of motherhood so that Milk and Love would fountain in abundance? Nettie fell back wearily against her pillow and watched the two delivering oumas whispering to each other and bustling about the baby, who had forced its way out with such wayward enthusiasm, leaving what felt like a hole. Nettie's bruised body was like an egg drained of substance, no more than a fragile shell. No wonder she felt nothing for the baby. There was only terror, and she knew that to be a sin.

Lord have mercy upon us. Christ have mercy upon us.

The Anglican litany learned for Confirmation haunted her. When she left the Moravian mission station for high school in town, her father agreed that the English church would stand her in better stead. Over and over the prayer rang in her head—Lord have Mercy upon us. Christ have Mercy upon us—demanding to be uttered. Antoinette Murray could not do so.

Come now, Ouma Anna said sternly, as she laid the tiny damp

creature on Nettie's breast, you've got to feed her. Nettie feared
that her empty frame, the eggshell, would shatter, but she nodded and looked away, so that the ouma had to get the little mouth
affixed. Then the baby sucked vigorously, making the mother
wince with pain. How would it manage to extract milk from
such emptiness? If only Nicholas were there to advise, but he was
kept out of the room by the oumas, who took no little pleasure in
lording it over Meester. These were things he had no knowledge
of. He had been shown the little girl, now he had to keep out
whilst they cleaned and bound the mother's body, smacked and
swaddled the baby, and got her to feed. But Nettie lay listless,
silent, until he appeared and assured her that the Lord would
indeed have mercy, that Mother Nature worked hand in hand
with patience.

Nicholas picked fresh lucerne from the cow's pasture and having packed it liberally on brown bread and butter, persuaded her
to eat. Whoever's heard of eating cows' food, the oumas protested, but the hole at the heart of Nettie slowly shrank and thin
milk trickled into the baby's greedy mouth. Nettie stifled cries of
pain as the gums clamped on to her cracked nipples. The oumas
recommended Borsdruppels, so aptly named for the chest, but
Nicholas, forgetting to be polite, said that was nonsense, that antiseptic Friar's Balsam would do the trick.

Never again would Nettie rely on Mother Nature. It was her
own efforts, her own stoicism that healed the wound and the
nipples, and trickled substance into her body, so that caring for
the baby, a girl, brought a wary kind of love. As for the child's
name, yes, they would have to rely on God's mercy, but Mercy
seemed to her too abject, too poor-sounding with a two-syllabled
surname. The variant Mercia was just the ticket.

The second child was much delayed. Nettie would not admit to it, but she did everything in her limited means to prevent

pregnancy. Nicholas advised that she should stop feeding the little girl, but the child fortunately was thin as a stick insect, so that Nettie claimed the milk to be a necessary supplement. More than three years later, when Nicholas, anxious for a boy, would tolerate no more of her nonsense, the morning sickness announced another pregnancy. The birth saw Nicholas trick the oumas out of their privileged roles. Of course, he would say that the baby had given him no chance to summon the midwives, that it came charging out of the womb as if pursued by demons, but the oumas pursed their lips. In his pride he let slip that the pots of boiling water and strips of linen had been at the ready. The oumas were outraged. What could Meester possibly know about the secret rites of bringing a child into the world? Too proud to have his son delivered by old Namaqua women, that was it. It was poor Nettie, subjected to the indignity of a man's gaze, his clumsy attentions, deprived of women's knowledge and care, with whom they sympathized. They muttered their curses. Meester's know-all pride and arrogance must come to a fall.

This time Nettie was prepared; she had no expectations of Mother Nature. She also chose to believe that Nicholas had no choice, that the baby was so quick off the mark that there was no time to worry about the oumas' absence. Push, he urged, his hands clamped on her shoulders, claiming that the baby's head was there, that it was a matter of minutes. Besides, he said, one could not be sure of the old women's cleanliness. Nicholas, the autodidact, had done his homework; it turned out that there was nothing to it that common sense did not dictate, and he delivered the baby with skill. A boy, they both exclaimed with delight. And relief, for that meant they could put behind them the business of reproduction.

Nettie said tactfully that he should leave the rest, the rituals, to the oumas, who had turned up regardless, to which Nicholas agreed—it was a live boy with everything intact—but not before the old women had washed their hands properly. The cheek of it, offering them a basin of hot water and soap! Ouma Grieta knotted her doek decisively and bit her lip. Ai Goetsega! Such arrogance would not go unpunished, and barely had she muttered the words when a bolt of unseasonable thunder rumbled. Within minutes a mighty storm was unleashed, and as the baby, smacked, washed and swaddled, drew his first mouthful of milk, rain drummed steadily on the zinc roof, drenching the arid land, and Nettie sank into grateful sleep, cradling the boy. They would call him Jacob, after her own father, and in honor of God the Father who had blessed Jacob of bygone days with productive dreams and a handy ladder. But Nicholas thought otherwise; he did not want to argue with God, but Jacob's treachery, deceiving his father and brother, should not have been rewarded; and his mother should not have connived with her son. So he suggested what he called the French version. Why not Jacques, since Nettie had after all been a Malherbe? They would call him Jake for short, and that should placate her father.

The little girl, Mercy, who at the age of nearly four felt the vastness of the world swirl about her, whose loneliness brought language tumbling willy-nilly, chaotically from her voice box, was over the moon about the boy. The baby was soft and round with a plump face in which she buried her own thin cheeks. He smelled of clean fresh water. He was hers, her very own baby whom she would love with all her heart. She spoke with him in the funny prattle that her parents did not understand, warbling her voice like a bird, knowing that he understood. It was as if a switch had been flicked and all around was glorious light suffusing the dull days. The baby opened his eyes, large and black, and smiled at her, flooding her heart, and Mercia promised baby Jake that she would guard him like the angel that her father said she should be.

There would be no more children, Nicholas said, confident that he could handle the tricky business of contraception. Nettie had done her duty, producing one of each, so there was no need to saddle themselves like poor and ignorant coloreds with a large brood. The children would be raised to the glory of God, and that could only be achieved by strict discipline and chastisement. To that end Nicholas and Nettie pulled in their belts and, turning each coin this way and that, assiduously squirreled away the cents for school fees.

When Nettie died, as quietly as she had lived, Nicholas was puzzled. Why had she said nothing of her illness? Why had she suffered the pain alone? For pain there must have been. When finally she collapsed into her bed and the doctor was summoned, they learned that she had no more than a week or two left. The cancer had consumed nearly all her organs. Her frame was no more than an eggshell. Nettie did not wait for the second week; she made the tremendous effort to speak of the children, to say that Jake should learn Latin, or that was what Nicholas thought she said. And then she was gone.

Mercia was twelve years old. She tried to summon her mother's spirit, but discovered that there was no such thing. Nettie was simply dead. Jake said that their father had killed her—the words of a grief-stricken child. But no, Jake said, he had overnight stopped being a child, he knew what he was talking about. Mercia, who had her nose buried in books, knew nothing. Old Who-art-in-heaven had killed their mother—of that he was certain.

Would Jacques have turned out to be such a reprobate, such a failure, had Nettie remained alive? Nicholas did not want to know the answer. But he could not help feeling resentful. Why had she died? He had done everything: he had chastised the boy; he had sacrificed and provided. Nicholas had an idea that cancer was something resistible that you let into your own heart, that you allowed its crabbing into your organs. Why else had Antoinette said nothing of her pain? Why had she not allowed him to gather Jantjie Bêrend that grew in abundance all around, the cancer bush that would certainly have cured her? Never again would he put his faith in a woman.

Mercia woke to the clatter of Craig opening the wooden shutters. Sad October light flooded in, licking the corners of the room. Pulling the duvet over her head, she buried her face in the pillow, protecting herself against the shards of icy sunlight. Glasgow was by no means the deep north, but it would be the death of her all the same.

Come again? Craig said. Naked, his arms raised, and holding on to the window frame as if holding up the golden day, he stood distracted, his back to her.

I want to kill myself.

It's a gorgeous day. Let's go out, Craig said.

If you won't come and live in Cape Town, I'll kill myself, her muffled voice came through the down.

We'll go to the Pots of Gartness on Endrick Water. The salmon should be there by now, back from the Atlantic trip. All that way they've been, to the bountiful Norwegian sea and now, shining silvery and plump, are on their way back home.

As a teenager Craig had cycled for miles to fish on the river, and in autumn there was the spectacle of the salmon leap. He hadn't been since then; there was no longer the urge to get out of the city, or rather, to get away from his family. The ice-bright day brought back that adolescence, set him off about his mother, who would not let him be, who went on and on, gnawing away in the hope that something would slip out—what did he think? what did he feel?—wanting something he could not give, something he most probably didn't even have.

Why, Craig asked, as he struggled to drag off the duvet that Mercia clung to, does this remind me of my mother?

Mercia came up for air. Oh stop. You're a grown-up, so stop whingeing about your mother. Or, be different—whinge about your father for a change.

How often they competed for center stage. Mercia wanted to talk about the melancholia that descended on her in October, how it took years in the Northern Hemisphere before she realized that the sadness came regularly at autumn. Thus no need to whinge.

I am at one with the universe, with the rhythms of the season, she mocked. Just as I am tuned in to the circadian cycle and must mourn the death of each day.

Aye right, with a glass of bevvy. And that, Craig said, shaking his head, was what made him sick of women, made him think of his mother. All that nasty business of the female psyche. Nothing that a good day of fishing in the rain wouldn't cure.

I have a lecture to write, essays to mark, a paper to finish, a new course proposal to submit tomorrow. Too much to do, she sighed, to go out gallivanting with a mother-hater.

So what's new. You always have too much to do. But it's criminal to allow a rare sunny day in autumn to pass you by, especially when the salmon are doing their high jumps. Come on, we won't be long.

Mercia staggered out of bed. Shocking, but by now she too thought of the chilly autumnal day as beautiful. Let's live in proper sunshine, in Cape Town, she howled all the same. Craig was busy making sandwiches and a flask of coffee.

Let's go, he said. And another thing about women, they always need padkos. As for himself, he could go for hours without something to eat.

Mercia punched his bottom with both her fists, pleased that he remembered the Afrikaans word.

So you'd rather have the good old pub, hey! Let's remember that Scottish pub food is disgusting. And whoever's heard of sandwiches without butter? That's what you get these days.

In the icy sunlight they set out through the city, on to the open road where the hills rose in the distance, the Dumgoyne a sharply outlined lump clad in tweedy autumnal color. They argued about the window. Craig said it had to be open, to savor the loveliness of the autumnal day, of the burnt-red summer bracken snuggling up to the purple haze of heather. Past the Glengoyne distillery.

My father's generation would have stopped for a wee dram, Craig said.

Mercia wasn't listening. If she feared the season, she has always loved the written word, autumn, its disdainful letter M ignoring the N, until it takes a suffix, another syllable for the letters to nuzzle each other, bound in articulated intimacy. Au-tum-nal, she said out loud.

They parked on a lane from where the roar of water could be heard. How could she have forgotten the dizzying beauty of a cold bright day? The hedgerows (oh, hardly hedge-rows, little lines of sportive wood run wild) having lost their summer lushness, now hosted valedictory vetch in weak purple and heads of tired honeysuckle holding out valiantly. And there was the starred triumph of autumn—berries. Polished red of oval rose hips, hawthorn, purple opalescent sloes, and clusters of bright black beads—surely too late for elder?

All eyes and ears for the water, Craig nodded absently; he

didn't know; like a frisky retriever he bounded down the steep, slippery steps to the falls.

There it was, the breathtaking Pots. The order of a banked river all broken, its waters parted, smashed up with jutting planes of black rock over which white water roared with fury and boiled into icy maelstroms below. Where the rock was less jagged, water cascaded in beaded curtains and, here and there taking the gradient in its stride, settled into still pools. And all within a single sweep of the eye. The trees along the banks had already taken color. In the autumnal spectrum of yellow through to burnt red, beech, oak, and elder huddled together, waiting to be lashed and stripped by the wind. But the day was still, and where the water pooled quietly, brushstrokes of reflected leaf color quivered on the surface, inverted.

Craig, who had been rushing along the path in search of familiar landmarks, came to a sudden halt. There, he whispered, taking her hand, look. Salmon seemed to float effortlessly upstream, then, bracing themselves, gathered speed in order to scale the rapids. As they rose in the light their scales glinted the mineral silver of the sea, the trophy of travel, of having managed the crossing from river to ocean, but alas, the return was not going to be easy. The healthier fish hurled themselves defiantly at the broiling water but their arched, curved bodies would fall back, thwarted—then, only the briefest rest before tackling the rapids once more. Heroic, yes, but Mercia felt embarrassing tears prickle as the indomitable creatures were repeatedly beaten, some cut by the rock as they fell back, leaving trails of blood. In the quiet pools the less vigorous salmon flopped about, exhausted, before taking up once more the quest of that circular journey now so near its end.

Craig explained about the redds upstream where months ago

the fish were spawned and to which they now tried to return to make new redds and do some spawning of their own. Clever, yes, but how repellent, Mercia thought, the endless repetition, not only the biological imperative to reproduce, but the need to return to origins, to the very same stream, to make their babies back home. After all that travel and the dodging of dangers—far more radical than any Homeric adventure, as their very organs adapted to the crossing from fresh water to the salt of the sea— this was surely disappointing: the circularity of their lives, and the return all tainted with October blood. Really, she should not have been applauding the few, should not have been rooting for the salmon to perform the spectacular leap, the momentary disappearance in the white spume, before surfacing in a triumphant arc above the rapids, in the calm of the stream where free of the fury they could head upstream. Not yet triumphant, since there would be more rapids to negotiate, more endurance tests before reaching the old spawning grounds, but hopefully none as trying as these at Gartness. Did they remember the reverse journey, the carefree, dizzying tumble downstream through the rapids?

What happens, she asked, when they get home, to the fond ancestral streams?

Well, it's not only the end of the odyssey, it's the end of their lives. After the female digs her redds in the gravel of quiet waters and the male does the fertilizing, they're just about pooped, ready to die and make way for the next generation.

Oh, midst the splendor of water and words like autumnal, she could kill herself after all. Mercia could no longer bear to look. Call it a tourist attraction! It was indecent; the place should be fenced off; humans should be sheltered from Mother Nature's cruel displays. How awful that return. She for one did not want to see it—the gravel redds murky with spawn and the self-satisfied rumbling of parents, turned into shallow graves where, exhausted by the business of reproduction, the salmon must lie down and die.

Well, they don't exactly die in the redds. There the new organisms will be growing into little smolts, the small fry, Craig explained.

She shuddered. Had he noticed, Mercia asked, young mothers steering prams in shopping malls or airports, explaining this or that to their little Johnnies in super-loud voices that declared the world a redd, a special place of spawning, of triumphant arrival. Craig laughed. That was not why he had brought her to Endrick, but he agreed. An object lesson in reproduction, base, primitive, animal, and he lifted her off the ground, spun round triumphantly in the slippery mud and declared that they were not ready to die.

Imagine, she said, making a song and dance about the wise salmon, when the wisdom is driven by reproduction, by the fetishizing of origins. No wonder salmon have pride of place in Glasgow's coat of arms.

Please, he said, no aspersions on Finn MacCool. That's my Irish heritage you're scoffing at. You should eat the salmon skin— best pan-fried and crisped—so that like my good self and Finn MacCool you too can gain knowledge of the world, become the oracle. Mercia would have to lighten up; she could see for herself that it was nonsense talk, this being in tune with nature—this wanting to kill herself, Craig said.

So off they went in the bright October light, back to the city for an invigorating bottle of red wine and protected sex.

It was presumably Craig's Irish heritage and all that crisped salmon skin that made him succumb. Mercia had been called by his sister, Fiona, who asked to meet for a coffee. She should have known; she and Fiona were not really friends. They sat at

Gandolfi's, where Fiona chattered frantically as if warding off an attack of some kind. She ordered too many cakes, which they pushed around on their plates. When finally it was acceptable to leave, as Mercia pushed back the heavy, carved chair, Fiona placed a restraining hand on hers.

Morag is pregnant, she said, and she would rather Mercia heard it from her, and sooner rather than later.

Mercia took a deep breath. When? she asked, ready to calculate the date of conception.

Fiona explained that it was a surprise to them, that the baby was not due until late November.

Mercia said a terse thank-you, and made herself walk out slowly. No running, and hold your head high, no not Johnny-head-in-the-air like her father had taught her; rather, as the Pilates teacher said, with a soft peach under the chin. That is what Mercia mouthed, over and over, as she walked tall through the Merchant City, through Queen Street station, to the Underground: soft peach under the chin. The trick was not to squash it.

So long it was, after Craig had left. Who would have thought that she'd have any tears left, but it felt as if the wound was being prised open. What exactly was Mercia crying for? If Craig had not taken the younger woman to Gartness, hadn't shown her the leaping salmon, what was it to her?

Such reasoning did not stop the pain.

🦋

Shards of autumnal light, the city leaved with October blood, yes, she remembers the day of the leaping salmon so clearly. When she gets back to Scotland, Mercia vows, she will return to Endrick Water. Many years have passed, and no doubt the path on the riverbank would be paved, and there would be signs prompting the tourist to press a camera button for the picturesque shot, alert her to the best place from which to view through a lens the crazed salmon glinting metallic above the water. She wants to be shot of Craig and his salmon, and since memory is so bound up with place, she believes that all such places must be revisited, the previous memory erased. That trip had left her with distaste for the iridescence of fish scales, for all things circular, for journeys that must end where they started.

Mercia is not home because this is where she started out; she is here in Kliprand, she reminds herself, because Jake wanted her to come. Now a wasted Jake seems to have lost his marbles, keeping out of reach, silent in a room dark and musty with the fumes of alcohol. She knows that she too is in a sense hiding from him, that she too wants to put off talking, put off the unknown decisions that talking will bring. In the meantime, the moderate October heat is comforting, and she does love the familiar view of gray-green scrub with flat-topped mountains looming blue in the distance. She loves that hot, red sand where ancient tortoises sit for days resting in the same scrap of shade as if the earth had not moved, or night had not fallen, tortoises whose purpose it would seem is to endure the passage of time.

So despite Jake, and Sylvie's horrible chatter, Mercia knows that this is home. There is a part of her, perhaps no more than insensate buttocks, that sinks into the comfortable familiarity of an old sofa. Which is nothing to do with three-legged cast-iron pots or roosterbrood; besides, the light slants onto the floor precisely as it does at the other end of the year in Glasgow—the world simply reversed. But here, is it not conceivable that Mercia could stretch out, boots and all, for a while at least, open her heart, let in the heat and light, and check to see how much of it has mended?

How very far you have traveled, Craig once said to her shortly after they met. She understood it as a tired trope and smiled, not

knowing whether to be offended. There was no point in saying
that traveling had brought very little, that apart from the civility achieved through money and self-regard the northern world
seemed much the same—there was only the business of growing
older and necessarily inching this way and that, scratching about
like a hen in the straw for a place in which to be comfortable. That
is the payoff, the compensation for the loss of youth, of beauty,
which is so wasted on the young, who do not know that they are
beautiful. As long as it has nothing to do with coming full circle
like a salmon, with the horrible notion of roundness and comple-
tion. But then, expecting to be comfortable in your declining
years, to shuffle into old age hand in hand with the beloved turns
out to be asking too much, is a sign of complacency that has to be
punished, and the punishment to be borne with dignity. Which
is to say without crying.

What, Mercia wonders, will happen to Sylvie? When all is
done and dusted will Sylvie go quietly, launch herself into a new
condition of single motherhood and ugly poverty? Or will she
throw her head back and bray at the unjust world? Tear out Jake's
eyes?

Nicky slumps in front of the television. His mother bustles about
with a feather duster, muttering to herself, or rather ambiguously
talking to herself as well as to Mercia, whom she does not address
directly, and of whom she appears to expect no answers. Even
the question of a camera, which Mercia is about to answer. Sylvie supposes that Mercia would have brought a camera, so why
then has there been no sign of it? But she does not wait for a
reply. Her strange discourse segues seamlessly to the child, to his
deprivation, of how he'd be better off without having to know
such a father, to Meester's camera that has disappeared, no doubt

sold by Jake for a bottle of plonk. A disgrace, and such a good camera that Pa had expressly said was for Nicky. Ag, to talk and talk about things, what does it help, Sylvie says self-reflexively; she admonishes herself to stop, that it does no good, and then she is indeed quiet for a while, before starting up once more. Mercia thinks that she could grow to like such interaction, where someone else's loops of consciousness wash over you, making no demands on you to speak, where your presence is enough.

As it happens, Mercia does have a camera, a brand-new Panasonic, which in a foolish moment at an airport she bought in the belief that she ought to have a hobby. She has brought it along, but does not even have the inclination to read the instructions. The ubiquity of cameras, the deferral of looking and experiencing as people snap instead, preferring the image, the chosen angle to savor at another time, has always been distasteful to her. The truth is that she is too embarrassed to carry the thing about. She ought to say to Sylvie that the boy could have hers. Why doesn't she?

Christ, the woman will sit there in the doorway soaking up sunlight and say nothing, stare like an idiot into space. As if there were no one else about, as if she, Sylvie, the one who dusts and sweeps and stirs the pots, were not there. That's what these grand people are like, the Murrays and their kind. If that's what education brings then thank you very much, she would happily do without abc-ing. She too could sit around with books, magazines, but what a waste of time that would be, getting yourself all het up like a teenager about people you don't know, dressed-up people who have nothing to do with you. No more than a kind of busybodiness that passes for being clever.

And why has Mercia said nothing about the camera? Sylvie's days of photographing herself are over; she would rather not think of that time; she doesn't know what happened to that old camera. Did she not give it to Kytou? But it's different for the child. Nicky, who knows no better, bless his heart, had gone through his auntie's bag, had brought out the camera to show his mother, and of course he has to learn that one does not look into other people's things, so she had to give him a good smack. Especially a cheeky child like Nicky, who said that he found the camera in his room, so why couldn't he look?

It is just as well that Nicky is there. A child is a handy thing for breaking the ice, so she says to Mercia, who starts—just as she thought, as if no one else is about—that the child tore his trousers yesterday. She wonders aloud whether Mercia is any good at nee-dlework, at invisible mending. That might just give the woman a much-needed something to do, something practical.

For a moment Mercia recoils at the idea. Mending, darning, letting out the dreaded hems—that she could not countenance, but almost at the same time she revises the thought. Why not? Why not do something with her hands, besides, will it not sound snooty to say that she can't?

I didn't do needlework at school, and my mother got nowhere in her attempts to teach me, she explains. But you know what it's like when you grow up; you want clothes, fashionable things. When there isn't the money and you wouldn't dare to ask anyway, you've got to get round it. So I tried to teach myself; I learned to knit and also to sew, but really I wasn't much good at needlework. I'll give it a go, but don't hold your breath.

Sylvie tosses the child's trousers to her. She doesn't buy that stuff about being poor. She remembers Mercia, an older, distant figure, always looking nice, and wearing good shoes. What non-sense, the Murrays had plenty, although the old man was accord-ing to Jake mean, and Sylvie knows exactly what he means.

Mercia examines the damage. The trousers are worn; the ripped fabric has frayed, so that sewing a new seam would not be

strong enough. Anyway, there's no such thing as invisible mending. She says that if there's an old pair that he's outgrown, she
could use the material to patch this one. She understands Sylvie's
frown. Faux-poor is the prerogative of the wealthy. The woman
cannot but fear that her child will be laughed at, so Mercia explains that patches these days are okay, ripped trousers twice as
cool and not at all a sign of poverty.

Sylvie's voice is adamant; she won't have her boy go about in
rags. It will have to be your fancy patches then, even if it makes no
sense that people should want to pretend to be poor. Imagine rip-
ping perfectly good trousers to look cool. She knows that Mercia
is making it up, no doubt trying to get out of doing the job, but
she finds fabric for the patch. Perhaps, she laughs triumphantly,
you could fix your brother's trousers as well. He's turning into
a right skollie, staggering about to the bar with his clothes all
ripped, making people say how she is a bad wife when there is no
need for him to wear torn things. No need at all, given that she
does everything, has the washed and pressed clothes hanging up
neatly in the cupboard, but no, he must get the kekkelbekke in
the village talking. There are plenty of those, just jealous that she
has married a Murray, and now ready to gossip about the slight-
est thing.

Well, if people once were jealous they will no longer be,
Mercia says. It clearly is not such a wonderful thing to be married to a man who's a millstone round Sylvie's neck if ever she
saw one—even if he is lying in his bed. But Jake will have to pull
himself together, get out of that bed, otherwise she, Mercia, will
drag him out herself. Sylvie snorts, easier said than done. It's time
to get the dinner, she sighs. A piece of fish would make a nice
change, the fish that Mercia said she would get. But Mercia, immersed in a tricky chapter that morning, had clean forgotten. She
is so sorry; she'll go right away; there is still time.

Forgotten to get the dinner? Sylvie says nothing but looks at her with incredulity. How can anyone, a woman, forget such a thing? Did that Scotsman of hers, that Craig, did he not expect better of her? No wonder the man left.

※

Mutual friends were careful not to invite Craig and Mercia to the same events. People were kind. Mostly Mercia, the one in need of kindness, would be consulted first, and she declined all but the most irresistible invitations. She knew that Smithy and others would also have to get used to the new couple, Craig and the woman whose name she could not utter. Soon, of course, a baby would keep them indoors whilst she, Mercia, would go about unencumbered. Pathetic, and though she thinks herself above it, it is the case that she braces herself for being viewed as one who has missed the boat, as people once said, one in need of kindness.

Nonsense, Smithy said, your heart will mend, and then you won't care. Then you'll see how people will envy you for coming and going as you please, happy as a lark. But that made embarrassing tears stream down Mercia's newly lined face. I'll be fine, she said, as long as I don't walk into them, or even into Craig.

Inevitably, she did. One Saturday morning early at the Fish Plaice, where mercifully Craig was on his own, and Scott the fishmonger, believing them still to be together, shouted his usual banter of No need for Viagra, fish'll do the trick. Yous having a party? Half price for three kilo, can't say fairer than that, pal. And his mother laughed, Yous should be so lucky.

Under his breath Craig said, Has Fiona told you? It was an accident. We didn't—

But Mercia interrupted with a terse Congratulations, and left without the salmon that Scott was filleting for her.

Mercia returns her cursor to a new page in the Home file. No harm, she thinks, in larking about, but the words about the self, so bound up with Craig, elude her. She would have to resort to the corny creative writing exercise: a day in the life of a penny, or an oak leaf in autumn, or a salmon . . .

who has crossed the boundaries from fresh to salt water, from river to sea, from sea to river, my scales glittering with guanine crystals, my kidneys primed with Italian wine, my skin bleached by sunless skies, I am the one flailing in the shallows, the one who has not managed the leap.

This she deletes and replaces with: the one who has declined the leap.

She ought to delete the lot.

This is also the story of Nicholas Murray, and the crucial role of bootstraps in the making of him. It is the story he did not tire of telling, one that marked him as outsider midst these idle Namaqualanders who toast themselves in the winter sun without a care in the world.

When Nicholas left his home in the Klein Karoo, it was not that he did not heed the fifth commandment—Honor thy father and thy mother that thy days may be long in the land which the Lord thy God giveth thee. Rather, as he explained to his pa, one cannot make anything of life as a plowboy. Granted, these commandments were given to Moses on tablets of stone, but if you thought about it, thought about the fact that Moses had led his people out of the land of Egypt, out of the house of bondage, then Pa would see that God intended for people to move on and to free themselves from oppression.

His pa, who believed that the earth should be tilled by those born to it, was not convinced. Besides, it was vainglorious of the boy to think of himself as Moses, and as for the argument that the earth he cultivated did not even belong to him, well, the earth belonged to none other than God. It was his ma who coaxed, who arranged for Nicholas a place to stay in the dorp where he worked by day as a messenger boy and went to school by night. He had given himself only six years, Nicholas boasted, in which to put himself through Matric and teachers' training college, and to take home to Pa a pay packet of crackling paper money.

Kliprand was Nicholas's first post. When he arrived—a young man—in the summer of 1955, he could not have guessed that he would spend the rest of his life in that place. Being from another part, from the Overberg district, a land more lush, where a vegetable garden could flourish and where cattle grazed contentedly, he believed that Kliprand was not a place for staying.

The advertisement in the *Government Gazette* spoke of a primary school in a remote settlement where he knew he would not be answerable to anyone. That was the kind of freedom he strived for—Nicholas would not be watched and bossed about by white people. Although he would have to teach all the classes in one room, the numbers were manageable, and since the heuristic approach was in any case the best education, his strategy was for the older children to learn their lessons and practice their English by instructing and testing the younger ones. Even the little ones, sitting in a circle in the shade, took turns at being teacher.

Only rarely did an inspector turn up to check on Meester, and not only were his books and registers in order, but the children, more or less clean, chanted their times tables enthusiastically, sang "Uit die blou van onse hemel," identified the Tropics on the battered old globe, knew the history of the country by rote, and could recite rhymes in English. The inspector knew nothing about Meester's after-school activities, the garden where children learned their natural sciences from the mealies, pumpkins, and watermelons he conjured out of the dry land. And from the goats and sheep that multiplied and soon constituted a sizeable flock. The people shook their heads in surprise and admiration: Ai Goetsega, that Meester was now a first-class kind of a man.

That was what the people of Kliprand called him—Meester,

but it was also his status as stranger that earned respect amongst the Namaquas, for strangers must be honored. He was an outsider and so necessarily better, a man who would teach their children, give help and advice with ailments, read and write their letters, and deal on their behalf with white authorities. When dominee was ill, they could rely on him to step in at a moment's notice to deliver a stirring sermon. Meester was in charge of the new drug against tuberculosis, left in his custody by Dr. Groenewald, who was not always inclined to travel to the township and so relied on him to administer the weekly injections. He also purchased from Dr. Groenewald a supply of anti-inflammatory tablets, the new drug which would rescue the sick from the very clutches of death.

Yislaaik, the women exclaimed with pride, this Meester was both teacher and doctor; he could do the needle as well as the pen. And when a minor problem arose for any family, they could rely on him for food, or to help out with a loan. These functions set him apart as a stranger, better off than themselves. Meester was a good man, and a good man was hard to find.

Nicholas was not going to scrape a living as a schoolmaster. The bootstraps by which he had pulled himself out of the world of goat-herders and plowboys, where three of his brothers remained, would lever him above the meager living of a village schoolmaster. He would also keep livestock and sell his own produce. His children would go to school and to university in the city. Nicholas was fortunate in meeting the lovely, God-fearing Antoinette Malherbe, demure in dress and demeanor, and raised in the respectable mission station of Elim. She was just modern enough to stop at two children. Boy and girl, that would do, one of each, she promised, although he would have preferred the boy to be the elder. Nicholas could not help feeling that not being the older contributed to Jake's fecklessness. A boy who is an ouboet would not shirk responsibility, but being the younger, the baby as Antoinette persisted in calling him, Jake had somehow been spoilt.

After all these years, was the place where he had been raised, the small holding in the Overberg valley where his family lived from hand to mouth, still home for Nicholas? Could that be home when he had not been there for so long, remembered little more than the youthful urge to leave the place? These were questions that plagued him once the children scampered about the stony wastes of Kliprand.

No, Nicholas came to love this land where he had done so well, and where he planned to stay until his dying day. He was nothing but loyal to Kliprand, his place of domicile, but saw no need to abandon his position as outsider. Here, in this remote outpost of Namaqualanders, he could not very well belong. Nomad blood seemed still to course in their veins, for why did they not till the land? Why were they content to toil for low-class Englishmen in the gypsum mines?

How he hated their speech. The dragged vowels and especially the use of ga and hitse, surely Hottentot words, he considered barbaric. How could knowledge be acquired in such a tongue? These people were too—and he appeared to search for the word each time—well, too indigenous, refusing to wash away the stamp of Hottentot origins. In fact, did they not use the excuse of brack water for not washing as often as they should?

Here in Kliprand a few of the old people sang, of all things, hymns in a savage tongue that Jesus surely could not condone, and the young men smoked local dagga and danced the kabarra, a word pronounced with a clicking tongue that Nicholas knew he would never manage. Flushed with shame, he watched the askoek dance, as some preferred to call it. A dusty affair, performed where the fire had died down after the grilling of flatbread, by men leaping high off the ground as they clicked the sides of their feet together, ash flying. His role as Meester was clear. The hotnos ways, the memory of clicks and kabarra and ash, had to be beaten out of the children. To this purpose he lined them up in military fashion, got them to march stiffly in time to his bellow of links-regs, left-right, up and down the dusty rugby field, starting the day with exercises that required straightened limbs and heads held high. Only thereafter the recitation of the alphabet, of times tables and unfathomable poems committed to memory, and the children were soundly thrashed for faltering.

Thus if Nicholas, as his father had taught him, was at one with the land, knowledgeable about its flora and fauna, knew its every undulation, its mounds and troughs, every outcrop of rock, the sparse shrubs, the memory of winter streams in the washed earth—there was nothing dramatic about this landscape—he was not of the place. Yes, he tilled the earth, but holding on to his bootstraps, he also cultivated a necessary distance, an unbelonging. By such means the distant memory of European blood could be kept alive.

The Murrays were of old Scottish stock, people who had settled before the Europeans were corrupted by Africa. A good old colored family, evenly mixed, who having attained genetic stability could rely on good hair and healthy dark skin, not pitch-black like Africans, and certainly nothing like sly Slamse from the east, who were not to be trusted. The Murrays had no further use for European blood, no need for more mixing; they were proud colored people who kept their distance from others. Nicholas shook his head contemptuously at the people of Kliprand who did not mind at all if one of their girls arrived from the white dorp with a blue-eyed baby, the product of cheap relations with a master.

Antoinette too, having been a Malherbe, was of good stock. If theirs had come to be an Afrikaans name, well the Malherbes knew better, knew that it was fighting Huguenot blood that coursed through their veins, infusing them with wholesome Calvinism. When, as a teenager, Mercia tried to correct her father about sly Slamse, pointing out that the slave blood of Cape Malays was also part of their heritage, he dismissed it as foolish ANC propaganda.

Nicholas did not tire of telling his young children the story of how he had pulled himself up by his own bootstraps. That he was one of a large family, of a father who was illiterate, was neither here nor there. The important thing was that that father was visibly of European stock, that he was a God-fearing, clean-living man of the land, even if that land belonged to a boer. For all his disadvantages, he had built with his bare hands a decent house for his family, fed and clothed them, and had never been in debt. Through hard work he gathered an adequate herd of cattle; in other words had set the example of pulling himself up by his own bootstraps. The Murrays, Nicholas said, were a tall and erect people; they held their heads high, and therefore each generation prospered beyond their fathers.

As the children grew older they secretly mocked Nicholas, who checked their postures, and was not past flicking his aap-stert at their legs with a clipped Head up, shoulders back. This pulling up by the bootstraps, Jake sniggered, did not make sense. It would surely make of the Murrays a crooked clan, bent over, always fiddling with their boots, anything but erect. He did not fancy the idea of prospering in that contradictory manner. The children noted that Pappa Murray's grandfather, the great Scotsman, was never mentioned, except in terms of the blood that he had brought. No doubt short and crooked with eating too much oats and lack of sunlight, and a drunkard to boot, Jake conjectured. Clearly Pappa didn't know him, otherwise there would surely have been aggrandizing stories. Most likely the Scotsman had another legitimate family, besides the children fathered upon his black slave.

Years later, after Jake had lost his job in the wine industry, he taunted Nicholas, drunkenly holding a bottle of wine by the neck, tilting his head and swigging directly from it. Look, he said, no slouching here; I've learned to keep my head up. Good Calvinist habit, he laughed, smacking his lips. I drink in honor of our Huguenot forefathers who brought the vine to the Cape, who established our flourishing wine industry on the backs of Namaquas and other qua-quas and slaves and the dop-system of weekly pay in flagons of cheap wine. Jake stumbled about in unlaced shoes. No danger, he declared, of pulling himself up by his bootstraps.

May God forgive you, Nicholas said, bewildered by Jake's madness. He shut his eyes, and his hands patted various parts of his person, as if in search of the aapstert that would cure all abomination. He spoke with difficulty, a Moses about to stutter his fifth commandment, but was it not too late for that? Instead, it was the story of Noah that would have to guide the boy, a story that Jake had clearly forgotten.

God sent Europeans to darkest Africa, he said, to teach us about moderation. Wine is to be drunk in the manner of Holy Communion, and drunkenness, as the Huguenots well knew from the story of Noah, is an abomination. Noah himself was of course blameless. How could he have known about the effects of wine? What God tells us is that Noah's son Ham laughed at his father's nakedness, and that Ham's descendants were blackened by the curse of Noah. Which places on us, the people of Ham, the burden of redeeming ourselves in the eyes of the Lord.

Nicholas's voice grew stronger. We may not have in English different verbs for animals' eating and drinking, it is too civilized a language, but just think, my boy, of the Afrikaans, vreet and suip, the gross words for the ways in which animals consume, words that we also use for the shameful excess of human beings.

Ja, Jake declared, slurring and swaying melodramatically, I am gesuip. And following the Latin conjugations that we learned from an aapstert, here it goes: You are gesuip / He/she/it is gesuip / We are gesuip / You are gesuip / They are gesuip. But tell me, he hiccupped, tell me, Grootbaas, do you know what Malherbe actually means?

Nicholas shook his head sadly. Who could have imagined such an abomination, such a disgrace? He was glad that Nettie was snugly in her grave. Nettie would know that he had done his best for the boy, that he was blameless, that in spite of regular chastising, the feckless Namaqua ways had infected the boy.

Now Nicholas is dead. Did her father die of a broken heart? Was that what his heart failure was about? Has he been killed by Jake's outrageous behavior? Had Jake found some choice words with which to strike a fatal blow? That, Mercia assumes, is what Sylvie means. If only she had been there to protect him, an old man who, having done his best, had to live with the disappointment of contrary children. Mercia sighs. Well, nowadays people know the risks involved in reproducing themselves. That the clone they hope for and groom may well turn into a viper. At least, Mercia has always assumed that that is what her own womb would produce.

It is more difficult than Mercia had thought, trying to work on her book, wading through the cant that clings to local versions of postcolonial memory, whilst waiting for Jake to rouse himself. Does she imagine that he will one morning rise and shine and over a cup of freshly brewed coffee discuss his condition or Nicky's plight with her? She chooses not to think that far ahead. But by midafternoon Mercia has had enough. She is bored with her summaries of existing arguments. The promise of new insights darts about, as elusive as the floaters that here, in the October light, assail her vision. So much for being home, where her eyes can no longer manage the moderate brightness of spring. Perhaps like grief these symptoms that appear one by one will pass, at least the ones that matter.

With little else to do in that place, the memoir presents itself as an option. In Nicky's little room, behind closed doors, she opens the file, flicks through the fragments. Mercia tries to persuade herself that the memoir, so much easier than critical writing, will fill the afternoon hours. As if she does not know better. As if she needs to see the cursor's tireless flicker at the start of a new blank document to know that no words, by virtue of being about real people and events, exist ready-made for committing to the screen. The words that have to be processed are yet to be found, retrieved from the teeming jumble, the cacophony that carries on in her head. How tired she is of this conundrum, of the unfound words that have fallen to her for processing. Tired too of the long imaginary discussions with Craig, the abject what-went-wrongs, and of Jake and the childhood he cannot throw off. Is she not also tired of the very living she makes, a profession bristling with words that generate more words? With more than enough words in the world, with the many commentaries on commentaries, the stories echoing each other, why the temptation to write another, to reproduce?

No, she must keep things in perspective. Writing about the dreariness of their lives in Kliprand would be, as she well knows, a redundant act. There is nothing extraordinary about the Murrays; in fact, are there any stories in the world that do not have a counterpart in another culture, that with a small measure of imagination are not easily transposed? Oh, she knows that this harks back to the now discredited notion of universality, but what to do, what to do when Jake, as wayward as he is in real life, won't be pinned down? Mercia closes the screen. It is a diversion from her work. She is a teacher and a critic, and that ought to do. If she is tired and despondent, unable to progress on her project, that too is a given; it is the condition of people in her profession.

The little room closes in on her. It is too hot to go out for a walk, and Mercia cannot face the possibility of meeting Sylvie on the stoep or in the garden. If only she had brought along the novel about siblings who return to the place of birth. These days her memory is not what it was; already she could do with re-reading the story she remembers as a version of theirs, echoed in another continent. Give or take a few transpositions, the different worlds are not so different, in spite of the genteel northern setting. Mercia having then settled into identification with the story, the characters—a child with a dressing-up box—wonders what it would be like reading the novel now, at home, where she grapples with being back. Although, being here in Kliprand is simply a question of a couple of weeks; bunking down boots and all is not an option. Besides, it is too late. Her father is dead.

Return has always been a tricky notion, teeming with thorns. Why, people often ask, has she not returned to the country after Mandela's release? She would shake her head, shrug, would not deign to answer. As if exile were a frozen affair in which you are kept pristinely in the past, one that a swift thaw could restore so that, rinsed and refreshed, you are returned in mint condition to an original time, an original place. Nowadays Mercia does not want to think about Craig's role in her condition, about how different things might have been had she not been enthralled by him.

If Kliprand is not home to Nicholas, it cannot be home to his children. They were born there, raised in Namaqualand, but no, they should not think of it as home. Physical geography is not everything; it is important, in the interest of self-improvement, to dispense with the notion of home. It is after all an excessive sense of belonging that leaves the people of Kliprand tied to the place, limited and ambitionless, bound by their past and its unspeakable customs. But they do not have the means to go elsewhere, the children protest on behalf of the people. Nicholas counters with the fact that as a young man he did not have the means to leave the Overberg. Only think of our forebears, he says, the adventurous Scots who left their home and braved the seas to make new lives at the Cape, or the Moravians who founded the mission station at Elim—there are examples of developed minds who were able to shrug off the outmoded, atavistic notion of home, way back in the nineteenth century. Thus his children should not think of this place of their birth, burdened as it is with the arcane complexities of belonging, as their home.

Instead, belonging is a given; it may be about the space where they live, but the self could belong any place at all where improvement presents itself. Belonging is sanctified not by place, but by blood relations, family. For the children, family is an idea imagined by their parents, bound up with the smell of yeast wafting from Nettie's baking, the curling wood smoke, the anticipation of warm brown bread on which her freshly churned butter will melt, and the prayer of thanks to God as they gather to eat. The grown-ups have no idea how oppressive the children find that family, that home. Nicholas has no idea how much Jake hates him, what he would give to be in the city where an odorless Duens loaf could be bought from the corner shop.

In Cape Town there are more Murrays, respectable brothers and sisters who have married well, which is to say spouses with good hair. If Nicholas's children long for company, for playmates, well there are cousins with whom they could correspond. The fact is that the children here in Kliprand do not wash their hands, he explains.

South Africa itself is a model, Nicholas claims. We can't think of this country as ours, because it belongs to white people, even to the English who claim to belong to Europe. Colored people can't support the Springboks; no, when we sit with our ears glued to the radio, it's the Lions or the All Blacks whom we cheer. So we are free, above geography. We're free to belong anywhere.

The children snort at his distorted idea of freedom. Mercia asks about their indigenous ancestors, the Africans who are their forefathers, but he brushes aside the question. The truth is that he wants to know nothing of them. It is important, he counters, to remember that the Murrays are colored people. But neither does he know anything of the colored revolutionaries of his age, the Dennis Brutuses or Cissie Gools or Alex La Gumas. What he knows is that respectable coloreds have nothing to do with whites and do not bow to such people, but that they do keep on the right side of the law, do not make a fuss. As for black nationalists, what folly from a people who can't read and write. When Mercia tells him of A.C. Jordan, he laughs. But the man's name shows that he's not African at all; he's colored. No, they are troublemakers, shortsighted people intent on destroying all that is civilized.

Mercia reminds her father of his sermonizing about Moses, who led his people out of slavery. Why did he not think people should work toward the overthrow of a government that oppressed them? Nicholas thinks her contrary. Moses was led by the voice of God. I am who I am, he says, ambiguously, pounding his chest.

Many years earlier, and shortly after Mercia announced her decision to throw in her lot with Craig, Nicholas wanted her to accompany him to Elim, the Moravian missionary station where Nettie had grown up. He said that Nettie had of late appeared to him in his dreams, that he could not rest until he had visited her old house and the church in Elim. It was important too that Mercia knew the place, that she did not lose sight of those roots.

Mercia was happy to go. They stayed the night with cousins in Cape Town, where Jake failed to turn up, and drove the next morning to Elim. Nicholas had been there only once before, many decades ago. He stood in the square orientating himself in the autumn sunlight, his head swiveling back and forth with amazement at time's tricks. The church, remembered for its cathedral-like proportions, turned out to be tiny. Beautiful, of course, in its simplicity, and above all, the purity of whiteness. There were the freshly whitewashed walls, and even the wooden pews, the austere pulpit, were painted white, and the sun streamed in through tall windows, bathing all things in brightness and purity. So that Nicholas fell to his knees and with tears streaming, prayed loudly to God, prattled about sin and forgiveness, prayed that Nettie, who now sat with the angels, too would forgive him.

Embarrassed by his display of piety, Mercia left to explore the square, where to her surprise she came across a monument celebrating the emancipation of slaves. She had not known of any such monument, of any acknowledgment of slavery in colored communities, and the inscription of 1938, some century after the actual emancipation, was puzzling. When Nicholas finally emerged, spent and presumably cleansed, he was embarrassed by the monument. No, he had known nothing of it, and no, Nettie had never spoken of it. These things he felt were best laid to rest. Let bygones be bygones. Would she, Mercia, not rather spend some time in the church? They were all sinful creatures, and never had he seen such a pure place, every inch of it white and dazzling with God's love so that having strayed from the straight and narrow they could bank on forgiveness. It required only humility to be folded in the arms of God.

Mercia did not say that the beauty of the church was for her spoiled by the talk of sin, dirty talk like muddy footprints across the ethereal white. She would rather cross the road and look at the church from a distance. Nicholas followed. What a pity, he said, that here where the majority of houses were so lovely in plain whitewash, some people spoiled it all by painting theirs in that salacious dark pink. Or, farther along the row, in a vulgar, bright blue.

Mercia disagreed. Yes, the white houses with their traditional thatched roofs were beautiful, picturesque, but really, one couldn't blame people for not wanting uniformity, for refusing to turn their village into a museum to be gawped at by strangers. There is nothing wrong, she said brusquely, with a bit of color.

Later, Nicholas was reminded by a denizen, leaning over his garden gate, that the pews had always been of dark wood, that they had only been painted latterly. By newcomers with their fancy ideas, the old man complained. Oh yes, he said, he remembered the Malherbes. Stuck up, they were, so that Nicholas said sternly that people could not be blamed for wanting to better themselves.

No, the old chap said, and paused, no they definitely can't be blamed, and he shook Nicholas's hand gratefully for the insight.

Across the square the village hall was buzzing with activity. As it happened they had hit upon a Saturday bazaar. Nicholas was struck by the orderliness, cleanliness, the inventiveness of produce for sale. Melon konfyt in pretty little baskets made of colored card and crinkled paper; bottles of homemade ginger beer; cupcakes artfully decorated with icing—nothing of the slovenliness of Kliprand here, so that Mercia sprang to its defense.

Actually, she countered, he had no idea how people lived there, he did not go to the village celebrations, where much the same stuff was made for sale.

No, he said, those people don't wash their hands; one can't risk eating their food. Here, Elim certainly had its share of poor people, but they at least were clean.

Mercia laughed at the poor-but-clean usage. How shocked her father would be by the filth of the well-off. How shocked she was visiting fellow students' flats in Europe, and then their family homes, where she found it hard to drink coffee from stained cups hastily rinsed under a tap. Cleanliness seemed inversely proportionate to privilege, as if people no longer able to pay others to look after them had failed to learn to clean themselves. Perhaps it was an inevitable outcome of social mobility that those who in the past had cleaned, women, were no longer prepared to do it for themselves or for others. It had been a source of contention between her and Craig. Mercia would have a cleaner; she worked too hard to do it herself. What could possibly be wrong with giving work to an unemployed person as long as you paid her a decent wage? But Craig was embarrassed, finally giving in on condition that his own room was left untouched.

The cleanliness of Mercia's childhood was nothing short of oppressive. If people complained of the ubiquitous sand that threatened to invade their houses, of the grit that stung their legs when the wind rose in the afternoons, then sand was also their salvation. For all its being the antithesis of the scarce commodity of water, the two elements cooperated in cleaning rituals. Pots blackened by primus flames had to be scrubbed first in rough sand, then polished with steel wool, inside and out, before being rinsed with hard-to-come-by water. A daily war was waged against soot that had to be scoured, first of all with sand, from the Jewel stove. In the damp riverbed they scrubbed their feet and smoothed their cracked heels with sand.

Once a month the entire family was cleansed internally. They fasted all day, and flushed out the unclean with castor oil, so that their digestive tracts felt sandblasted, later to be laved by the thin vegetable soup they supped in the evening. How could her father be oblivious to the cost of that cleanliness? Mercia remembered the horror of Saturdays when the chores assigned to her were specifically for her training as a girl. With the washing of the family's handkerchiefs left to her, no one could have been more pleased with the advent of paper tissues, but Nicholas thought it an extravagance they should do without. How she gagged at the slimy mucus that had to be dislodged from the cloth. The grit of sand helped, a barrier between her fingers and the excretions of others, but the handkerchiefs had to be wrung, twisted this way and that to rid them of the slippery stuff, and then rinsed of the soiled sand.

Why were the nasty chores reserved for her? It was also she, Mercia, who had to empty the chamber pots, and if she can barely remember her mother, Nettie's inspection of the pots on Saturdays remains indelible. A daily rinse was not enough. Once a week the enamel pots had to be scrubbed with sand to ensure that no unhygienic deposits adhered, and all before rubber gloves had found their way to Kliprand. Grown-ups were exempt from these demeaning tasks, and so was her brother. Mercia knew that questioning her lot would achieve nothing more than a sting-ing smack—such was the nasty world of grown-ups. Had her own mother not rebelled as a child? And if she had, why was she repeating the practice? Not only would Mercia never give her own child such tasks; she knew from an early age that she would rather have no children to bully. Mercia never traveled without rubber gloves in her suitcase, just in case something nasty had to be handled.

Then, as she watched her father steeped in borrowed nostalgia, stumbling about the village of Nettie's childhood, affectionately recollecting the hardships of their early marriage, Mercia felt a rush of sympathy for their ineptitude as parents. She could hear Jake's cynical reprimand, that it was in her own interest to believe that the old folk did what they did because they believed it to be for the best, to be in their children's interest. How could you buy that shit? he asked scornfully.

Mercia does not understand why Jake has hardened his heart, why he seems angrier than ever. Surely people grow more relaxed about their parents' faults as they grow older. After all, Nicholas and Nettie would have been damaged in turn by the weird beliefs of an earlier generation.

Mercia can no longer think kindly of Jake. He is a monster, not the nice brother of the novel at all.

Nicky says that he is not tired, that he does not want a nap as his mother has ordered. Could they not instead go for a walk and explore? Mercia smiles at him, pleased that he wants to be with her, or rather, she amends, pleased that he wants to go out. If it turns out that she'll have to take Nicky to Glasgow . . . no, there'll be a way out; she must not allow herself to be bullied into anything like that. All the same, she is pleased to take the boy out for a walk. Besides, she can see no reason why a child should sleep if he is not tired. But wary of repercussions she says that if he lies down quietly for fifteen minutes, they'll go for a short walk. It will be cooler then. She makes another condition. They will speak English for the entire walk. She has ascertained that the boy understands well enough. What he needs is to practice speaking. Nicky looks uncertain; he doesn't think that he'll manage for such a long time. Perhaps, he suggests, they could speak one language on the way there and another on the way back. That would help Auntie Mercy with her Afrikaans. Mercia laughs, It's a deal.

Settled on the uncomfortable sofa, Nicky falls asleep instantly, and wakes up half an hour later, still raring to go. With the help of a tossed coin, English chooses itself as the language for the outbound walk. Nicky hopes that they'll go to the cave, or find more caves with chincherinchee in the mountain.

Is such conservatism typical of children? Do they all want to do the same things over and over again when the wide world of newness is waiting to be explored? Mercia startles herself with the thought that that will have to be beaten out of the boy, which, of course, is no more than an idiomatic expression, nothing to do with physical assault, but it pains her all the same to have thought in such terms.

No, she says, it's too dull to do the same things. Let's explore other places, see what crops up.

They set off across the field where the sheep graze, toward a disused road where Mercia remembers lorries bumping along the gravel with their cargoes of gypsum from now-defunct mines. The mountains are too far, although they could drive there another time, she promises, but today they have to be back before his mother gets home. Yes, says the child, she will worry about him being taken by the troll.

Nicky's English is better than he thinks, although Mercia has to supply several words and also at times correct the Afrikaans pronunciations, but the concentration slows down his chatter. He promises to learn some from his father when he gets better; he knows that you can't be clever without English. Mercia explains that it is simply good to know more than one language, that it allows you to talk to different kinds of people, and living as he does in South Africa he should also learn Xhosa. Perhaps they already teach it at school? she wonders aloud, but Nicky says he hopes not, and rushes ahead chanting to himself. Christ, there is no question of her being able to stand in for a parent. Not only the formidable task of raising a child, but also, there is so much for him to unlearn.

They stop to look at ants' nests, track the ambitious insects struggling with impossible loads that seem beyond their means. But no, there appears to be always a way out as by hook or by crook the desired object is eventually dragged down into the excavated

earth. Mercia, ever the teacher, has to stop herself from offering
the behavior of ants as a homily. Nicky, with unbridled enthusiasm, is detained by all kinds of things, his pockets stuffed with
stones, a dead insect's carapace that he says looks like a Volkswa-
gen, various leaves. Why? Why? Why? he asks continuously, and
she wonders how parents have the energy or patience with so much
talking, so much explanation of a world that barely makes sense to
her. The responsibility is oppressive. If only she could turn back,
announce that she's had enough, for she is assailed by alarming
heat, wave after wave of hot flashes that leave her breathless. When
the heat subsides, she realizes that the child has taken her hand,
that he has stopped talking. But it takes no more than a wan smile
from her for the barrage of questions to resume.

Mercia is unable to identify all the flora; she could swear that
these plants did not exist when she was a child. Together they
marvel at leaf structures, at thorns and succulents. There is an extraordinary single green leaf that grows directly, without a stalk,
out of the ground on which it lies flattened. Why, he asks, will it
not sit up nicely like the fresh green of sorrel that is now bursting
into flower?

Mercia doesn't know, distracts him with the flowering sorrel
that she had to gather as a child for making soup; she encourages him to chew at the long sour stalks packed with vitamin C.
Nicky is enthralled by the history lesson on the Dutch sailors
who, on their way to procuring Eastern spices, stopped at the
Cape to cure their scurvy with sorrel. He likes the word scurvy,
rolls the R extravagantly and chuckles—to him it sounds like a
swearword. She explains that scurvy led the Dutch to gardening
and refreshing themselves at the Cape, that it could be seen as the
root of all the country's troubles. Nicky the parrot repeats after
her: the root of all our country's troubles.

Mercia is surprised that the boy knows nothing of the fields of multicolored daisies that cover the land at the beginning of spring, only a few miles farther north, in the heart of Namaqualand. But Nicky does not think that sounds so good. Much more exciting to find things that are hidden, see what crops up, he echoes, and off he scampers, giving himself a break from the exhausting English.

Yissus, he screams, gou, kom kyk, then corrects himself hurriedly to repeat in English. Mercia catches up and laughs to find that he is excited about a tortoise. It could hardly run away, she exclaims. Has he not seen a tortoise before? Oh yes, but he has never found one himself. They keep still so that the tortoise sticks out its ugly head and swivels its eyes about before withdrawing, this time tucking all away, head, legs and tail, so that it is dead still, pretending to be a stone in the sand. They admire the shell with its border of black and yellow triangles arranged around the twelve hexagons, themselves marked in black and a deeper yellow. Mercia thinks that the age can be told from the markings, but she can't be sure. The child wonders if it is a female and whether its babies might be nearby, kept hidden in the shade of a bush. He would search for them, see what their markings are like.

Oh no, Mercia explains, the female simply scratches out a nest, lays her eggs, and wanders off so that the hatching takes place all by itself. The baby tortoise picks its way out of the eggshell and manages on its own, makes its way in the veld all by itself, finding its own food.

Nicky is sorry to hear that. He wants to know why. He would not like to be left by his mummy, left to find his own food. His mummy wouldn't just leave him in the veld.

No, of course she won't, Mercia says, taking his hand, because you're a boy, not a tortoise. But you won't stay with your mummy forever. Perhaps you'd like to come and stay with me for a while in Scotland?

Oh yes, he would, now that he can speak English, and blowing up his cheeks with the sound of a propeller, he shoots off at an angle, diving sideways. He would drive the airplane himself, he shouts.

When he returns from his flight the tortoise has wandered only a couple of feet. Nicky worries about its inability to run away from its enemies. Mercia knocks on the impregnable shell, turns the tortoise over to show him its undercarriage, and teaches him the words, carapace and plastron. See, she says, how it is protected from its enemies? It can always run indoors just by pulling in its head. The tortoise carries its house on its back.

Nicky would like to take it home. The tortoise won't mind where it lives if its own home is on its back. Can we eat it? he asks. Mercia is horrified. Is that really what humans are programmed to think of, of destroying other creatures, of eating them? The thought makes her sick. She manages to say quietly that if he, Nicky, would not like to be eaten, the tortoise surely would not like it either, and that that is always a useful test. The child agrees, but then says triumphantly that if it has no children to care for, and if it carries its home on its back, it would surely not mind being taken home as a pet? Mercia says that they do not know what a tortoise likes to eat, what it likes to do, or whether it has friends it might miss. If it lives in the veld, that is where it prefers to be, so no, the test still holds. Would he, Nicky, like to be taken away as someone's pet?

The child laughs. Yislaaik, he would fight his way out of a cage. Like this, and he demonstrates his fighting moves, thrusting his fists and rolling in the sand.

As they set off back home, he wags a finger. Now, he says, it is his turn to teach Auntie Mercy some Afrikaans. It is so much better to speak more than one language.

The child seeks her out, seems to look to Mercia for diversion. Come, let's play, he says. She is panic-stricken. How? she asks. What is she to do? Nicky is on all fours, growling, expecting her to follow suit or to come up with something amusing. Mercia has no idea what such a game might be. Well, she says, playing for time, I don't think I'd make a good lion. How about writing? she asks. Today he could learn to use a pen and to write his name. But Sylvie is worried; she wonders if Nicky is not too young to be burdened with schoolwork. Is that, she asks, the right thing to do at his age?

Mercia frowns. Actually, she doesn't know; she imagines that children learn to write at different ages, so that there could be no harm if Nicky seems interested. It is simply a question of entertaining him with the alphabet, of offering an alternative to television. There surely is no need to think of reading and writing as labor if the boy enjoys doing it, she says. There is much laughter from Nicky, who screws up his face in concentration and tries with all his might to follow with colored pens her faint outline of the letters. He crows with delight as he gains control, as the wobbly lines spell his name. Then they sing together the alphabet song that Mercia summons from who knows where. She claps and sways along with him.

Now the child is indeed exhausted. His eyes droop, his head lolls as he slowly slides down into the cushions and slips into sleep. His arms are flung out on the old sofa, and he snores like an old man. Sylvie has gone to work, and Mercia does not know how long he should be allowed to sleep.

There probably is more to raising a child than common sense allows, and if Mercia is going to have any influence on him, she might as well start investigating. She looks about the room, hoping that a book on child care might be lying about. Jake has surely at some stage taken an interest in the boy, would have wanted to know what to do with him. She checks the corner, under the television, where books and papers are neatly stacked, but no, they are mail-order catalogs, magazines, and old newspapers. A large brown envelope slides out of the pile of disturbed papers; it is not sealed, and Mercia hesitates for a second before peering into it. They are photographs, which she cannot resist looking at. All of Sylvie as a young woman, taken at various intervals, some fifteen years or so ago, she guesses, before she put on weight.

Mercia frowns at the images, so radically different from the woman she knows, or rather from the current Sylvie. She is barely recognizable, but no, it is the same high Namaqua cheekbones, the narrow eyes and angled planes of the proffered face. The girl in the photographs is not only youthful and slender, but seems also unbelievably vain. She looks brazenly into the camera. The pictures are carefully posed, and clearly all taken by Sylvie herself. Dozens of pictures taken over a few years, Mercia surmises, nothing short of an autobiographical project, which for all her boldness makes the girl at the same time look vulnerable, exposed, and yes, she must admit, beautiful, with all the beauty of youth that is taken for granted by the young. Mercia has thought her to be a simple, uneducated country girl, one who talks too much, prone to whining, but modest all the same. Here, however, gathered in the envelope, is evidence of a confident, bold young woman brimming with self-awareness and striking various extravagant poses, a Sylvie transformed by the eye of the camera.

The brightest of the color photographs, one with patches of purple daisies, leaps out at Mercia. There is Sylvie in all her vulgar self-regard, the country girl's take on glamour. The pose in cheap sunglasses and tight trousers is self-conscious; the ill-fitting shirt has sprung a button, presumably just before the click of the camera, so that the girl's brassiere shows. But her head is tilted defiantly as if she has just been reprimanded by the aunties to stop her nonsense. It is true that she is slim, youthful, and surprisingly comely, the delicate face lifted to the sun. But what on earth could have possessed Jake to fall for the little tart?

Mercia is embarrassed by her reaction to the girl, or rather, to the pictures. Once upon a time one was able to say: I take back those words. Now that we know how our thoughts and utterances betray us, they can no longer be taken back. Unlike the evidence of fingerprints, they cannot be erased. If only the word tart had not entered her thoughts. Mercia remembers the day, some years ago, when Jake told her that he was going to marry the Willemse girl. She could not hide her dismay. Now there's a surprise, she said, but why marry?

No, you're not surprised. And marriage is not the issue. The truth, dear sissie, Jake cackled, is that you disapprove. You're no different from the old man. You don't even know Sylvie, but you do know that she's not your kind, not good enough for your brother. You've become European, too grand for us; you don't belong here anymore. How bourgeois you've become, Mercy, a fine liberal you are.

Mercia stared at him, tongue-tied. Once upon a time she used to think of bourgeois as a dirty word. But the truth was that over the years the label of bourgeois like a garishly colored garment had faded into something less offensive, something perfectly wearable. Acceptable, because she was wearing it. Considering who she was and how she lived her comfortable life, would it not be dishonest to claim otherwise? Mercia's head spun. She would stand her ground.

Certain aspects of the bourgeois I won't deny, she admitted. Social and economic security is after all of value because it brings tolerance of the other, which can only be a good thing.

But which, Jake said triumphantly, you have just shown to not be the case. You are your father's child, and Sylvie belongs to those other people who can't be tolerated.

Jake was right, she conceded, and her view of the girl was inexcusable, so that she would make every effort to get to know Sylvie and rise above her prejudices. She put her arms around him and said that she hoped he'd be a good husband and keep off the drink.

So once again Mercia falls short of her promise, knows that she cannot delete the word, tart. But it is not only the pictures of Sylvie that interest her. There is for her nostalgic recognition of the Willemse house, the whitewashed raw brick and its patch of veld fenced off with chicken wire that serves as a garden. Culture sliding into rude nature, for whilst the vygies have been planted, arranged in the enclosure, they are barely different from the flora beyond the fence. And around the so-called garden, in stiff competition, is the less garish, yellow sea of common gousblom that has drifted from the roadside. But it is quite eclipsed by the two patches of vygie in fluorescent purple that anchor Sylvie's provocative figure.

As a teenager, Mercia found that house fascinating. It was the only one that had, if not a stoep as such, something of a verandah, a rough assortment of corrugated strips balanced on stilts, that threw its shadow on the broom marks of the patch where old women sat in the afternoons. Then it was by no means a garden since the enclosure, so much larger in those days, also held two hens and a bantam cockerel with a plume of glossy blue and green tail feathers, who strutted the perimeter, pecking his way, up and down, up and down, amidst what she remembers as straggly lucerne. Was there not an outlandish plaster gnome with a painted red hat that she admired from the distance?

Mercia remembers the old women, two of them she thinks, and the child, Sylvie, who lived in the wobbly-walled white-washed house with gingham curtains. No hollyhocks, of course, but on the stoep with its makeshift verandah there was a painted paraffin tin with something growing—was it a vygie? or a malva?—something that may or may not have flowered. There was certainly the little girl, Sylvie, barely a toddler, who skipped about chatting and singing to herself, her head like that of the cockerel bobbing this way and that. Her bonnet tied under her chin hung by its slack straps on her back. As a child, Mercia had not dared take off her own bonnet with its stitched, starched brim framing her face to keep the sun out, and the pleated flap at the back for protecting her neck. Her mother had sewn a pretty picot edging all around the bonnet, so that there was no question of not being grateful, but how she admired the child who had tossed the thing off her head, in spite of an aproned Willemse auntie scolding from the doorway. There was often an old woman sitting in the doorway, elbows on parted knees and chin propped in her palms, surveying the world.

The full thorn at the end of the lane that features in Sylvie's photographs was the only other tree in the area. Mercia, the child, assumed that it had been planted by the auntie who worked in town. That was what any association with town brought— something different, something desirable like the dappled shade of the thorn tree where goats gathered to munch at mimosa balls. So much more leafy than her father's tree at the dipkraal. Mercia cannot remember the names of the Willemse sisters, the women whom others gossiped about. She has an idea that there was sometimes a man under the tree, beavering away at something or other, so that she would not go closer, but all was recollected in the yellow fragrance of mimosa that kept her transfixed then, and now drifts about the photographs spilled out of the envelope.

Father said it was rude to loiter and stare; he said that she should keep away from the Namaquas. Mercia would nevertheless wander the length of the lane—really it was the bed of an ephemeral stream that seldom carried water—hoping to see into people's houses. She would slink past, as close to the open doors as she dared, hoping not to be seen, not to encounter anyone. Once a Willemse auntie whom she had not seen sitting in the dark interior called out, but she took fright and darted off. What she had glimpsed was shelves of painted enamel plates on white paper, possibly newspaper, hanging down a few inches and prettily cut out, so that light from outside picked out the white lacy pattern.

There must have been something about the little girl's carefree darting about the yard, bare-headed, the tinkle of her voice as she scolded the bantam cock, that Mercia envied, that made her own circumscribed days seem all the more oppressive, every day being like a Sunday, the day of prayer and of wearing shoes. There is still something of that carefree child in these photographs, something that stirs pity for the plight of the older Sylvie. Mercia feels her chest tightening. It does no good peering into the past, stirring spurious feelings of nostalgia. Then, inexplicably, something of Nettie enters, something of her own mother, and it takes the jolt of the photographs, the many faces of Sylvie cascading to the floor, for Mercia to start, to bristle against the nostalgia for that which never was.

For Nettie's love was distant, concentrated into picot edging or a scrap of frill on the clothes she sewed for her daughter. At the time of her mother's death Mercia felt little more than puzzlement, for in death Nettie seemed not much more remote than she did in life.

Nicholas insisted that the children look at the corpse, at the face that once was their mother's. Mercia's answer of no, that she had no wish to see, was squashed by her father's yes, it was required, the paying of respect to the dead. And it was grotesque— the stillness of the waxy skin and the orifices plugged with cotton wool against corruption—that face like a photograph of Nettie. The stranger, already a ghost, was not her mother, was an absence felt through an image, and the very place where the corpse lay, the place occupied by someone who once was Nettie, ceased to be real, drawn by the corpse into its absence. The twelve-year-old child felt the thrall of placelessness. Ghostly and vague as it was, it whispered the promise of escape from the dreariness of Kliprand and the vulgarity of apartheid.

Unlike Jake, it was impossible for Mercia to summon the tears she was expected to shed for her mother. For him Nettie's death was devastating. How, he sobbed on Mercia's shoulder, was he to live with the old man without her? Jake was too young to be motherless, and whilst Mercia for a while tried to indulge him, the demands of adolescence and of political resistance took over. By her late teens she had all but forgotten about Nettie, indeed other than in the role of progenitor, dismissed the very idea of a mother as being redundant. Mercia shrugs. It worked for her, so she will not now be bullied by nostalgia into believing otherwise.

Mercia picks up the photographs, the many faces of Sylvie, shuffles them into a neat pile. How sure the girl seems to be of herself, of her own attractiveness. Has Sylvie never had any doubts? Heavens, the painful self-consciousness of Mercia's own teens seems not so long ago. It was only in her nineteenth year that she began to think of herself as passable, that she dropped her shoulders and lifted her head, still barely presentable, and peering out through the disguise of a pressed fringe held fixed at night with cello-tape, saw in the world something that could after all be managed. Yes, given the right tools, she began to see her way clear to glorious escape. All that guilt and fear of childhood, the unwieldiness of adolescence, that was where ugliness lurked, that was what she would put behind her as generic, for really, now as a student, free of her family (she would see them only occasionally), the possibility of beauty beckoned at her. Like the night—she sang, drunk with poetry—that covers all defects in the mystery of darkness, she would walk in beauty, and keep fear at bay. If it was perhaps the other way round, if it was the promise of escape that bestowed beauty, what did it matter? She would not be bound by place; she could and she would get away; motherless, she was free to do as she pleased.

And now, how that self-belief wags a mocking finger. The scholarship in Scotland that was meant to be no more than a break from the oppressiveness of home led to Craig and lifelong exile. From the start Craig was for keeps. After all the short-lived, disappointing dalliances with unsuitable young men, she knew that this was different. And Craig was not afraid of saying it out loud, as he playfully—touch wood—knocked on her head: we are for keeps. Which even allowed her a year of research in the USA and for him, traveling in Europe. Theirs was not the kind of relationship that restricted each other. And fortunately for both, having groped their way through childhood and adolescence, they were sure that they wanted no children of their own.

Apartheid meant that there were no discussions about where they would live, about which one of them would give up his or her home. Thereafter, Craig was evasive about emigrating. It was only sensible to wait and see how things developed, and Mercia, by then engrossed in her work, was patient, and did not note how time had crept up on them, for they were what is known as a happy couple. What then had gone wrong? Where and how had she failed? Mercia has gone over the questions too many times. She must accept that the condition of having been left is about being left with unanswerable questions. Like flies to wanton gods etcetera, or plain old shit happens, as they say these days. She is sure that the question of how things had gone wrong would not have detained Craig. His concern was the setting to rights: the new woman, necessarily younger, who had somehow slipped into his life, and made the old intolerable, expendable. All he needed to worry about was the mechanics of replacement, how to sever things in a civilized, sophisticated fashion, without the messiness of tears and howling hysteria. Mercia thinks enviously of Sylvie, who, when she finally accepts her rejection, will hurl herself at the heavens, rail and rage and tear Jake apart. How satisfying, how cathartic that must be.

Mercia sits up straight. She must not think of herself as an abandoned woman, an old woman, whose thighs have spread and who sits with her legs comfortably apart, hands folded on her stomach. It is that image that drives her, reluctantly, to the gym. It has irritated her that even Smithy has read her visits to the gym in terms of a quest for a new man.

Don't be ridiculous, she snapped, there are ways of overcoming loneliness without burdening yourself with a strange burk. I'm warding off osteoporosis, that's all. Oh, and a potbelly too.

Well, that's wonderful, Smithy said with her usual clapping together of hands, no need then for me to have a sign made for the rear window of your car: Abandoned woman at the wheel.

Together they had laughed at the ludicrous warnings on cars. It was important to Mercia that Smithy, a bona fide mother, agreed on the Child on Board signs. What on earth could such complacent parents have in mind? How naïve the belief that otherwise reckless drivers would slow down in deference to their parenthood. Did they not know that it made any sensible person want to crash right into them and their precious brats?

Mercia flicks once more through the photographs. It is not, she consoles herself, like reading someone's letters, which she would never do. Photographs are already public, already an objectification of the person, meant to be looked at, so that she cannot see why anyone should mind; indeed, Sylvie presumably wants them to be admired. These pictures are all of Sylvie, taken by Sylvie herself, as if she is alone in the world, not lonely, just the only one left, having shooed everyone else out of the way to celebrate her aloneness.

There is one of her in a butcher's shop surrounded by sausage that she surveys with pride, pleased as punch at the fine career of butchery ahead of her. Mercia stops at another of the girl leaning against the kitchen wall that had been painted in bands of sky blue and grass green, no doubt, from the flaunting look, her own, recent handiwork. The old Willemse sisters must by then have been too tired to care. Provocative, all the pictures, with a pouting sexuality and devil-may-care stance that cannot be imagined from the careworn Sylvie of today. Mercia looks more closely. Yes, there it is in the corner, the edge of a set of shelves clad in lacy fabric. It does not seem like newspaper cutout; rather, white oilcloth she thinks, with pretty scalloped edges, nicely referencing the old newspaper.

Mercia is about to shove the photographs back into the envelope when her eye catches one in black and white, a curious picture, taken at night, with the girl in a white T-shirt rising ghostly out of placeless darkness. The foreground on the right is a solid black blur, probably a rock on which the camera has been positioned, for a jagged stone edge, having caught the lens, is projected as a shadow onto the girl's white T-shirt. Sylvie is positioned behind an old wire fence just visible on the left as a few hexagons of chicken wire. Loosely strung above it is a slack line of barbed wire, which cuts across her chest. Her torso is slightly angled; her right ear catches the camera's flash, as do her teeth, shown in a stiff, artificial grin.

Out of the darkness behind the girl, the only form picked out by the flash is the outline of a tree, so strange and stark and otherworldly that it appears as the negative of an image, its bare branches bearing unreal clusters of broad leaves here and there. Might it be a wild fig? Above the tree, to the right, and at the top of the photograph is an effulgent patch of light in the sky. Mercia does not know enough of the night sky; she would like to think that it is the heavy luminosity of the Milky Way.

The photograph is extraordinary. It is of a Sylvie whom Mercia does not know and cannot fathom. A strange young woman in knowing performance who claims for herself an iconic presence in the ethereal light, then subverts it with a grin. Or is it an ironic grimace? The light in the sky, resonating as it does with the eerie, flashlit figure, might almost be an aureole cut adrift, carelessly tossed into a painterly scene, and askew in its ascent to heaven. Sylvie's loose white T-shirt, rising out of black rock where the camera must have been placed, displays below the barbed wire the outline of a target printed in black lines across her chest. For all the girl's lack of education, the photographic figure is imbued with language: I am alone in the world; I cannot be touched; I am transfigured.

The barbs of the wire bore through her T-shirt, sink into her flesh, into this representation of Sylvie the saint who will pluck out the barbs without flinching. Sylvie the invincible.

What is it that the girl knows? There is more than self-reflexivity, something beyond the knowing aesthetics of representing the self. There is knowledge that crosses over from the ghostly world of the photograph, that flicks across eerily into the real, now a flickering shadow across Mercia's heart. A shadow of fear and awe. Who is this apparition who rises out of the darkness, whose bright, ironic grin haunts the viewer? Who is Sylvie?

Mercia shoves the photographs back into the envelope just in time. She has not heard the click of the gate, the crunch of footsteps, until the girl struggles noisily, heavily into the house with a newspaper parcel that she draws out of a shopping bag. After the ethereal picture, the solid figure and drawn mouth seem to exude a bitterness that makes Mercia flinch.

A lekker brawn for tomorrow, Sylvie announces. Some tripe and trotters.

Does the girl think of nothing but food? No wonder she has grown so heavy. How can it be that there is no trace of the extraordinary figure of the photographs? Then Mercia screams involuntarily as Sylvie unwraps the newspaper parcel and triumphantly holds up a scraped sheep's head, its eyes staring glassily out of the mottled gray-black skin. Sylvie throws her head back with laughter. It's only a sheep's head. I'm going to cook it with the trotters for brawn. Very nice, flavored with a bit of curry powder, and it's something that Jake really likes. You'll see how he'll jump out of bed for brawn. She looks up at Mercia's frozen face. What's the matter, she says, you must have seen a sheep's head before? There is unmistakable scorn in her voice, so that Mercia does not trust herself to reply. Then, seeing the child asleep on the sofa, Sylvie shouts, Ag no, man, this is no time to be sleeping. She shakes his shoulder until his eyes open. This reading and writing business is too much for him, too tiring for a small boy, she says.

Nicky sits up muttering; he rubs his eyes, and looks around bewildered. Mercia takes his hand. Come, she says, we're going to help your mummy to make brawn.

Just then Jake shouts from the room: Sylvie, come. Where are you? Sylvie, come, quick.

Mercia wants to plug her fingers into her ears. This, the sound of her own people, this is what she needs to get away from.

❦

Mercia is sent out of the kitchen by Sylvie, who says that she doesn't need any help, that it won't do having a child perched on a chair with a knife in his hand.

It's a blunt dinner knife, Mercia protests, but Sylvie the mother says, Whoever has heard of a child chopping onions? She helps Nicky down and turns on the television, with a warning that he is not to fall sleep.

What is happening to Mercia, the carnivore, here in Kliprand? Is this the measure of her distance from the place, from her home, her people? The smell of meat and onions boiling in her mother's old cast-iron pot from Falkirk makes her gag, so that she goes out to the very end of the garden where Sylvie has planted a frangipani. It is still young; its stark bare branches like amputated limbs against the evening sky conjure up the legendary demons and ghosts of long-dead slaves from the east. From some of the puckered stumps, clenched fists of flower have pushed their way out, the perfume of the young buds still locked away. Mercia wills a remembered fragrance to drive off the smell of sheep's head and trotters. Which can't be so different from any cut of mutton cooking, but the smell is inexorably linked to the image of the hideous head.

Is Mercia growing fastidious about meat, about the killing of animals? She doesn't know. This is home; everything is topsy-turvy here. She would like to think that it is only the head, the face that is after all so like a human's, that is repellent. She remembers, as a child at Sunday school, the picture card of John the Baptist's severed head on a plate, which made her stomach turn. Hideous and barbaric, she thought, and squeezed shut her eyes, although the afterimage of curly hair and beard, and glassy eyes, would not go away. Even years later, in Italian museums, she winced at the paintings, Caravaggio's and others'. Botticelli's held her in frozen horror, foregrounding as it did a sweetly smiling Salome holding the head on a plate. Focusing on the richly adorned rim of the plate, Mercia understood that it was indeed the plate, that statement of cultural refinement, that doubled the horror.

No danger of a gilt plate tonight. Sylvie will cook the head with onions and spices, and the meat floating in the jellied liquor will be picked from skin and bone, so that there could be no picturing of the head in the brawn. But it makes her gorge rise all the same. Transformed in the cooking it may be, but Mercia knows that she will not be placated. The problem is how to get round it, how not to offend Sylvie.

She returns to the question of why she finds meat difficult to eat here in Kliprand. It is not only the head. The faint nausea that has gripped her over the last couple of days is undoubtedly linked to meat. Is it connected with Sylvie, the butcher girl?

Back home in Glasgow, Mercia had no such misgivings about meat. She would pound ginger and garlic with cumin and cardamom in a marble pestle and mortar for her signature dish of Moroccan lamb, having herself pickled the lemons, quartered and salted and packed snugly in their own juice some months before. Lately, she has made a point of continuing to have friends round to dinner; she would not retreat into lone spinsterhood. Besides, there was the relief of having no Craig to appease, Craig who so loved dinner parties, but always, always complained beforehand. Always complained that he'd had enough, that he hated the fuss and bustle, that it was too much trouble, that they should think of an excuse to call off the dinner party. Please could she say that he had pneumonia. Or a brain tumor. So that she shut him out of the kitchen.

Cooking for friends was a pleasure she would not have spoilt by Craig. Mercia would turn up the music and dance to Karoo blues, whilst stirring and waiting for the spices to fry slowly, on the gentlest of heat. Ek will huis toe gaan, she crooned along with David Kramer, ground her hips and dipped her shoulders hotnos style, waving her wooden spoon defiantly. Or hummed and shimmied along to a Klopse tune where Ibrahim's piano allowed, where the beat picked up, and the cuts deferred to Basil Coetzee's sax. Then, as the smell of fried cardamom rose, repeated its aroma and weaving through coriander and paprika revised its fragrance, she savored a bittersweet homesickness.

And always the moment of hesitation—should fennel not be given its rightful place with coriander? Always the sound of her father's voice that could not be dislodged: soos vinkel en koljander—like fennel and coriander. The recipe does not call for fennel, but Mercia cannot imagine coriander without a dash of its twin. They were lookalikes, meant to go together, inseparable and, according to the Afrikaans idiom, interchangeable. Like the collie dogs Nicholas gave to Mercia and Jake, the puppies already named Vinkel and Koljander with their identical white collars, so that the children would not argue. Jake said that they were sheepdogs for Nicholas's own convenience, but Vinkel attached himself to Jake, so that even he could not resist the adorable creature.

Craig, for all his bad temper beforehand, would be the life and soul of the party. He boasted about Mercia's Cape dishes, her use of spices, learned, he announced to guests, at her mother's knee. Mercia did not correct him. Did not say, no, that she learned from Jane Grigson's recipes, the inventive English cook who borrowed, gloriously freed by the fact that there is no oppressive tradition of fine British cuisine which demands slavish adherence. Instead, Mercia dredged up stories of Lusitanian navigators, the Cape as refreshment station, the Cape of Storms turned Cabo Esperanza in the establishment of a spice route. Vinkel en koljander brought to Cape shores in exchange for scurvy-fighting fruit and veg. Once she spoke of slaves from Goa, Malaysia, East Africa, sizzling their spices in the shadow of Table Mountain, which was not nice, so that Craig explained that Mercia had had too much to drink. No one said that eating meat was not nice.

Ag, it's the time of day, the dipping light that makes her vulnerable to sentimentality. All this nonsense about food when she should be thinking about her work, or rather, about Jake. Mercia, who has never had any difficulty in meeting deadlines, is anxious about the scholarly work that has given up on her. It is only October, but the temperature seems to have risen today and she simply cannot think, cannot come to grips with the argument. It is in her interest to leave Jake alone, to wait for him to come round and to observe in the meantime how things are with Sylvie and the boy, but without her work she is growing impatient, enraged by his slide back to drink.

The icon of the memoir beckons from the desktop, offers itself as diversion from the awfulness of being in this house. Mercia thinks of this writing as private, but she can't help wondering what Jake would make of being translated into these words. Still, how else is she to get through the days in this place called home? How is she to manage sly nostalgia that creeps into the hole left by Craig? It is infuriating, this need to recollect a past that cannot be considered without irony. Is it in fact nostalgia? So layered are the fragrances of the past, so spliced the memories of places, that nostalgia will have to do without an object. This home where Jake snores and Sylvie squeals is not a place to yearn for a dubious past.

If memoir is driven by nostalgia Mercia finds it embarrassing that she is driven by the zeitgeist. It is, she consoles herself, because there is no Craig to tell, because that daily decanting of events into words must find another form.

The table is set for three. Mercia prepares herself for a vaudeville performance, for cooing appreciatively over the food before doubling over with a bolt of invented tummy ache. But there is no need. Sylvie explains that the brawn is not ready. The infusion of spices takes time, does its work whilst the dish is still warm, then it must cool down completely and stiffen into a jelly. Which is why she's fried some sausage for tonight. But look, she says, how Jake's delaying her with his demands. Now she has to leave everything and go out to get him some potato chips. He doesn't want sausage. Also, he says, a bottle of brandy, for which the chips are of course an excuse.

Mercia leaps to her feet. She is curt, insistent in her instruction. Sylvie must go about her business and pay no attention to Jake.

But he'll scream the house down, she says, there's only twenty minutes left before closing time.

Mercia says no, he can no longer be indulged. She storms into his room and tells him that Sylvie is getting their dinner, that Nicky is hungry, and that if he wants any he should join them at the table. Like a child he pulls the covers over his head and turns to the wall.

That means, says Sylvie, that he still has some drink left. That he's just wanting to stash up for tomorrow.

Jake has eaten almost nothing since Mercia's arrived. Mercia wakes up in the night and hears him stumbling into the kitchen.

A squeaking door, a band of light from the fridge, the rustle of paper and a clatter of containers of some kind make her sit up and throw off her covers. Vinkel en koljander—the smell has driven him out. The smell of Nettie's spiced tripe and trotters and the brawn they loved as children. No refrigerators in the old days, but their mother had a cooling contraption of chicken wire packed with wet coke that evaporated in a draft so that the brawn remained set.

You're hungry at last, Mercia, who has tiptoed out in bare feet, says triumphantly.

No, not really, er . . . just checking, he says. Jake rubs his hands together, embarrassed, drags them through his uncombed hair. He is unsteady and has to lean on the cupboard.

Checking? she laughs. To see if your wife keeps the fridge well stocked? How would she manage that, Jake, on her wages?

Jake will not look at her; instead, he tries to make his way back to the bedroom. But she stands in the doorway. For God's sake, Jake, why try to avoid me? You summoned me, remember? Now I've come all this way and you won't talk to me. Why not tell me what's wrong? And why not eat if you're hungry? There's bread, and butter, and by now yes, the brawn will be set.

No, I want nothing. I'm sorry; it's all a mistake. I shouldn't have written to you. I must've been drunk, he laughs. Then with surprising strength he pushes her out of the way. Why don't you go back home and leave me alone, he says, I want nothing to do with any of you. He returns to his room and bangs the door shut.

What kind of character is Jake in her memoir? Mercia fears that he holds little interest, lying as he does in the fetid, darkened room with so little to say. He is not even good at playing the tortured drunk devil. No consular musings under the volcano, no clouds boiling, no mescal-induced thunder. What a dull pair they are—Jake thirsting after alcohol and she, Mercia, cravenly leaving him to his own devices whilst she bangs on about Craig.

The next day as Sylvie prepares to go out for brandy, Mercia intervenes. It is time to act. In her clipped, lecturer's voice she forbids Sylvie to buy Jake drink, says that enough is enough, she will deal with him. Sylvie screws up her face. Does Mercia not know what he is capable of? That he is stronger than he looks? That it's all right for Mercia, who is of another place, but that he will kill her and the child?

Nonsense, Mercia says. But you should go, keep out of the way. Take Nicky and stay with your AntieMa for the night, she orders. This is no sight for a child. She, Mercia, will see to Jake right away, get him to eat, take him to see a doctor and find the best route for rehabilitation. That is why she is here. It will be easier to manage on her own. She'll call Sylvie when it's all in hand.

Sylvie is uncertain. She does not think that this namby-pamby woman could handle Jake, who has on occasion leapt out of bed in search of the butcher's knife that she has had to wrestle off him. She is his wife. It is her duty to stay. But Mercia has turned into a mad Murray; she is determined; she has not come all this way to be defeated. Sylvie tuts, hurriedly grabs her things. Actually, she has had enough, could do with a break from these people. Even AntieMa's darkened rooms seem like a haven, and she will make warm roosterbrood for the old woman, who at least will appreciate her efforts.

Mercia pats Nicky on the head and does not know what to do when, like a cat, he rubs his head insistently into her side, as if to drill his way into her belly.

There, there, she says, patting mechanically, you go and see your granny, and when you get back, we'll . . . we'll have a picnic. And play.

In the veld? he asks. In the veld, she replies.

When they are gone, Mercia charges into Jake's room, yanks at the curtains and flings open the window. Jake is enraged. He calls for Sylvie, the doormat wife who will do his bidding.

Get Sylvie, and get out of my house, he roars, or rather, tries to roar, but his voice does not manage; it peters out into a sob.

I'll get my own, he cries, as he struggles out of bed. Jake is unshaven, bedraggled in a torn T-shirt and crumpled boxer shorts. Mercia gasps at the sight of the swollen legs that struggle to carry him. Rising with Jake is the effluvia of sweat, alcohol and an unwashed body, so that Mercia turns away in disgust. He shakes violently, stumbles as far as the kitchen and falls into a chair. It is clear that he will not make it any farther. He breaks down, sobbing. And with the slyness of an alcoholic stammers that he can't think, can't speak, cannot tell her what's wrong without a drink to calm him down.

You should keep out of this, he warns, you'll be sorry. Just get me a drink, he cries pitifully, and then go home, leave us alone like you've always done.

Mercia ignores the jibe. No point in explaining herself, and besides, it is probably a device to get his way. So she says no, that she'll drive him to the doctor's, and that his rehabilitation will start today. They will try to find a suitable clinic. No need to be melodramatic, she says. Alcoholism's an illness, and it can be treated. You've done it before. Why not have a shower now and the doctor will give you something for the craving.

M-Mer-cy, Mer-Mercy, Jake stutters comically, please, Mercy, you don't know what they've done to me, that bitch and . . . and . . . ; you mustn't hear this; you don't want this—this punishment, just get me a fucking drink. Or get me a gun. I can't tell you what they've done, you mustn't know. A fucking drink, and then a gun. I should have killed him. I want to die. They wouldn't let me die.

Stop this childish nonsense, Jake, she says. If there's a story to be told, it should be let out, like bad blood, Mercia soothes. It can only do good to let it out. And then we'll see about getting you back on your feet.

Jake cackles weakly. If only she would get him a drink. He doesn't care about blood, good or bad. He must have a drink. How can he talk, let bad blood out, without a drink? Mercia's eyes swim as she stares at him. Her little brother. A pitiful figure on the floor, where he beats his head against the chair from which he has slid down, sobbing. She swallows hard. In this order, she says: a shower, a drink, your story, and then the doctor. Jake must promise, and she will hold him to it. She has a bottle of duty-free whisky in her bag.

Mercia is sorry that she has let Sylvie go. She is no nurse, but now there is nothing to be done but to help him to the bathroom, grit her teeth, and get him out of his clothes. Jake, shaking violently, slumps on the tiled floor, incapable of soaping himself. He won't be touched, and Mercia does not want to touch him. There is nothing to be done other than hosing him down. She fetches washing-up liquid from the kitchen, shakes it haphazardly all over Jake and directs the jet of water at various parts of his body whilst he squeals like a child and rolls into a ball, covering his nakedness. Soap that backside, she says. I won't stop until you're clean all over.

They sit across from each other at the kitchen table, an emaciated Jake wrapped in Mercia's silk dressing gown. The glass in his hand is empty. He has gulped down his whisky and water, and reaches out with somewhat steadier hand for the glass that Mercia poured for herself, still untouched. She waves him on. What does it matter?

Mercia needs water; she is unable to speak. Like a child she probes with her forefinger in the cavity of her mouth, taps along her parched palate. It is a terrain of sun-baked mud, cracked, absorbing sound as if it were moisture, so that, try as she may, no words issue from her lips. Mercia does not have the strength to fetch water from the tap. She gulps repeatedly. When the words finally make it, they are strangled. She cannot look at Jake. She gropes for his hand, but he shakes her off.

How, she asks in a stranger's voice, do you know all this? How do you know that it's the truth?

Fanus, he says. Fanus let it out one night. We were drinking at Aspoester. I suppose he had too much on his plate. Their child had died of pneumonia a couple of days before, and he was bitter. Also, he was drunk. The Baatjies brothers were there also—we'd all been drinking—and I can't remember what we were talking about when he said how could I be sure that Nicky is my child? Then it all came out. Everybody else was quiet and I knew at once that it was true. Actually I've known right from the start that somehow something was wrong.

Who's Fanus? Mercia asks.

Are you mad? Of course you know Fanus Lategan. He was in your class at school. Have you forgotten everything about us, about home?

Mercia wants to say the word, home, after him, but it refuses to be uttered, offers its own pretentious substitutes. Pays de natal. Mal pays.

And who else . . . here . . . in Kliprand . . . knows about it?

Jake stares at her. Dunno. Who cares? So that Mercia answers her own question: everybody, I imagine.

Once Sylvie had confided in one person there could have been no stopping the story from circulating, gathering detail and digressions, subplots, salacious frills, and codas as it passed from person to person. Or perhaps people just knew, in the manner of "just" as used in those parts, bypassing source or reason, stories like that having lain dormant for years, knowledge embedded in the sinews of a community shunned by the Murrays, lying in wait for the moment of exposure. Oh, she shudders to think . . .

Will you stop, Jake shouts, stop thinking of yourself. This is about me, the wrong done to me. I don't care who knows what. All I know is that he was a dirty vark, a sanctimonious pig, and I should have had the courage to kill him.

Jake is trembling violently; his fists held aloft are clenched, and with his wild, unkempt hair and open mouth he looks like something out of a historical painting. Mercia summons an image: Absalom caught with his head trapped in the oak, raging helplessly, whilst a mule with raised hooves slips out from under him. It is the shadow of the mule, stark in the bright light, she holds on to, a helpful image for Mercia, who does not, will not, think of this Jake as real. So she is able to say calmly, lingeringly,

Ac-tually, Jake, was it really only some weeks ago that you heard this nonsense from Fanus? I wonder if you hadn't heard it a long time ago, that that was why you married her—Sylvie. For revenge?

Jake's open mouth snaps shut as he stares at her, before beating his head on the table, his face turned away. He is, of course, drunk.

Fanus, Mercia says, is patently wrong about Nicky. One thing is sure, the child is pure Malherbe, unmistakably Nettie's grandchild. One need only look at those eyebrows, the entire brow is Nettie's, just like yours.

Jake does not reply, does not lift his head. Horrible choking sounds escape from his throat. That is what Mercia must focus on, on Jake, on Fanus, the messenger. She must not think of Meester, Grootbaas, Nicholas. Her father. Or of the girl.

At school, in the seventies, Fanus Lategan had been the brainbox of the class—a clever boy, equally brilliant at the sciences as he was in the arts, and with a formidable, enviable memory. The midseventies was a breathless time of revolution, with Mercia and Fanus working together on Black Consciousness leaflets. Someone had tried to set the school on fire, and her father, who knew nothing of the clandestine ANC branch they had helped to establish, warned her against the savagery of dangerous, lowdown types intent on self-destruction. Mercia nodded meekly. He was of a generation who had pulled themselves up by their own bootstraps. He could hardly be blamed for his ignorance, his political naivety; indeed, she pleaded as Fanus spat contemptuously, he was like so many grown-ups a victim of apartheid propaganda. Hell-bent on being respectable coloreds. No point in wasting time arguing with his kind.

Halfway through 1976, through their Junior Certificate

year, news of the Soweto uprising rippled through Namaqualand. Mercia and Fanus, not yet sixteen years old, bonded more closely as they listened to the official news, the brazen lies of the SABC, the savage killing spree of the Defence Force, and their resolve strengthened. They were black South Africans who with the dispossessed majority would bring the country to its knees. The following year Steve Biko was killed, and when Kruger, the minister of police, boasted to the world that he didn't care about Biko's death, Mercia wanted to know what her father thought of his words. Nicholas stared at her in silence. When she screamed, What do you think? What do you say? he left the room.

Devastated by her father's silence, Mercia rushed off, turned to Fanus, clung to Fanus, who put his arms around her awkwardly as she listened to his pounding heart. For a couple of days there was an awkwardness between them, a quivering shyness that made their speech rustle helplessly. For many months they remained close friends, but Fanus would move away abruptly as she leaned toward him, would hastily withdraw the hand that she brushed against. Mercia was puzzled; she thought that they loved each other, that such intimacy was nothing less than love. Then it stopped abruptly. Fanus arrived at school one Monday morning speaking in clipped tones, his voice grave as he looked her straight in the eye. No, he was no longer interested in bourgeois poetry, and he waved away the anthology she had promised to bring along. The time for concessions, he said, was over.

From then on he avoided her, and Mercia, devastated by his coldness, wrote many a letter, none of which she sent to him. Had she imagined their special relationship? There could be no return to their former camaraderie, and she could not ask, could not bear the What-do-you-mean reply she was sure to get. There was no point to the letters, no real addressee, for the Fanus of old was a phantom. But the writing helped to mend her broken heart.

It was later that year, in the spring, when she heard from others that Fanus would not be going to university. So much cleverer than she, he was, but the Lategans were poor, the father a farm laborer who would not manage to pay for higher education. They struggled to get their five children through school, and Fanus, as the eldest, had to find work to help with school fees for the rest. It was only fair that they too should have secondary education. Guilt-stricken, and hoping that her father might have a solution, Mercia spoke to him about Fanus, who by now had fused in her mind with the image of a Guguletu schoolboy, arms flung aloft, as the bullet struck.

Hokaai! her father said, raising his hand into a stop sign. He suspected the boy of political involvement; he would not be surprised if Fanus had chosen this route in order to further his seditious plans, and if that were not the case, the boy, if he had any backbone, would later, through his own efforts, put himself through university. That, after all, was what he, Nicholas, had to do. Had to work as a delivery boy whilst attending night school, and as an adult paid for his own teacher training. Terrible, he tutted, that the poor go on having so many children.

Mercia felt a second stab of blinding hatred for her father.

There was no question of speaking to Fanus, who avoided being alone with her. Only once, when in her presence he said that he might not bother with the Matric exams, Mercia interrupted, Ah, but if you were to decide on the day to take them after all, you'd still run off with the prize. Fanus was scornful. A silver trophy! Who cares about that? There's a fascist regime to be overthrown, work to be done, he said, without looking at her.

That was, of course, not what she had meant. They would all have refused the silver cup that Dr. Groenewald had bequeathed to the new Colored High School, and she burned with shame. She thought of refusing to go to university until her father paid

Fanus's fees, but what after all would that bring? Fanus would certainly not have accepted, so that all she could wish for was to leave Kliprand, to put behind her the guilt and shame. And she did. In the heady days of political struggle at the-home-of-the-left university, of falling in and out of love, Fanus and Kliprand faded and merged into a place left behind, a place to which she would never return.

And it turned out, said her father a few years later, that Fanus, just as he suspected, had no backbone after all. Having passed the Matric exam with flying colors, he failed to pull himself up by his own bootstraps. By the time he had helped to get the younger ones through school, and was a leading figure in the seditious UDF, he was working as a manager of sorts in a builders' yard in Kliprand. Some intellectual! Meester snorted.

So Fanus did not manage to get to university, and Mercia, whose heart was fully mended, assumed that he had like most young men in the village succumbed to drink. In the years that followed, it was not difficult to avoid him during the vacations. Still, she wondered about him, and the trace of guilt persisted for years. Now she cannot help feeling that Fanus has got his revenge. How he must have hated them, the Murrays, who took for granted their privilege.

She must have said it aloud, for Jake sits up and says, Look, this isn't about Fanus; it's about me, about us, our family, and the vark who fathered us. And you shouldn't hold anything against Fanus. He always asks after you, always wants to know how you're doing at that university of yours; he thinks you're dead smart.

Mercia groans. Oh no, he doesn't. He knows only too well that he was much cleverer than I, that it's a world in which I had an unfair advantage. Too late now for the Fanuses of South Africa, too late for a generation lost to drink. For all the shit in this New South Africa, for all the complaints that the country is going to the dogs, at least for the likes of the Lategans their children have free schooling. At least Fanus's children will have more of a chance, won't be ground down with crap work and drink.

Oh yeh? His child is dead, Jake all but shouts. Look, Fanus has more reason to despise me, he says, for having made nothing of my so-called advantage. But I'm glad, do you hear me, I'm glad I left, that I didn't take the money that the old bastard—and he puts on a solemn, sanctimonious voice—scrimped and saved and sacrificed himself for. Control freak—obedience and gratitude weren't enough, we had to be his clones. Siss! Puffed up with his own pathetic achievement, with the bloody old bootstraps ballad. Siss! What a pity he didn't just support Fanus instead, but no, he was fixed on the idea of family that he could mold in his own form, the filthy old hypocrite. Dirty vark. May he squirm in his grave. May the worms gorge themselves and puke in disgust.

Mercia hangs her head. She cannot bear it. She shuts her eyes against the image of their father's face that drifts up into her vision. The dead old man's disgrace, like a swarm of blowflies, has invaded her body, so that every organ buzzes with shame. She hears again his voice, the ardent prayer to be a good God-fearing father, and the words he so often quoted: Solomon loved the Lord, walking in the statutes of David his father. Holy, filial love, that was what he set store by. She feels a rush of pity, which she knows to keep to herself. How Nicholas has let himself down.

As if he senses her pity, Jake says, Listen to me: he was evil. When he brought me back here to Kliprand—I was in bad shape then—he might as well have put that bitch on a platter for me. Oh yes, he said we'd have to get someone in to help. Sylvie this and Sylvie that, and she *was* wonderful. My legs were swollen; I couldn't walk, but oh Sylvie was the one with healing hands. So she nursed me back to health with her massages and her chicken soup and thereafter her boerefuckingwors and homemade ginger beer. All his doing. What kind of father is that, passing to me his leftovers when I'm on my knees? Dirty bastards.

Jake turns away in disgust, gropes for the bottle, from which he takes a draining swig, and announces that he is off to bed, that she should go, far away from him and his dirty mess. Drained as Mercia feels, she reminds him of his word. She'll drive him to Dr. Swemmers; he can have a sleep while they wait to be seen, and she says nothing of the rehabilitation clinic where she hopes he'll be able to go that night. Jake nods. He is too tired to resist; he'll do anything. He does not question her fumbling in a drawer for clean pajamas, tossing his things into a shopping bag.

Mercy, he says, I'm sorry. I shouldn't have written. I wanted to keep all this from you.

Jake is shaking; his bleary eyes are awash. Mercia knows what it has taken for him to tell. She puts her arms around him and his head drops on her shoulder. Sweetheart, my poor sweetheart, she says, and is alarmed to hear in her own voice that of the woman on the bus ride to Edinburgh. Poor Jake, she revises, over and over as she leads him to the car, bundles him into the seat.

❀

Mercia swithers about Fanus. Should she speak to him, perhaps even meet up with him? The awkwardness of their teens is still there, a ghostly guilt, but there is always the possibility that he has invented it all, for reasons so base that she knows it to be a foolish hope. Still, she would prefer to hear for herself the story, find out his source (has Sylvie told him?), and check for herself how Fanus has, as one does, translated it through his own history. So that she in turn can retranslate it through her cloud of shame and pity? Oh, she doesn't know; she is tired of speculations.

There is no question of speaking to Sylvie directly, and that is that. She has not rung the girl, and Sylvie would not expect to hear from her until later that day. But it is her responsibility to ascertain as best she can what really happened. The sins of the father have to be borne, but Mercia cannot bear the girl to know that she knows.

Fanus, though, will have nothing to do with that responsibility. When she looks up his number in the directory and calls to ask whether she could meet with him, he is clipped, firm. He does not beat about the bush. If it's about Sylvie, he says, yes, he knows he has spoken out of turn; he is sorry, he should not have said anything to Jake.

It was cruel, he concedes, but now that he has spoken, there is no more to be said. He wants nothing further to do with it, with them. It is the Murrays' business, not his. Still, he hopes she is well and that Jake is recovering. He heard he was ill.

Fanus's civility is cutting. Is there no possibility of checking whether, having spoken out of bitterness, he is not now brazening it out? of asking how he knows? But Mercia knows that it is the truth. There is no need to ask, to invite unsavory detail. Perhaps she has hoped to see him for her own purposes, to put behind her the guilt of the past? Now she must choose to believe that Fanus is indeed interested in Jake's health. She gushes, tells him how lucky they've been. Did he know the new sanatorium only eight kilometers out on the N road going north? Well, there was a bed available and Dr. Swemmers managed to get Jake admitted that very afternoon. She, Mercia, has just returned, and yes it won't be easy the next few weeks, but at least she knows that he is in good hands. Jake has after all done it before, recovered from alcoholism.

Yes, Jake is lucky to have you home, lucky to not rely on state resources, Fanus says, and wishes her good night.

Sylvie, the precocious child, is fearless. The child of three mothers and no father pays little heed to the old women's sighing and complaining. She keeps out of their way. Out of their sight she practices theatrical laughter. There is plenty to keep her amused as she prises her way into the world that they try to keep at bay. She thinks nothing of crawling under fences, climbing over gates, tearing her pinafore across barbed wire, dismissing the bark of dogs with a mocking woof-woof. The soles of her feet, tough as leather, withstand all but the most vicious of thorns. As for the common, multisided thorn, she brushes that off without wincing. Sylvie is the tomboy who shares with Meester a love of sheep, who as a child ran along to help him herd them into the old concrete dipkraal where he clipped their ears. Sylvie did not fear the stern man as other children did; she held out her hand for him to take, to help her skip across a runnel, a man whose own children were somewhere far away, so that there was no obstacle to swinging the little one onto his shoulders, a child so eager and old-fashioned for her years. Or perhaps that was how he preferred to think of her.

One afternoon, having scaled the chicken-wire fence at the end of the lane, Sylvie found one of Meester's ewes. The sheep teetered drunkenly, bleated bitterly as if in pain, before collapsing in the sand. Blood came from her rear, and the child watched fascinated, saw that the ewe was in the throes of giving birth. Under the animal's smooth coat was the unmistakable shape-shifting of a creature desperate to get out, so that Sylvie instinctively played the midwife. She tugged at the tiny, slippery hooves, and helped the lamb to find its way out as the mother shuddered her last breath. With the lamb cradled in her arms she rushed to Meester's house. He dribbled milk into its mouth, and together they drove off for a baby's bottle and teat for Hansie. Meester said she could have it—the orphaned hanslam with its adorable black head and hooves—as her very own.

Sylvie held the lamb tenderly in her arms as she fed the little thing, its tail wagging with pleasure. AntieMa said she was not to call the lamb her baby; it was old-fashioned, sinful even, for a girl to think of having a baby. But having delivered the lamb, having seen it all, Sylvie didn't care. She knew she was Hansie's mummy, and better than the rag doll that Ousie had made for her, he loved her loudly with a plaintive baa. And she made sure to report to Meester about Hansie's antics.

Sylvie did not say anything to Meester about Blinkoog, the orphaned kid that Oom Hansie had given her when she was only six. Then her mothers complained, tried to return the gift, but so pitifully did the child wail that they gave in. When Blinkoog was barely a fully grown goat, Ousie sold her to the butcher, for how would they keep her fed in the winter months? Blinkoog's was not a story to be told.

Why, Sylvie asked, was the old dipkraal there, why did they no longer dip the sheep?

Meester said that all had changed, that the fat-tailed Afrikaner sheep, prone to blowflies, needed antiseptic dips in late spring. Now, in the modern days, the old Afrikaners, herded for centuries by Hottentots, were no longer farmed. No, he laughed, just as we colored people have made progress—we no longer need the fat rumps of the Hottentots to see us through the lean months—better sheep are being bred, ones that don't succumb to pests and disease. Meester explained the crossing of Blackhead Persians with the Horned Dorset, and how the new Dorper breed was chosen from those with black heads and white bodies. And that Sylvie should not like some backward, uneducated people think that this went against God's will. Oh no, it was clear that

God had sanctioned the breeding. Dorpers were Chosen Sheep. Chosen for this arid veld where they'd eat anything, chosen for their fecundity, and for being such good mothers. Besides, they did not need shearing, and even the rich sheep farmers were no longer interested in wool. Who needs wool when people prefer the new, more convenient fabrics like nylon? The Dorpers grew so fast, and their mutton was so good, that clearly the breeding had been sanctioned by God.

Sylvie had no fear of contradicting Meester. She did not think that Hansie's mother had tried hard enough. Without her, Sylvie, the old ewe would have kicked the bucket without caring about the baby desperate to get out. Also, nature had not always done so well by the Dorper. Look she said, how their coats are shed in early summer. She laughed, pointing at the weird-looking old ram who was kept tethered away from the ewes. His woolen hair had fallen out from the legs upward, and what remained was a tattered karos that seemed to have been flung carelessly over his back, making him look ugly and foolish. Not ugly at all, Meester said, involuntarily patting the bald patch at the back of his own head. Mother Nature knows what's good for him, and I daresay there's a beauty in such a practical arrangement when it's still cool in the evenings, and something flung over the shoulders is just what he needs until the temperature is right. Then he'll shed the last of the wool and look as handsome and dignified as any shorn ram.

How the child loved to hear Meester's stories about sheep. Sheep, he said, were the favored animals in the Bible. On the Day of Judgment, when the Son of Man comes in all his glory, he will separate the nations, one from another as sheep are separated, and he will place the sheep at his right hand.

So, will goats be cursed, will they weep and gnash their teeth? she asked. Meester wasn't clear about that. He shook his head and tutted; he said it just wasn't worth bothering with the less advanced creatures. These Namaqua people won't develop until they give up goats. He may have started out with goats but it is clear that Dorper sheep are the way forward. Sylvie understood that Meester did not include her in the backward people, and to show her discernment she reminded him of the wolf in sheep's clothing. She would know the difference, she said confidently; she was no Red Riding Hood.

She liked hearing Meester's story of the foolish Dutch king, William of Orange, who sent the first woolly merinos to South Africa—that's how they landed here—and then the next year asked for them back because, he claimed, they had been sent in error. What kind of king was that who changed his mind? Or who made mistakes and then thought the act could be undone? And now, who needed merinos when scientific knowledge had produced the Dorper?

The child quipped, Who needed kings? Perhaps kings, like merinos, were out of fashion. That's why they didn't have a king in South Africa. But Meester said that that was going too far, too immoderate. That a grand country like England had a queen. Which was altogether a different matter. The child could imagine being a queen with a shiny crown, one who would never make a mistake.

Sylvie would not for all the world miss the slaughtering of a sheep in Meester's yard. Then she would hold one of the hind legs and watch him wield the sharp knife skillfully, score just beneath the skin, before kneading with a fist so that the flesh gave way cleanly, separating with a warm sighing sound from its skin. Meester said she could take home some intestines, trotters, and a couple of neck chops for her mothers, also fat for kaiings, all in exchange for scraping the stomach into clean tripe, and Ousie said that the Lord would bless Meester for his kindness.

Please, Sylvie begged AntieMa after school, please could she go with Meester and the boys to the veld, where they would gather melkbos for winter feed. She would take along a bag for collecting wood, and Ousie said yes, that it was good of Meester to take an interest in her. Perhaps he would help to put her through college one day. Yes, Sylvie said, echoing Meester, education was the only way out of backwardness. But Sylvie did not care about days in a distant future. Scampering into the world before sunrise, she loved each day as it broke in a rosy glow, loved being in the open veld with the vast blue dome overhead. She leapt with the boys onto the back of Meester's bakkie, helped for a while with gathering and chopping melkbos, then would wander off looking for birds' eggs, chasing after unfamiliar goggas, or sat stock still in the valleys, listening to strange animal cries cutting through the silence.

And as the girl grew hips and breasts under the old check shirt and cumbersome skirt, as she leapt tomboyish onto the back of the bakkie, AntieMa and Ousie and Nana did not think of protecting her against Meester, who after all was like a father to the child. Besides, they thought that the younger boys, Jakkie and Kytou, always went along, were picked up on the way. Had Sylvie not told them so? They did not imagine that alone, away in the secluded kloofs with only sheep to keep an eye, Meester might one day see that the child was no longer a child, that she had grown hips and breasts, and that perhaps she no longer wanted him as a father.

No, he was not her father. For Nicholas, the days of fathering were over, his children gone. He took her hand; he would show her a protected bower where the thorn trees clumped together on the bank of the dry riverbed. He told her to unbutton her shirt and free her new breasts, small as green apples. He spoke in a new voice, which the girl knew had grown deep and hoarse for her alone, of the beauty of the body, of her breasts. The delicious warmth of sin glowed purple through the dappled leaves, through the crown of thorns above, coursing through her new body.

Sylvie had been taught not to undress completely, to wash herself in AntieMa's darkened room with a cloth and a basin of warm water, one part of the body at a time, the rest kept decently covered, and her skirt not to be removed at all. Under the trees with the dappled light on her breasts, she stretched out her arms and thrilled at the warm air lapping at her bare skin like so many tongues, thrilled at the pleasure of being looked at and admired. Meester said that God had made Eve to be adored and looked at by Adam in all her naked beauty, that there was nothing for Sylvie to fear.

It was Oom Hansie sawing under the thorn tree who put down his tools as Sylvie tried to slip by. He mumbled that it was too hot an afternoon for the veld, that she would be better off resting under the tree. It was hoeka time for coffee, could she not make him a mug of coffee? It was better for Meester to send a man to look for sheep; he, Oom Hansie, would be happy to go after they'd had a little chat over a mug of coffee. He had some ginger biscuits in his bag.

Sylvie laughed. Oom Hansie was an old man who hammered and sawed and dozed in the afternoons under the tree. Who did not talk. What did he know about sheep? No, she lied, she was waiting for Kytou and Jakkie; they would be branding the new lambs today.

Why, she asked her mothers, does Oom Hansie sit at their gate? Could they not tell him to go? Ousie said that there was no reason why he should not, that he worked with his hands, and actually it wasn't their gate. The large old thorn tree belonged to everyone, and even if he were a foolish man, Sylvie should be careful not to be rude. Oom Hansie should always, at all times, be treated with obedience and respect. Meester agreed with Sylvie that Oom Hansie would not be able to run after sheep, and that the sheep would not respond to his call, as they did to hers, her magical tok-tok-tok which always made them turn their heads.

What else was there for Sylvie to do after school? Even the homework took her no time at all. The previous day part of the flock had not returned to the kraal and Meester relied on her to come along to find them. Then they would clip the ears of the new lambs, in case they strayed into the Boer's adjoining camp. Oh, Sylvie ached to be alone in the veld with Meester, who said she was clever and beautiful. He knew everything about plants, about the red earth, the minimal variations in the vygies; he alerted her to the drones of insects, the paths washed by rare rainwater, the clouds in the sky with their fancy names.

Say after me, he said in English: cumulus, cirrus, stratus, and she said after him, as he stood behind her, his hands on her shoulders, steering her to the east. He relied on her sharp eyesight. There, he said, look to that ridge. Are those not sheep on the horizon? Then as she squinted into the sun, his hands slipped down onto the brand-new breasts. So that was what they were for. His fingers were like the tapered flutes of Jan Twakkie flower at the edge of the dry vlei, bright against the blue sky. And she loved his words, spoken like a dominee, hoarsely: I have come in sin. I must ask for forgiveness, but you are so beautiful, so very beautiful, and his voice, his body, trembled with appreciation for her. What did she care about silly old sin that AntieMa trotted out on Sundays? She had a new, quivering body and here was Meester, her very own father, dressed in sin, ready to attend to that body.

I am here for you alone, he said, and, steering her to their bower, unbuttoned her shirt, unbuttoned himself in the purple glow.

Sylvie could see no wrong in it. No, she was proud to have an admirer in Meester; she was his precious whom he would not hurt. Her pressed hair was nothing to him; he said she was beautiful and brave and clever; he cared about her purity; he would guard her, he said, with his life.

It was the meddling old man, Oom Hansie, who spoiled everything. Who knocked at the door and castigated AntieMa for her airs and graces and for allowing Meester to take advantage of the child. AntieMa, boiling with rage, ordered him off her premises, but when Sylvie came home she thrashed the girl, with the help of Nana, who held her arms pinned down. Sylvie would not confess to anything, but she was barred from going to the veld, and from that day her mothers kept a strict eye on her. But oh, she found ways of seeing him. She would walk miles, wait for him under the thorn trees with breasts bared in the purple light of sin.

Neither her mothers nor Oom Hansie said anything to Meester. Years later, Sylvie wondered why they hadn't, why they assumed that it was her, the child's responsibility.

It was Meester himself who, after many months of clandestine meetings in the veld, drove up alongside Sylvie one afternoon as she walked back from school. He sat stiffly in his seat, barely turning his head toward her to say that he had had a vision. He looked past her at the sky as if God were keeping an eye. God in all his glory, flanked by angels, had come to him in the night, spoken to him in a terrifying voice. They were not to meet again. Not ever again. God's grace had thus far kept them out of trouble, but now He has spoken. She, Sylvie, should keep away from him, should no longer tempt him, lest her own soul be damned forever.

Sylvie wept for weeks. She could not eat. She grew listless and frail, and failed her standard five exams. Her menses that had started only the previous month now would not stop. AntieMa said she was pure evil, that there was no question of her staying on at school. How lucky they were that old Lodewyk was prepared to employ her.

Until the day she started in the butcher's shop Sylvie believed that Meester would rescue her. For all God's warning he was surely still her friend who had promised to protect her, but no word, not even a sign, came from him.

What kind of God was he who interfered so cruelly?

The answer: a cruel God. So that Sylvie owed him no allegiance. With her arms plunged into the alchemy of sausage meat, she stopped crying; she bought lipstick and cigarettes, took up her hems, and in tight jeans went dancing with boys from the high school. Her mothers shook their heads sadly. Why had they expected anything else? The sins of the fathers must after all be visited upon the children to the third and fourth generations. But Sylvie would hear nothing of fathers. It was all too late, she said. Having three mothers suited her just fine; she had always appreciated their delicacy, so she hoped they would not now burden her with dreary stories, with fathers. AntieMa was outraged. How right they were to send her to the butchery. If it were not for her pride she would ask Lodewyk to thrash the girl, but Ousie said no, pride was also a good thing, and the girl would grow out of this rude phase.

One night Sylvie drank a whole can of beer and allowed herself to be dragged off to the dipkraal by one of the Dirkse boys, who later boasted about his conquest. The truth was that although she had cast off all thoughts of Meester and God, by now a composite, her body would not obey. Much as Sylvie wanted to lose herself in the embraces of perfectly nice young men, her flesh revolted at the final act; she simply could not, not even after a second can of brave beer. Fortunately for her, none of the young men were prepared to say that he had failed, and so her reputation as a loose goose grew. She reveled in the role. A loose goose had privileges. A loose goose was allowed to hang out, smoking and drinking with men, slapping her tightly denimed thighs, and tilting her head back to crow with loud laughter. And if they went on a jaunt to Rooikrans, she leapt nimbly onto the back of a bakkie, standing all the way with her thumbs hooked in her jeans pockets, keeping a posed balance as the vehicle juddered over corrugated roads.

Old Lodewyk too must have got wind of Sylvie's looseness, for he lurched at her one day as she was preparing chops, a hand already groping at her shirt before she realized what he was doing. How thrilling it was, the idea of raising the axe, of severing a hand cleanly, and watching warm red blood rush from the cut veins, watching it spill down the wooden block. Entranced she was, Sylvie the wild one, Sylvie the butcher, who would wrap the old, liver-spotted hand in newspaper that they kept for cheap cuts, and hand it to him. Then frightened by the vision she took the axe, held it aloft, and with her left fist shoved the old man away. There now, she said quietly, we wouldn't want that bad old hand chopped off and parceled up as soup bones, would we?

There was no question of old Lodewyk trying anything on with her again, but how that hand, those fingers seem to point at her, mocking the girl stuck in a butcher's shop with an axe. That image of herself flickered on a rough wall; the Kool Kat talk with which she inflated herself echoed as if she were trapped in a cave; it was as the apostle said, all noisy gongs and clanging cymbals. At school, Sylvie had learned by heart the text in Corinthians, but where, she wondered, was the love the apostle spoke of? He might as well have spoken in the tongues he raged against, for she knew that there was no escape. Overhead the sun bludgeoned its way as it did every day across the unwavering blue of the sky. At three o'clock the easterly wind rose to sweep stinging sand across the dry plains. There was no escape.

Ousie, sliding down heavily in her chair, held out a hairbrush at Sylvie, who brushed and plaited the thinning gray hair. Ousie carried a small shriveled potato in each pocket, but the arthritis in her arms and hands would not desist. As her mothers declined, Sylvie grew more tolerant of them. She choked on a lump in her throat when she caught herself humming along to Ousie's hymn: Jesus sal a-al jou so-onde weg was, jou so-onde weg was . . . Was her life to be mapped out in the manner of her mothers? If there was no escape, the Kool Kat would at least resist for as long as she could.

For a while she thought that escape had arrived in the shape of Fanus, with whom Sylvie became friends. Much older, more sophisticated than the milksops she had been seeing, the young men who sat hungover in church on Sundays, Fanus was wry and cynical and did not go to church. Which appealed to her.

What a brilliant life of boerewors you're managing here for yourself, he mocked, as she wrapped the sausage in greaseproof paper.

Sylvie laughed; she knew they would be friends. She could talk to him about the dreariness of being trapped, of her fears of taking up the baton in the manner of a relay race from her mothers. But her mothers were content; they didn't complain.

No, Fanus said, they have God.

So, should we try to find God? she asked. The sound of clanging cymbals rang an ominous note of God.

Too late, he said. It's no longer possible to get mixed up with superstition when there is a real world crying out for radical change. Fanus explained to her the work he was doing for the ANC, got her to help with distributing leaflets and organizing tea at meetings. For all his gravity, he understood her wildness, laughed at her loose-goose posturing, appreciated her need to dazzle on the dance floor, so that it seemed inevitable that they would drift into each other's arms. But Fanus said she was too young; he spoke of his ambition to go to university one day. Which Sylvie understood as an excuse. He would go away and leave her behind in a butchery, so that she listened quietly, nodded respectfully, and sealed her heart. She should go to night school, he said, but Sylvie was fearful, skeptical of the benefits of schooling. She would rather not know things; knowing, she feared, was not all it was made out to be. We see but in a glass darkly, Sylvie quoted.

Fanus said, nonsense, that she should put all that nonsense from the Bible behind her. Sylvie knew that he did not love her, would never love her. Once Fanus left she stopped leafleting and making tea for firebrands who failed to see the hands that served them.

Sylvie thought of Ousie, who must have felt trapped, who had left, and then returned. Ousie, the mother, with a real live baby in her arms, refusing motherhood.

Mercia puts the mobile in her handbag, looks about the room, and slinging the bag onto her shoulder, knows that she cannot stay there. Not in that house. Not in Kliprand. She does not have the courage or the strength to face Sylvie, but above all she cannot bear to be in that place. She has to get away. Grabbing her keys and computer she locks up and drives off. She should be in Cape Town before bedtime.

At the petrol station she sends Sylvie a clipped text to say that Jake has been admitted to the clinic and that she, Mercia, is on her way to town. That she'll be in touch. It may be shameful but she has to keep moving, get away from this place called home. She must not think of her father, will not be destroyed by him. He too is departed, is dead, thank God. Mercia need not brood over him and his actions. No need to go over their last days together. There can be no point in pondering over what it means to love, to have loved a man, a father who is capable of abusing another child. She has in any case no language for such an exercise, no escape route via metaphor. This crime—and the word brings a sharp pain—has to be fully faced, but she does not know how.

He is dead; he is dead; he is dead, she says out loud. And she, Mercia, must live, will live, as long as she can get away. Out of Kliprand. Out of the country. For the moment Jake is being cared for, but she cannot think what to do about Sylvie. She does not want to see the girl, for in her heart Mercia can find not a scrap of the compassion that the girl undoubtedly deserves. Of course it is shameful, but vacillating between guilt and disgust, she does not know how to manage, how to fulfill her responsibility toward Sylvie. How will she conceal her revulsion? Oh, she knows that it has unfairly been transferred from Nicholas, but it is revulsion all the same. Somewhere in her heart she must find compassion for the child abused by an old man, but her heart is tired, recalcitrant, and will not do the mind's bidding.

A check—that will have to do, but later, all in good time. Right now Mercia does not want to think of them, her people. To live, she must think of a life elsewhere. Yes, she is driving to Cape Town, but she has to propel herself into another time, another country. She would rather think of the absence that is Craig.

🏵

Throughout that cold summer in Glasgow Mercia had shivered in a coat, an unfashionable gray coat she had not worn for years, which she wrapped around herself, belted, to keep out the chill of being unloved—an actual chill—to keep pain from spilling out into everyday business. Was there no end to grieving? How long, she wondered impatiently, would she go on feeling sorry for herself?

Mercia mulled over the many words and expressions for being abandoned, through a range from the hurtful "dumped" to the far-from-neutral "being left," and settled for a euphemism that is also said of the dead. Craig had departed. At the time, she claimed that his departure came out of the blue, a bolt that struck at a perfectly happy relationship. Thus, if Craig's departure came as a surprise, she had not been vigilant, had not kept a close enough eye on things or, even more distressing, had turned a blind eye to signs of his disaffection, for signs there must have been. Why, for instance, had she insisted on an Easter break by the sea when he so hated that kind of holiday?

Now it strikes her as shameful that she, a woman devoted to the close reading of words and actions on the page, failed to keep track of events in her own life. Blinded by grief, and perhaps, she must confess, by the condition of having been left, for she has not always been able to separate the two, she has not arrived at an explanation for what happened.

If the time has come to reexamine the preceding months, or as Mercia is forced to revise, the preceding decline, it must mean that she is recovering. So once more she picks over Craig's departure as one does a scab, even as she fears from the previous, barely acquiescent flake that it is too soon, that blood will once again ooze, that a new scab will form to protect the wound, and so delay recovery. But the thinking person must press on. There is some satisfaction to be found in the crumbly bits willingly prised away from the healing wound to reveal queer new flesh that will grow accustomed to air and light, that must eventually merge with the old, leaving a barely visible vestige of the injury. It would be prudent to stop there, to leave alone the rest that is not ready to be picked at. If she claimed at the time that her heart would never mend, it is the case that the scab is smaller, that there is less of a temptation to pick at it prematurely.

The ready-made belief in time-will-heal is after all not to be scoffed at. One day, in its own time, the remnant scab too will depart, leave of its own accord, simply flake off unnoticed, and disappear, leaving in its place the shiny new skin. But Mercia cannot remember ever being caught out in that way. No, scabs are attention seekers. There is usually an eager itch that begs for a helping hand, even if it is premature, a false appeal. Thus the metaphor brings a warning: she must be careful in picking over their last months together. If she is committed to conscientious close reading there is also the danger of probing prematurely or too deeply for her own good. A woman of a certain age must be careful not to destroy herself.

And neither will Mercia be destroyed by her father.

🍥

Mercia had wanted Craig to go home with her, but he was adamant that the Cape was too far, too expensive, would take up too much time. He hated long flights so that she looked for somewhere closer where they could go for a week.

Hell no, Craig said, who wants to laze at a resort for British tourists reddening in the sun, fanning themselves with the *Daily Record*? Do I need a holiday? Anyway, what's wrong with the cottage on the Solway?

It's too cold. Besides, you don't read the *Daily Record* and you *are* British, so . . .

Beg your pardon, hen, I'm Scottish, he interrupted.

Well, just because you're a tourist, doesn't mean that you have to eat burgers and chips at McDonald's, and swill beer at the Irish pub. There's plenty of scope to be different.

Good old considerate Craig had forgotten that she was the one with a full-time job, the one exhausted by teaching and the pressures of publishing, who needed a break. No wonder her tone was sneering. The next day she wheedled, Oh come on, Craig, I'll die if I have to wait for a sun that may or may not show up. We've been to the Solway, now I need to get away, farther away.

What's wrong with you? Why can't you stay put, enjoy leisure without thrashing about in airports? Are you not getting too old for this wanderlust? You know that banging on about sunshine is an excuse. You just want to be on the move, get to as many places as possible. Tick them off. Conspicuous consumption of space, eh?

Mercia laughed, let it go. Except she would insist on the sunshine. It is the case, she said, that black people need more sunlight, that here in Scotland the expats—oops, I should say immigrants—are developing rickets.

Craig picked up his guitar and started humming to a poor execution of "A Hard Rain's A-Gonna Fall." Mercia knew that if she arranged everything, every detail, paid for the flights, he would succumb. Which swung it. So, why did she not go on her own? That, she decides, is an unreasonable question. And why, after all those years, twenty-four to be precise, did they have separate bank accounts? Neither of them wanted to be married; the apartment was bought in both their names, but why the pitiful calculations for a kitty as prices fluctuated, the counting of pennies like students in a rented house? Yes, that was what they examined—bills and receipts, rather than their lives.

When they first moved in together Craig said that as a feminist she would want to keep separate finances. Then they would not, like children, have to ask each other for permission to buy anything, he said, as she demurred. For Mercia there was no question of not being independent. Now it seemed absurd, an overvaluing of money, and bugger all to do with independence, equality, or feminism. Why would common finances involve her asking for permission to spend? Surely as responsible adults they could have trusted each other, even indulged each other. As it became clear that Mercia would earn more in her senior position at the university, the issue of finances was not revisited. Perhaps it would not have been possible for Craig, the poet with a part-time post, to raise it.

Now Mercia winces at the vulgarity of waiting a year until

Craig could manage to overhaul the heating system, afford his share of an expensive new boiler and radiators, and she blushes at the arrangement of contributing 65 percent to the gas bill since it was she who wanted heating during the summer evenings. How did they arrive at the figure? Did neither of them notice that instead of simplifying their lives, separate finances brought endless dreary consultations and calculations? How, she wonders, could a relationship survive such tedious, such shameful arithmetic? Neither of them was after all a spendthrift or a gambler. How much simpler, more civilized, it would have been to throw all money into the same pot and help themselves as and when the need arose.

Mercia did not choose Lanzarote. Rather, it was the fact of a direct flight as well as the reduced cost of apartments in a fishing village some distance from the designated resorts that decided their destination. There was no time to do any other homework on the island, so that they were both delightfully surprised at the beauty of the place. For all the island's inhospitable volcanic heritage, Father Culture was kept well in check, forced to doff his hat respectfully at Mother Nature. Surely the Lanzarotian architect and artist César Manrique should be proclaimed an international icon, should have been a Nobel laureate, Craig enthused, for managing tourism so strictly and sensibly, for the architectural restrictions he imposed, and above all for his aesthetic development of natural phenomena and disused structures. Why has the rest of the world not followed suit?

They lounged and basked under a moderate sun and argued companionably about the merits and demerits of stifled individualism. Craig was emphatic. If people are allowed to paint their houses in their chosen colors, with no regard for the collective appearance, you should expect the triumphant ugliness of English streets. At least in Glasgow there was uniformity in

tenement colors. Aesthetically pleasing, the black window sur-
rounds and woodwork against blond or pink sandstone. But
look at your country, he said. It's criminal, the lovely coastline
wrecked by rich people with no taste, who have the freedom to
design and build monstrous houses with no regard for the collective outlook. Is there no town planning? Are there no architects
in South Africa?

Ah, but there are strict regulations for RDP housing for the
poor, plenty of sad uniformity there, Mercia said.

It was true that on the island the uniform white of the houses
with their green paintwork inland, or blue at the seaside, was
lovely, and that adherence to traditional low-rise buildings made
for picturesque towns. Three cheers for Manrique, Craig called,
and filled their glasses with exuberant bubbles of a bargain Veuve
Clicquot that he had bought at the airport. She had fortunately
stopped herself in time from asking whether he could afford it.

We drink too much, Mercia said, but Craig said no, they
didn't drink enough, that another bottle was better than following the awful middle-aged trend of giving up alcohol for health
reasons. Imagine being teetotal in order to extend impoverished
drink-free lives. Mercia reached out for his hand; she couldn't
have agreed more. They would siesta on the private balcony. The
Mirador del Río could wait for another day.

It was then she asked, In Scotland, does the word yes count
as a greeting? Or is that just used in Glasgow? I don't remember
coming cross it in the south.

What do you mean? Where are you greeted with yes?

In public places—shops, restaurants, libraries, dentists'. The
person at reception, often a woman, will ask in a rising tone,
which is to say a puzzled tone, or even something of a bark, Yes?
As if you had stumbled into the wrong place. And that before
you've got round to saying anything. Perhaps it's not said to men?

Well, I can't say I've ever heard it. Could it not be a friendly tone? Perhaps it's your paranoia—you really should watch yourself, not watch out for the imaginary slight.

In some ways they might as well have gone home to the Cape. Mercia was surprised by the familiarity of the island, the wide plains of dry earth and sparse growth. Apart from black volcanic rock and the black dust through which determined flora burrowed its way out, the place was uncannily like that of her childhood. Good old Kliprand, she exclaimed. But no, distinctly more lush: fields of prickly pear for the cultivation of cochineal; ghanna bush hardly recognizable with plump parcels of rolled-up leaves; and gray old Jan Twakkie sprayed green, with branches tapering into elegant fingers of yellow flower, but familiar all the same in the way that prosperous relatives are familiar. Mercia had a vision of her entire extended family appearing on the horizon, scrambling over black rock: Murrays and Malherbes of the malpaíses. There's no escaping us, they chanted in chorus.

Craig nodded sympathetically; he had after all met some of that weird clan. Well, we are so close to Africa, only a hop and a skip away. The Canaries must have been used to ships from the Cape popping in for a bite to eat and drink, he said. Bet the islands had a reputation for being hospitable. That's what seafarers would have needed them to be, even as the natives turned their backs and clung for dear life to their fruit and veg. Pretty Polly, pretty Polly, he twittered, such hospitable canaries.

Actually, Camões has many stories of treacherous natives who thought nothing of plotting death for their visitors.

Ah, but did they show hostility, or did they smile treacherously, was his riposte.

Mercia remembered that Craig did not like being corrected by her. There surely is a difference between canaries and parrots? he asked.

Dunno, she said. She hoped they would not argue about parrots.

See, he said, stabbing at the map, here in the south it's called Papagayo, that's parrot. A Papagayo beach for nudists and French writers.

Craig had found in a cupboard a raunchy French novel about Lanzarote with which he had struggled for a few hours. She pretended to have dozed off.

Mercia wandered off, impatient with Craig's enduring desire for sitting in cafés, drinking coffee. Actually, they argued about coffee. She thought she had gone off it—another sign of aging—never again would she touch coffee, but Craig said that such physical responses should be resisted, that the pleasure of sitting in cafés was more than the enjoyment of the drink. Mercia could see no sense in that.

The malpaíses, arid wastelands of volcanic lava, a moonscape of broken rock hosting nothing other than dry lichen, stretched ahead as far as the eye could see. The smooth curves of volcanic mountains in the distance seemed to disown the jagged terrain they had once upon a time spewed up. A long way below an icy blue Atlantic thrashed against black rock, the same stuff that the elegant Mirador was crafted from, and Mercia, shivering on a promontory, buttoned up her inadequate jacket and clutched at her lapels. In spite of the cold these badlands were strangely familiar. The windswept malpaíses felt uncannily like home. Gazing down at a series of socos, semicircular windbreaks built of volcanic stone where farmers coaxed who-knows-what into growth, mollycoddled against the wind, Mercia's eyes watered. Was it self-pity for the child who escaped from the sand-scouring easterly wind, who hid behind a thornbush, telling herself tales in which Nettie was cast as the wicked stepmother? The icy wind batted her between past and present.

How to keep ice out of the heart! No dead metaphor, that. Like the newly arrived arthritis that gnawed at her wrists, there was a clenching sensation, a ripple of pain through what she imagined to be her heart, presaging this very day, the now of picking over Craig's departure, looking back across volcanic runes, where scabs of lichen spelled out a future. How could the islanders take comfort in the outcrops of lichen? According to the brochure those scabs of barely live organisms promised, simply by being, by tenaciously surviving, to break down through eons of time the rough crust of volcanic lava into crumbly earth where life will one day, once again, take root. Some distant day, it promised, ghanna and Jan Twakkie and prickly pear will triumph, and transform that wasteland. Flooded inexplicably with the misery of the badlands, Mercia shook her head in disbelief. She was no artist, no poet like Craig who could imagine such a time. She rushed off to the next venue, Manrique's house, where he had captured forever the flow of black lava. There it appeared to spill over a window ledge, lured into culture's space of pristine white paint, and remain suspended in a building called home.

An indefatigable tourist you, that's what you are, Craig said the following day, playfully tugging at the cord of her trousers. Why not stay put today, lie on the beach, drink minty mojitos in the sun?

But no, Mercia needed to press on, tick off Manrique's architectural sites that simply had to be visited. Craig flicked through the brochure.

Jardín de Cactus? Nope, he said, that's where I draw the line. Being conscientious is not my thing. I've seen enough cacti without even looking, and what's more, I happen to know that you bloody hate cacti too, so what's with the spending good euros on a garden full of the vicious stuff?

Mercia went alone, driving fearfully, gingerly, on the wrong side of the road. Craig was the driver, that was the deal he'd so casually reneged on, but she'd be the last person to mention it. Besides, the garden was worth the troubled drive. An old quarry at Guatiza had been transformed into an exquisite circular structure, an amphitheater with terraces of cacti from all over the world. Once again she admired the now familiar use of volcanic rock crafted into a pattern of crazy paving, paths that wound dangerously around the tiers in defiance of health and safety rules.

In that warm, sunken space, protected against Atlantic winds, large mammillaria of thorn and robotic limbs of vicious prickles stood starkly against the blue sky. Here Mercia found, as she knew she would, the species from home. Euphorbias from Transvaal, quaintly labeled in the old geographic names of the trekkerboer, and the very melkbos from Kliprand—here sporting fleshy flowers—turned out to be another type of euphorbia. She thrilled at seeing the name given by Portuguese seafarers: Cabo de Buena Esperanza. Her own Cape of Good Hope, words printed on the municipal exercise books and rulers of her childhood. How often she derided that childhood. Yet, she could not but savor the memory of a little girl riding on her father's shoulders as he taught her the homely names of plants.

Mercia thought of the Swiss mercenaries who in bygone days, hearing the sound of cowbells, fell ill to the new name of nostalgia and languished for home. Was she here in the Jardín de Cactus being pricked into Heimweh? Was there no telling the difference between Fernweh and Heimweh? Did the former lead to the latter? Only a small matter then of shifting prepositions? Was there no choosing between the contradictions of longing for and longing to be away from home?

Pull yourself together, girl! she admonished. Mercia had to remind herself that she preferred the lush flora of the Northern

Hemisphere. Could Kliprand be aestheticized like this volcanic quarry? She feared not.

On her return, Craig was not to be found reading his book on the balcony, with lunch prepared, as they had earlier arranged. There was no note. For a moment panic struck as she swiftly checked the bathroom and kitchen, and foolish tears threatened. Something ominous had happened. Had Craig left? packed his bag and gone? But no, his bag was there. Mercia took a deep breath. No doubt he had wandered to the beach for a swim. She splashed her face in cold water, grabbed her swimsuit, and walked down briskly to find Craig just emerging from the sea.

You'd better not go in, he said, as he offered his pale lean back for the rubbing in of sunscreen. A notice has just gone up, and he pointed to the board. Medusa has arrived, so swimming is not recommended today. He mimed the waving of jellyfish tentacles. Anyway, it's lunchtime. I thought we'd have tapas here at the café. My treat, he grinned.

And I'll see if I can find you a *Daily Record* and flat Scottish beer, Mercia said. Was he not going to ask about her driving?

Funny how Craig did not seem to hate that kind of holiday after all, seemed to take to lounging about in the sun like a duck to water. So that it came as a shock when on the fourth night he said he had had enough. Even of Manrique. That Mercia should excuse him from further sightseeing. He stayed at the apartment with his laptop, writing or sulking on the balcony in the sun.

Mercia found that driving on the wrong side of the road was not as terrifying after all. Dinners in the evenings were civil, even pleasant, since she was determined not to admit defeat. There was no question of probing. Craig had surely already met the new woman. Had he been pining for her? Mercia had always thought that she would know instinctively if Craig were to be unfaithful; she is ashamed of having had no idea.

Mercia thinks she should forgive herself the cowardice. She must have sensed that their days were numbered, that probing would hasten the end. Now, driving along the deserted national road to Cape Town, burdened with knowledge that she would not like to pass on to anyone, she feels something lift, feels relief that Craig has gone, that he has found someone else, left, departed, dumped her—whatever. Wincing at the thought of her abject questions, Mercia is grateful that he refused to supply any details of the new relationship. He was right: she is better off not knowing, and thus not having any basis on which to imagine his new life. Now that she is freed from telling him about Nicholas, Craig can surely no longer be mourned.

Here, approaching the city, with a garishly lit Table Mountain growing closer and the cool coastal breeze in her hair, the briny air brings a strange calmness. Mercia notes that she is speeding. She takes her foot off the accelerator.

Much as Mercia would like to discuss Nicky with her dear friend Bella, who after all has raised three children, she is relieved that Bella is still visiting her own family in Port Elizabeth. They both arranged to return at the beginning of the following week, but fortunately Mercia has keys and may come and go as she pleases. And fortunately she left a suitcase at Bella's. She has not brought back her bag from Kliprand, does in any case not want to wear the clothes tarred with the nastiness of uncovered history.

Mercia is just in time to pick up bread and coffee at the 7-Eleven store. Funny how she has returned to coffee since Craig has left. She looks forward to a bath, imagines the effluvium of shame taking form as a grimy ring left on white enamel. Mercia hopes to hole up for the weekend, or rather, settle in the shade of the garden with the problematic chapter of her book. She expects it to be a struggle, but away from Kliprand she might well return to writing. It would be good if Bella could look over that chapter. Bella is a social scientist who is amused that after all these years Mercia still writes about South Africa. They have been reading each other's work ever since their student days, and Mercia's absence leaves her more in need than ever of her friend's local take on home affairs.

The alarm system bleeps as she opens Bella's front door, and then her mind goes blank. Damn, she can't remember the numerical code, the bloody code she used only a few days ago. Now there is the usual drama of the security company arriving, the usual absence of neighbors too fearful to investigate the blaring alarm but peering through the blinds all the same. Fortunately Mercia remembers the code name to cite to the uniformed security guard who arrives armed to the teeth, a name that will legitimize her entry. As it happens, she was there visiting when Bella moved into the house and had the alarm installed.

Let's have Cedric Visagie as the code name, and together they laughed, remembering the handsome, charismatic young man from their student days who had had the audacity to date them simultaneously. He had fabricated for each a story about having to keep their relationship secret, something to do with his role in what they inferred to be MK, and the young women, feeling the thrill and privilege of their brush with the armed wing of the revolutionary movement, were eager to comply. Although not bosom friends at that stage, they had rooms in the same student house, each conducting her secret relationship. Until Mercia grew suspicious. She thought that she had seen Visagie's car drive slowly past the house just as Bella came in and babbled about being out with a cousin at a new club in Woodstock. Fabulous new band, she said. Mercia should come along some time.

A couple of nights later Visagie gave Mercia a lecture on Adam Small, whom he thought to be wrongly dismissed by the commissars of culture. Take *Kanna hy kô hystoe* he said, no less pertinent to the struggle than the banned Dennis Brutus's resistance poems. He urged her to read it. Writing in Kaaps, he said, was the way forward to claiming their indigenous culture and valuing their roots. He gave her a dramatic rendering of

en Moses was 'n hakkelaar
ja Moses was 'n stamelaar
en Moses was 'n moordenaar
maar God was in sy elke aar.

Mercia thought of the slim book in a brown paper bag hurriedly swept up by Bella on her way out to meet her cousin. She waited for Bella to appear for breakfast and repeated what she could remember of Moses the stammerer, Moses the murderer. Bella blanched, put down her half-eaten boerewors roll to stare in amazement. No, she shrieked, it can't be, and they fell upon each other with laughter.

Now the burly security guard dressed up in his paramilitary uniform and patting the gun in its holster looks up from his cell phone with incredulity.

That *is* the code, isn't it? Mercia says.

He laughs. Yes, man, but it's mos also my name, so for a second I thought you making fun of me.

It's the name of a famous bullshitter, so just you keep on the straight and narrow, she jests, wagging a finger.

The man does not leave before telling her gruesome tales of attacks on lone women.

And what makes you think I'm alone? she bluffs.

He taps his nose and leaves.

Mercia shuts the door, relieved to be in Bella's lovely house. She laughs out loud at the memory of Cedric Visagie as the two women turned up together for the next date. How she marveled at his composure. No more than a flash of panic slid across his handsome face before he explained that his job was to recruit both of them. It was simply the way in which the revolutionary movement at times had to achieve its aims. They were clearly not ready for the sacrifices demanded in those difficult times.

Heavens, how they laughed. But Visagie called after them all the same, Don't forget to read *Kanna*.

Mercia finds it difficult to fall asleep in Bella's house. She cannot rid herself of Jake's disclosures, of the injustice done to him. It is on Jake that she must focus. When she drifts off momentarily, she is assailed by nightmares, by lewd images of Nicholas. She wakes up screaming with an image of her own clubbed head, of blood trickling into her gaping handbag, of her father looking on.

Mercia finds Bella's old dressing gown; she will not go back to bed. She opens the file on her desktop—Home. Might it not help, as the therapists say, to write up the grim story? If Mercia has no pretensions as a writer, no aspirations to write stories, might a plain telling, a brief account in visible black marks on an illumined screen, not do the trick? With one thing leading to another as is the case with writing—for she does not believe that the writing up of events can be any different in practice to critical writing—one story generating another, she may well find the distance, and thus clarity and the much needed compassion. Memoir might be a misnomer, but why, after all, has she returned from time to time to the file?

Mercia types the sentence: Nicholas Theophilus Murray was a good man, a decent man. She stops. She does not have the courage to bare her bosom to the screen. She shakes her hanging hands like a shiatsu masseuse so that the toxins might exit via her fingertips. If memoir prides itself on fidelity—for why else would one want to rake up the past?—has Mercia not also seen how an indulged memory grows fat and multiplies, spawning brand-new offspring? But there is no one to tell. Not Bella and not as much as a longing for Craig.

Mercia stares at the keyboard. This is a father-son story into which she has stumbled, nothing to do with her, and thus not fit for memoir. She cannot find the words; she would have to skirt around their story, around the father, and how then would she avoid the fiction that telling begets? Mercia wants nothing to do with artfulness; besides, having snaked its way into their lives, the thing must be laid to rest. It must not be given the chance to take another shape.

She shuts down the computer.

It may be madness, but there is nothing else to do. The decision to come to town has been impetuous; to return in the small hours may be equally rash, but Mercia knows that she has run away in cowardice, that she must return, go home right away to deal with Sylvie and the boy. They are her responsibility, her inheritance.

With Table Mountain now a ghostly cutout shape behind her, Mercia drives through the city's silence to pick up the national road that will take her back home. She does not register tiredness; instead, the questions mill through her head:

What kind of person am I? What kind of woman am I? The answer cannot be refuted. The kind of person who finds it hard to think and feel beyond her own loss. The kind of woman who does not forgive another woman for being a victim. And should self-knowledge not bring release from such self-absorption? Apparently not. But for all her desire to remove herself from them, from her people, from the place of exile called home, she cannot, and it irks. Has she gone crazy, driving right back to that place? To that desert she had thought of as dead, but where like any suburban home swathed in shamefaced lace curtains blood has been racing and pounding, and boundaries have been ruthlessly trampled. Worse, more wicked, for offending in the veld—God's own country, mythopoetic home of wholesomeness, home to kalkoentjies bursting blood red into a new vernal world, home of healthy, simple pleasures seasoned with the plentiful salt of this earth.

The schoolgirl's song of spring echoes in her head: Al die kriekies kriek daar bu-ite, Elke springkaan spri-ing. Such Edenic pleasures at home, where simple people are supposed to live wholesome, frugal lives amongst frolicking crickets and harmless locusts. But there is no such thing as simple people. The good folk of Gray's elegy have long since departed, doubly dead; besides, that knowledge, rich with the spoils of time, has neatly sidestepped the carnal. And Mercia should have known that bucolic innocence, the stuff of the pastoral, is refuted in country matters that blindly pursue their own carnal laws. The lamb with his fleece as white as snow is the issue of a thrusting ram, a tupped ewe. The coming of the Lamb of God—his mum up the duff.

Mercia glances at the speedometer. She must slow down. She must not think of it. But for all her years, she is a child. The concupiscence of the parent—let alone this, this business—it is not for the ears and the eyes of a child. Sylvie was a child. For all Mercia's atheism, it is the word SIN that lodges itself in her thoughts. He, Nicholas, her father, has sinned against the girl whilst his God turned a blind eye. And the iniquity of the father will be visited upon the children until the third and fourth generation. Dear little Nicky's burden—and rage engulfs her on behalf of the child. She may have thought of it as Old Testament nonsense, but how will the child avoid suffering his grandfather's sin, the wrath of an unjust God?

At least Mercia has done with crying. She may feel relief at not having to tell Craig, but if he had still been there, would she have told him about the shame that now is hers? Could she tell anyone that this home has been burned to the ground, that she would rather choose to suffer the dark and icy north with its plentiful water for washing away the sin that now is hers? Ag, she resorts too readily to melodrama. Why bother with the idea of home, a notion that has been turned inside out, like an old garment in preparation for mending? Thank heavens there is no longer any need to explain herself or, as they piously say these days, the need to share. She says out loud, dipping her voice: Allow me to share my shame with you.

If Mercia is past crying, it is also no time for irony. As for Jake, poor Jake for whom it has been so much worse, who has thus far borne it on his own, will there be a second chance? This poison is more potent than alcohol. If only she could carry some of that burden for him. She should feel rage on his behalf, but it is too late; she does not hold out much hope for his recovery.

Thank God for the ease of driving in the small hours. Mercia tells herself that she will overcome her self-pity, that the mind will strike a deal with the heart, allow it to throb to a new beat of compassion. She is on her way back to Kliprand. She does not want to see Sylvie, but she will; she must try to make amends. As for the problem of the child, who surely should be removed from the poison of the past . . . well, she doesn't know. He ought to be taken away, ought to be relieved of the burden of home and the legacy of shame. She ought to give him a new life in the gloom of Glasgow where he could warm his hands at a hearth glowing with the uniform pellets of smokeless fuel. She does not see her way clear to doing so.

When Mercia arrives in Kliprand after five a.m. she feels for the first time the exhaustion of having driven all that way and back. Even the car seems to sigh deeply when she turns off the engine. She gets out quietly, stretches, and tiptoes to the stoep. There is the same stirring sky of her childhood, with fading stars and a paper pale half moon bowing out to the faint glow of the day's arrival—the surge of light that tugs at her heart. The view of flat-topped mountains in the distance is the same as that of the house in which she grew up. She ought to be sipping coffee, her mother's mixture of coffee and chicory that Mercia imagines the Huguenots to have brought to the Cape centuries ago. In this house there is only cheap instant coffee, and Mercia has thought it impolite to buy her own. It would only have confirmed

Sylvie's view of her as a snob. Better to say that she does not drink coffee.

In the morning air there is a strange smell of cold ash that makes its way to her mouth, so that she imagines tasting it. It is the spent smell of cinders; it belongs to the outside grate where Sylvie does her braaivleis and baking, where yesterday's fire for grilling roosterbrood has died down. Mercia has an inkling that she has somehow offended Sylvie, but really there is no point in pondering where and how their words clash or miss each other.

As the red deepens and the sun appears on the horizon, Mercia unlocks the front door and tiptoes in. How strange that Sylvie, an early riser, is not yet up. Mercia goes to the kitchen; she will die without a cup of coffee. Or so it comes to her, the fear of facing Sylvie, so that she puts on the kettle, searches for the jar of instant coffee. The sound of the lavatory flushing through the house makes her brace herself for what lies ahead.

It seems like an age before Sylvie comes in. She sits herself down at the table in silence, as if for an interview. Mercia has her back to her, holding an empty coffee mug. Thank God for Nicky, who stumbles into the kitchen in his pajamas.

You're back from Cape Town? he asks, evidently pleased.

I'm back, she says, and turning round, smiling at the boy, says that she'll make coffee for them, that she needs another mug. For an instant her eye catches Sylvie's.

So Sylvie knows. Knows that she knows. Mercia fears that Sylvie will speak, offer explanations or details, but of course the child is there. The girl bows her head while Mercia chats with Nicky, but then she rises, supported by her left hand placed flat on the table. She looks up, willing Mercia to look at her.

How will all this be paid for, this treatment of Jake's? she asks.

Mercia assures her that she will deal with it. In fact, she says under the girl's frank gaze, what they should do today is open an account in Sylvie's name so that she could handle the expenses herself. Mercia will make monthly payments into the account. There will be enough for Sylvie to see to the mortgage, to ensure that they do not get evicted.

Sylvie sits down once more, stretches her legs, leans with her elbow on the corner of the table. She stares listlessly ahead at the shafts of sunlight slanting above the lower door. She lifts her arm, then lets it fall, a guillotine through the swirling, dazzled motes of dust. Mercia waits until, eventually, Sylvie speaks. The girl is strangely composed, her face youthful, luminous, as she looks up unflinchingly, into the sunlight.

She would rather not have anything to do with money, Sylvie says with quiet dignity. If Mercia could arrange to settle Jake's bills herself, she would be grateful. It is best not to rely on her to make payments. So there is no need for an account in her name. She would rather not have that responsibility. For herself and Nicky there is no problem. She'll manage. As for the house, she knows that Jake will not come back, either to her or to that house, so there is no need to secure the house on her account. She and Nicky will manage all right.

Mercia cringes at the thought that it is Sylvie who so definitively has washed her hands of them, the Murrays, that she does not expect compassion, that she won't be bought off. Indeed, Sylvie rises swiftly, light-footed, as if divested of her burden, rolls up her sleeves, and says that Jake's room has not been cleaned for the entire two weeks that he took to his bed.

Mercia would like to show that she understands. A better person would put her arms around the girl, but that she cannot do, that is not possible. She turns to the child, pulls him onto her knee and with her arms around him says that she understands. That she will stop off in town to arrange the payments for Jake's care. Sylvie says that not once has that window been opened, that

Jake's room is disgusting. With a broom and mop, she sets about it, whilst a chastened Mercia sets about packing her bag. There is nothing else to do. She wants to support them, not only out of guilt, she realizes; rather, because they belong to her, because this girl who has risen above abuse and misery without any help demands her respect. Sylvie is her inheritance, but she cannot insult Sylvie with further offers.

Nicky, who has wriggled off Mercia's lap, helps her pack. He searches his pockets frantically, then rushes off to consult his mother, who arrives with his good trousers. From their pockets he extracts a piece of string, a glass marble and a pigeon's tail feather, whilst his mother looks on smilingly. Here, he says, he has found these presents for Mercia, but if he had known she was going so soon, he'd have got her something special like the porcupine quills he left at his ouma's house.

Mercia says that these are the best presents she has ever had. She swallows back the unexpected tears as she kisses him goodbye. It won't be long, she promises, before she'll be back for those porcupine quills. Then she remembers the camera. Here, she says to Sylvie, this is to make sure that you send me photographs of the two of you. She shakes Sylvie's hand, slides into her seat and is about to drive off when the woman puts a restraining hand on her arm.

You will, she asks in a strangled voice, take care of Nicky?

Yes, of course, Mercia finds herself saying, bewildered, not knowing what it means, what she means. Look, I'll be in Cape Town for a few days. We could talk on the phone, later. Then she amends it. Listen, I have to be back in two months to see to Jake. That gives us all time to think things over. I'll keep in touch. I'll let you know.

How bloody awful. How the woman must wish she were a fucking tortoise. Summoning from God knows where the

courage, the dignity, to free herself from them, the poisonous
Murrays, only to be thrown back once more into their clutches—
for the sake of her child. Is that what mothers have to do? Eat
humble pie? Prostrate themselves for the sake of their children?
Sell themselves? How wretched, how absolutely wretched for
Sylvie.

Home at last. The taxi stops behind her car, parked exactly where she left it two weeks ago. Mercia drags in the suitcase, shivers, and switches on the central heating. She wanders through the ice-cold apartment, sparse and elegant after Sylvie's cramped rooms. Something is wrong, a disturbance of some kind, as if someone has rearranged everything ever so slightly, so that she can't put her finger on it, can't say with conviction that the coffee table has shifted an inch to the left. Which is, of course, nonsense.

Is this where she lives? Is this her home? What does she do with all these things, all this space? What would any single person do with all this space? At the time Craig had argued for a smaller apartment, but she would hear none of it. The place had been a bargain at the price, and one room less would not have been significantly cheaper. She stands in the doorway of the vast living room with its ornate cornices and wall of tall windows. Her grand nineteenth-century Glasgow apartment, built by sugar and tobacco lords from the spoils of slavery.

Before her very eyes panning across the rug, the elegant leather sofas, the glass and chrome table, all these things assume the ghostly shapes of objects covered in dust sheeting, all wrapped up and parceled like a Christo project. Mhairi, the cleaner, had once asked her what the Corbusier chaise longue was for. Mercia shudders, shakes her head to free the furniture parcels of their wrapping. This is her home with the marble fireplace and mantelpiece at the far end. The cold hearth smells of Sylvie's outside grate. She will not light a fire.

Still clutching her coat, Mercia goes to Craig's room, sits down at his desk at the window, where she can see the man across the road sitting at his own window, reading a newspaper. A man for whom Craig had constructed an entire life in prize-winning free verse. The terra-cotta boxes on his window ledge cling to the corpses of summer flowers—a brown tracery of once-blue lobelia persists, and dead petunia stalks sit bolt upright in rigor mortis. There they will stay until next year, she remembers, lashed by winter wind and snow into bare, spindly stalks. Until spring comes babbling like an idiot, scolding the old roots. Until one Saturday morning in late April when the man will fuss about the window boxes with new trailing lobelia, new petunia plants that in good time will produce their blue and purple flowers. Just like every year that they have lived there, when spring comes down the hill. In April, not October. Would the man recognize himself in Craig's verse? There is something comforting about not knowing him, knowing nothing about him except for the business with window boxes.

If this home away from Kliprand and her family feels strange, it is only a question of time, a matter of half an hour at most, for the emptiness to be filled with what soon will be familiar routines. Like the gas boiler fired up, pumping hot water through old copper pipes, the warm tick-ticking of radiators slowly thawing into life, spreading invisible warmth. In this empty apartment Craig's absence hovers like the heat molecules rushing up, out of reach, to cling to the high ceiling. Mercia will not wait for the warmth; she will not call Smithy just yet; instead, she'll do her messages as the Scots say—a trip to the supermarket, which invariably means a conversation on the corner of Byres Road where she is so often detained by someone she knows. So many students who have passed through her hands. More of a village here than Kliprand. Does no one ever leave this city?

Dr. Ants in Her Pants. That's what Craig called her when he first flicked through her passport. Only five years old and already bursting with border-control stamps. Where have you not been? he asked, shaking his head.

In those brand-new days there was something of admiration in his voice. Craig had after university spent two years in London, with a trip each to Paris, Berlin and Amsterdam.

Look, he said defensively, I come from a country of folk who once upon a time rushed about colonizing the world, and so freeing those left behind of the horrible Christianity they took along to dump on others. Thereafter, folk needed only to move across the border, either to make good or to relish being in exile. Now, having recovered ourselves, we no longer have to do that, so I've come back to Glasgow and this is where I stay put. Healthy or what?

Mercia laughed. In those brand-new days their differences were a source of fond banter. She said, Let's be accurate: back to the West End of Glasgow. It's because you can't find your way in big cities, hopelessly lost in London, nose in the A–Z for the entire two years, no sense of direction; in fact, could you find your way to the south side of this city?

Mercia has always had that fifth sense, even in strange cities, where, after a cursory consultation of a map, she was able to move swiftly through a crowd, confident about her whereabouts. Like a springbokkie, her father used to boast, lifting its nose to smell the direction of the wind, pounding a hoof into the earth, before, quick as a flash, having found its bearings, it leaps off straight as a die to its destination. That is still how Mercia sees herself, propelled effortlessly through the world, eager to see yet another place. Not pathological restlessness, as Craig later diagnosed. She was after all prepared to stay put in Glasgow. In the city's West End with Craig by her side, she had no desire to move house, to try another city, or even another part of town.

Precisely, he said. So you have the comfort of a home, but rushing about being a citizen of the world means that you don't have to acknowledge it as home.

This home needs time to make itself more comfortable. As Mercia searches for a warmer coat, ready to wander down to the supermarket, the telephone rings. It is Smithy, darling Smithy, whose voice is like honey, except, that voice is unusually clipped as she asks Mercia to come over for dinner that night. Smithy seems anxious to get off the phone, so that Mercia knows something is wrong, wheedles the news out of her. All right, Smithy says. I planned to tell you later, but here goes: Morag gave birth prematurely last week. The little girl's been in an incubator for six days, but she's out now. Tiny, but absolutely fine.

Mercia is pleased to hear it in advance. Now, she says briskly, we need not talk about that tonight. But tears prickle, roll down her cheeks. The trick, she thinks, is to be organized. Instead of rushing out, she makes a careful shopping list of essentials that she could carry the short distance. She does not have the energy to drive.

There is no one to detain her on Byres Road, which is a pity, because the next trick is to have a conversation, at least about the weather. Neither does Mercia meet anyone in the supermarket, but the lady at the till with the elaborate hairdo greets her with a long-time-no-see that allows her to say that she's just back from Cape Town, that she's only been away for two weeks. Lucky you, hen, the woman says, it's all right for some, and she recites the week's weather forecast, unseasonably cold for the end of October. Already full-blown winter while you were sunning yourself down under.

Back in the apartment, where the heat now envelops her, Mercia treats herself to a long lavender bath. It will all fall into place—everything will be fine—everything in its place—a place where she is immune, where such news need not ruffle, she recites. She congratulates herself. So far she has done well, and besides, why wouldn't it be fine? It would be foolish, unrealistic, to think of herself as mother to a baby girl. That was not what she'd ever wanted, that she must remember. But neither was it according to Craig what he had wanted. It is another Craig who has become a father. A new man who, unlike Jake, will be a good father, who no longer has any connection with her. Again she corrects herself: fatherhood has not changed anything in relation to her. Craig left when he left. Departed. And she, Mercia, need not think differently about him. Not since he has left the woman who does not want children.

Mercia knows it is inconvenient; nevertheless, she arrives early at Smithy's. She promises to keep out of the kitchen, where there is mayhem with the smoke alarm ringing. Instead, she will help with getting the children bathed and ready for bed. The children are disappointed that she did not see lions or elephants in Africa. Not even a monkey. No, but she has seen a tortoise, and for a bedtime story tells them Achebe's fable about the leopard and the tortoise. Which they don't think much of. Little Ross says that she is mistaken. Making marks in the sand, scribbling, is not the same as writing, no wonder leopard doesn't understand what tortoise is up to. He, Ross, has been learning to write proper letters, capitals and lowercase. Unlike his sister, who cannot even write her own name.

Over dinner Mercia gives Smithy and Ewan an edited version of her time in South Africa. She will have to go back at Christmas, she explains, to sort out Jake, who hopefully by then would have recovered, but she omits her father's monstrous story and glosses over her expectations of adopting Nicky. Smithy says she is relieved that Mercia has not taken any rash decisions; she worried that Mercia might be bullied into foolish plans for Nicky. Would it not be better for the boy to be taken on by someone closer by so that he doesn't lose touch with his mother? Some people, she says, are born to be aunties, which Mercia finds wounding. Born to be, rather than choose to be? But that is not worth pursuing.

They offer no information about Craig's baby, so that it is Mercia who dutifully asks after her. They haven't seen her yet, so are unable to answer any questions, Ewan says, but they hope, when mother and child come out of hospital, to go round with a wee gift.

Mercia has no idea where it comes from, does not have time to wonder whether it is the word gift that unleashes her words, but as if jolted by its entry, she straightens her back to speak. She hopes that Smithy will help, act as intermediary. She has decided to sell the flat and let Craig have his half of it.

Ewan shakes his head. No need for that, he says emphatically. Why not take Craig's word for it: he doesn't want anything, doesn't want you to be uprooted or inconvenienced in any way, which earns a sardonic smile from Mercia. Living as he does with Morag—that grand apartment in Kelvinside was left to her by her parents—he has no need of the place. Besides, as Craig says, it was your deposit that enabled the two of you to buy the flat. Half the monthly mortgage that Craig put into it was less than paying rent, which would have been the case if he hadn't shacked up with you. He is the first to acknowledge that.

But Mercia is adamant. She cannot resist a sarcastic hope that Craig's modest tastes will allow him to live in such splendor, but no, jokes aside, she hopes not to have a distasteful conversation with Craig about money. She has thought about this carefully, she lies; she is determined to sell and it is only fair that he should have the proceeds, which after all are legally his. The apartment is registered in both their names so it is not a gift, she stresses. The deposit is neither here nor there, but if he insists, she'll subtract it from the profit. She trusts that Ewan and Smithy will deal with Craig on her behalf. When Craig left, she explains, giving up the flat made him feel better, less blameworthy about dumping her, but now that all that has settled, everything fallen into place, now that there is a baby, he will see that guilt or blame is inappropriate.

Mercia castigates herself. She should not so thoughtlessly have accepted his settlement, but she imagines that with a new baby the money will come in handy. Now, she says, it is her turn to feel better, to draw a line under all that lively past. The apartment on Elgin Terrace is, like the many places they visited together, a place of the past, a place that no longer carries meaning for her. Phew, that's all sorted in one mouthful hey, Mercia chuckles self-deprecatingly. Tomorrow, when I put the flat on the market, it will no longer be my home.

And where will you find a new home? Are you going back to live in Cape Town after all? Smithy asks.

Mercia says that it's unlikely, that she doesn't know. She hasn't thought that far. It hardly matters, she laughs. You know what a tortoise I am.

Actually, Smithy says, I don't. You've lived here in the West End for twenty-four years. And what, by the way, have you done with your shell?

Mercia looks bewildered. Really? Twenty-four years? As if she did not know. Well, I'll have a look at the estate agents' tomorrow, at what's on offer here, or perhaps on the south side, but the sale will take some time. I'd like something smaller, more manageable. Rent if necessary. Give myself time to see what crops up.

Something crops up the very next day in her e-mail. A message from Tim, her head of department, urging her to sign up for the university's personal development advisers' training session entitled "Facilitating Interactions." Every department is now required to have a PD adviser, and after her sabbatical she would be the ideal person, writes Tim without a trace of irony. Mercia howls with laughter. What kind of people dream up such hogwash? The training session may well be hilarious, but Tim cannot seriously believe that she'd come back with a party bag of self-help tips for her colleagues. She could make them up without going: to facilitate interaction, behave like a decent human being and do not throw eggs at your interlocutor.

Mercia presses the reply button and writes, Fuck off, Tim. But stops herself from sending it. Instead, she reaches for the "save" option, and wishes that like female protagonists in novels she accidentally pressed "send," with the entire department copied in. If only she could pack in the job, go somewhere where she does not know the language, somewhere where there is no possibility of interaction, where she can't read the script—China or Japan. And again, the very next day, something crops up in her e-mail. An advertisement for a professorship at the University of Macau. Christ, you'd swear she's skipped into a fairy tale. Just as well she's given up on the memoir. Who would believe that it's for real? But anticipating a third visitation, she receives no further e-mail surprises. Unless the old-fashioned letter in Craig's hand counts as something that crops up. Mercia tosses it into the bin, unread, then spends too much time prowling around the bin, begging herself not to succumb. She retrieves the letter, holds it to the light, ascertains that it is a single folded sheet of A4 paper, before savagely snipping at it with a pair of scissors. It is not enough. She would not put it past her, in the early hours, to reassemble the pieces. So once again she retrieves most of the scraps and with newspaper sets them alight in the grate. For a few seconds a homely fire flares in the hearth.

Mercia has been shortlisted for an interview. Which doesn't mean that she knows what she wants, she assures Smithy, but she may very well go, remove herself from the flat where in the small hours she hears Craig pacing up and down, burping a baby.

Oh well, a job offer could come in handy as leverage for promotion at our hallowed place of learning, says Smithy. But Mercia is adamant. That would not be her reason for going all that way to an interview.

No, of course not, Smithy says. That's not the way of a citizen of the world. Mercia starts. Have they, Smithy and Craig and who knows who else, been making fun of her? She must not be paranoid; she cannot afford to lose her friendship with Smithy, so she laughs it off.

Together they lark about, poring over a map. Neither of them has a clear idea where Macao is. Or Macau. Have these people not made up their minds as to what to call their place? Smithy asks. But that appeals to Mercia. Shows a healthy attitude to their place, their home as either this or that. Is it a country? A city? They Google the place, and one of the entries lists Camões.

Yes, that is the association Mercia remembers, Macau as a place where Camões sojourned. If she is not mistaken, *The Lusiads*, or part of it, was written there. Wouldn't it be wonderful, she says, if Macau were the place where old Adamastor was born. He, the monster of the coarse gravelly voice, who finds himself hugging a hillside, cheek to cheek with a boulder, instead of the beloved who mocks him from the waves. As for Adamastor's grave, proprietorial warnings to explorers that so exercise South Africans, she doesn't care. Nothing to do with her and her kind.

Aye right, hen, dinnae worry about your monster, mocks Smithy. I know plenty of real men hugging a hillside after the honeymoon. Nothing to do with unrequited love either, just the old story of being blinded by sex rather than thinking about a flesh-and-blood woman, another human being.

Already Macau sounds cozily familiar. Adamastor—let's say he was actually born in Macau, Mercia muses, a seed sprung in the mind of the one-eyed Camões, the poet in exile. I can just see him grumpily brooding in his grotto, an alien on a Chinese peninsula without a guidebook to facilitate interaction, one who transforms his monster into Table Mountain, towering over the Cape Peninsula. It would be like a homecoming for me. Of course it didn't occur to the poet that the Khoe who lived there had a different story for their own sea mountain, Hoerikwaggo as they had already named it.

No kidding, Smithy says, Professor, the job is yours. Adamastor must be recast right there in the place of his birth.

Yes, no kidding, and who knows what forebears of mine might hail from Macau, famous for its slave trade, Mercia jests. Who knows what happened to the children born to Camões's Chinese concubines?

And so she talks herself into it. She ought to stay put and deal with selling the flat; besides, she doesn't really dislike her job, but Macau does seem awfully tempting. Even providential, given that she has already decided to leave the West End.

But a flat, darling, says Smithy, is not the same as a city, or a country.

Mercia has spent a sleepless night, was up at dawn, and now before the interview has plenty of time to wander about the campus on Taipa with its assortment of buildings perched on a hill, modernist structures at various levels that, thanks to ingenious gardening, appear to grow out of the rock formations. She is grateful for her infallible sense of direction, since the place is a challenge, with floors numbered differently in buildings connected by walkways. These she explores, fascinated by the flora of Macau, which is everywhere on display. Gardens tumble out of rock faces, are exquisitely laid out on roofs, transform embankments, provide ornamental edging to the facades of stonework, are tucked between buildings, turning awkward spaces into lush displays. And so many of the flowers are those of the Cape: bougainvillea, hibiscus, poinsettia, oleander. Perhaps even jacaranda, which, like the frangipani she does recognize, is not in flower.

She finds on the northern side a bench on the fifth floor, or is it the second? from which to look out at the spectacular view of hazy sunlight on the water, the long bridge connecting Taipa island to Macau, and the hills flanking the city's glitzy casinos, from which light bounces. Mercia does not know what to think of living in a place like this. She ought to consider the possibility of a question about why she wants to come to Macau. She could not very well say that "Facilitating Interactions" has driven her there. And who's to say that Health and Safety and Personal Development Advice are not in any case already hiking their way over to China? Instead, will she say something limp about the weather, the heat, the flowers of the Cape? By virtue of being interviewed, there is a chance of being offered the job, so what in the world would she do if it were offered to her? She has no idea, but no doubt she'll soon find out.

Mercia's head spins. She has twenty more minutes. She rises distractedly, wanders down a flight of stairs, and catches a glimpse of morning glory tumbling over rocks. And so late in the year too, although the weather at the beginning of November is deliciously hot, hardly autumnal. A flash of blue trumpets lures her along a corridor that promises a hidden garden, until she realizes that she has lost her bearings, has lost the garden. If only she could get out into the open, out of this building, she would be able to find her way. And indeed, just before panic sets in, Mercia sees in the dark low-ceilinged corridor ahead natural light pouring in from a structure on her left. It is a turtle pond, situated both indoors and out, its far wall an ornamental stone structure of various levels, supporting another roof garden.

On that far bank of the pond in the morning sun the creatures are huddled together, haphazardly piled up on top of each other, as if there were not enough space, as if they have been hurriedly driven out of the water. Some are settled on a large concrete fish. Rising out of the water are two ghostly concrete structures, resembling mountains in old Chinese paintings, and on these are placed, in various crags, little figurines. As she squints to see what they represent, several turtles splash noisily into the water, as if they have just woken up. Mercia watches the ancient-looking creatures lumber in and out of the pond. She checks her watch. There is time, and although she is not sure of her whereabouts, the campus is small, and the garden on the right means that she'll get out, find her way once again.

She is drawn to the strange movements of a small turtle with yellow markings on its shell, the markings, she assumes, of youth. It swims in circles, apparently trying to gain the attention of a large, older turtle that clumsily turns away and moves off, only to find itself repeatedly confronted by the youth. With its left flipper it swipes in irritation at the stalker, whilst steering itself away. But the young turtle persists until it manages to face the elder squarely. It reaches out with its flippers—how like little hands they are, the bones between the webbing raised like fingers—as if to touch the face of the other, the splayed fingers quivering with excitement as they slowly shiver forward, but before they touch, the older turtle turns away, evidently repelled, and hurriedly makes off.

Mercia leans over to inspect more closely. The young one does not give up. It describes wide arcs around its quarry, then homes in. It earns a few clips around the ear, is rudely rebuffed, given the cold shoulder, but when the older turtle is lulled into dropping its guard the younger slips round and deftly confronts it once more, face-to-face. The prehistoric head turns away in distaste, and as its pursuer moves round to capture the eyes, the exasperated creature lifts its head out of the water. Give me a break, it seems to cry; give me space to breathe, but when the head drops back into the water the little face is right there, looking into the elder's eyes, supplicating. There is language in the movement of those fingers, shivering with passion, as they reach out to touch the face of the other.

I am here! Please, oh please. It is I!

That is what it seems to say. The trembling digits are about to make contact when the older creature swipes at them, cruelly lashes out, then plunges deep into the water and manages to get away.

Phew, what a performance. What could the little chap be pleading for? What does it want? Perhaps, unlike its land cousin, the tortoise, who can walk away from its eggs, this lot left against nature in the same pond, thrown together in the same waters as their parents, will not be abandoned. Will keep on circling the elder in abject supplication. Will stutter through those quivering hands, Acknowledge me, it is I I I I . . .

No doubt exhausted, the little one with its bright yellow markings gives up. It swims slowly to an oversized stone turtle sprawled on the slant of an angled concrete slab with its head raised above the water. The young turtle scrambles onto the lifeless back and lays down its head wearily, its delicate hands still stretched out. It might as well whimper into the concrete carapace: I am here. Acknowledge me. It is I. Perhaps it is resting up, thinking whether it should try a different grown-up next time.

Mercia has a vague idea of turtles having something to do with feng shui. What, she wonders, does the little chap make of that responsibility?

When she finds her way out, she is on a road. A taxi cruises by and she raises her hand, finds herself hailing it. She feels foolish, standing in the road miming to the driver a ferry taking off. Hong Kong, she says repeatedly, then worries all the way about the success of her flailing movements until they are in sight of the ferry terminal. In the taxi she sends a text to say that unforeseeable circumstances prevent her from attending the interview. She will, of course, refund the ticket.

Mercia thinks of the drive from Kliprand to Cape Town and back. Is she—a mad menopausal woman who has been left— losing her marbles? At the airport she avoids looking in mirrors. Why has she, who has never indulged in erratic behavior, rushed off? She cannot blame a turtle.

Back home in Glasgow she tells everyone, except for Smithy, that she was not offered the post, that she in any case found the humidity too oppressive.

A few days before Mercia is due to fly back to Cape Town, there is a call from Sylvie in the early hours. Jake has died. She has just heard from the sanatorium. They say that someone must have smuggled in a bottle of brandy, which he has evidently drunk in one go. Sylvie assures Mercia that it had nothing to do with her, that she knows how dangerous that would have been after weeks of detoxification. Besides, Jake did not ask her for anything.

Sylvie's voice is tired. From time to time she loses the thread. She says that she had been visiting, that it didn't seem right to leave Jake on his own. Mostly he didn't want to see her but she would take food for him all the same, nice warm roosterbrood, brawn, or curried tripe with beans, his favorite things, because in places like that the food is sure to be inedible. Funny how the previous day she took Nicky with her, and Jake looked so much better. He walked with them in the gardens and was quite nice, quite calm. He was good with Nicky, sat the boy on his knee, and he even spoke kindly to her. She thought he was definitely getting better.

Mercia says Sylvie should go ahead with funeral arrangements, that she will try for a flight that evening. But Sylvie is in no hurry to get off the phone. She says, as if speaking to someone who did not know him, that Jake had not always been bad and rude. He had been a good husband, and at the beginning a good father to Nicky. For a while it seemed as if one could put aside all the bad things of the past. She could not see anything wrong in that, but then the bad old things crept up on them. Jake suffered so much that she can't help thinking that he is better off now, but still, it doesn't mean she's not responsible for his death. Everything has been her fault. AntieMa has been right all along. For a long time she's had no truck with that kind of talk, but now she gives in. She, Sylvie, is shot through with sin.

That's nonsense, Mercia says firmly. Don't you believe anything of the kind. It is sad that Jake's died, that he could not find anything to live for, but I know, I can assure you that it's not your fault. If there is sin involved, it is you who have been sinned against. I'm sure that you need no reminder from me, but now it's time to be strong for Nicky's sake, and to banish all such foolish thoughts. There's plenty to do, organizing the funeral.

Do you think, Sylvie says, that I should slaughter a sheep for the funeral dinner? That's all I can do now for poor Jake. You know the whole of Kliprand will be there, wanting something decent to eat.

Mercia tries to banish the grotesque image of an animal on its back, its legs twitching and blood foaming from its broken neck.

Well, she says, yes, if that's what you want to do, if you think that's the right thing to do.

Mercia cannot cry for Jake; she is infused with loss, with the sadness of his ruined life. She finds the photographs of Jake as a child, the little boy in short trousers bunched around the middle with a snake belt. A laughing Jake restrained by Mercia, whose arm is around him. A young man with a huge Afro hairstyle to annoy his father. Jake in his businessman's suit. Always with laughter in his eyes.

Before Mercia goes to bed she finds the file, Home, still on her desktop, and without opening it, drags it into the trash bin.

· · ·

Until the day before she is due to return to Glasgow, Mercia does not know what she will do about Nicky. They have spent much time together, reading the books she has brought along. She has answered as clearly as possible his questions about his father and death. The child seems attached to her, and as she sits down to a breakfast of roosterbrood and a boiled egg Mercia decides to bite the bullet. She'll manage; things will work out, even if she does not quite know how. She must do it for Jake. She can see herself in a new, cheaper apartment in Glasgow, on the south side, with the bright little boy who is so like Jake. Mercia would, of course, send him back to spend summers with his mother, just a question of pulling in the belt, and if perhaps Sylvie would want to visit, well, she could handle that.

The child is still asleep and it is time to put Sylvie's mind at rest. Mercia starts in medias res: So, if you want Nicky to come with me, I'd be happy to take—

Sylvie leaps to her feet. Her eyes flash. What do you mean? How can you take him? Where to? she barks.

Mercia is flustered, and before she manages to speak, Sylvie pounds her fists on the table, screams. Nicky is a Murray but he is also my child, my own child. He's all I have. I'm a nobody, so you think you have to take my child away? That I'm not good enough to bring him up? You can't take him away. I won't let anyone take him away.

Tears of shame stream down Mercia's face. For a second she thinks of fudging, of rephrasing to cover up, but no, Sylvie deserves nothing but the truth.

No, of course I don't think anything of the sort. He is your child. Of course I can't take him away. It's a misunderstanding, a mistake. I thought . . . Jake wrote to say that you wanted me to take Nicky, and then you asked me. Just as I left last time. Remember?

Sylvie stands with her arms flung out, ready to take on the world. She gesticulates wildly. I asked if you would help out. It was difficult; I'd rather not have help, but his education must come first. I meant help with his education. Her voice drops as she says, I'll need money for that. Then she shouts, I'm his mother. Even a sheep screams when its lamb is taken, so how could I have asked you to take him away? What do you think I am? Jake was mad, poisoned by drink. How could you have believed him?

Mercia says please could they stop this conversation. She is sorry, deeply embarrassed. She should have known better. She would be very glad to help with Nicky's education, but first, would Sylvie forgive her. At which point Nicky arrives, rubbing the sleep out of his eyes.

Why are they shouting? he asks. And his mother says no, they are not. That everything is sorted out. Everything is fine. That one day he will visit Auntie Mercy in England.

PUBLISHING IN THE PUBLIC INTEREST

Thank you for reading this book published by The New Press. The New Press is a nonprofit, public interest publisher. New Press books and authors play a crucial role in sparking conversations about the key political and social issues of our day.

We hope you enjoyed this book and that you will stay in touch with The New Press. Here are a few ways to stay up to date with our books, events, and the issues we cover:

- Sign up at www.thenewpress.com/subscribe to receive updates on New Press authors and issues and to be notified about local events
- Like us on Facebook: www.facebook.com/newpressbooks
- Follow us on Twitter: www.twitter.com/thenewpress

Please consider buying New Press books for yourself; for friends and family; or to donate to schools, libraries, community centers, prison libraries, and other organizations involved with the issues our authors write about.

The New Press is a 501(c)(3) nonprofit organization. You can also support our work with a tax-deductible gift by visiting www .thenewpress.com/donate.